For  F

Acknowledgments

I am grateful to *Smashwords* where these stories first appeared as e-books and to *Polar*, the Crimes and Letters Magazine, which published *A Sound of Singing* in Greek, translated by Anna Darda-Iordanidou.

# 1 THE RUSTLING OF SILK

We were sitting in a private dining-room upstairs at Rules in Maiden Lane, not a restaurant that I could afford. But Harrington had done very well in the City and when it came to his turn to host our annual reunion dinner, it was to Rules we were invited. And a fine dinner it was, leaving all eight of us comfortable and mellow as we sat with our coffees and port. Eight of us, all now in our sixties, thrown together studying History at that small college more than forty years before. Harrington who had always been pushy and direct, Abigail, by far the most intelligent of us, who'd changed to Law in her Third Year and was now a Supreme Court Judge, Giles the newspaper editor, and the rest of us with our less illustrious careers. All of us taken out of our daily lives and allowed, for this one evening, to put our cares to one side and feel young again.

Unsurprisingly, it was Harrington who destroyed this feeling of trouble-free nostalgia by suggesting that it would be a splendid idea if we were all to tell a story, recount a tale, share some strange or curious event. There were a couple of groans and I saw Abigail half-smile as she looked down at the table. Harrington, however, would not be put off. He'd had an idea and he was going to stick with it. He was proposing to start the ball rolling himself. as he put it, when I surprised myself by interrupting him. Perhaps it was the alcohol or the pleasantness of being amongst old friends. Whatever it was, I'd decided that I might as well be the first with a story.

I have always wondered, I said, why M.R.James never wrote a ghost-story about Cyprus. He worked there, of course, for a short while in 1887 when he joined the excavations at the Temple of Aphrodite at Old Paphos. I think he was responsible for collating the inscriptions they found. I can't imagine him directing a dig, or even wielding a trowel. It's odd enough just to think of him at work on a Classical site. We know him now as a Medievalist and it would make more sense to us if he'd been been working with Camille Enlart, studying and cataloguing the medieval Lusignan buildings of Cyprus. I could imagine M.R.James with one of those old-fashioned surveyor's wooden measures, pacing out the dimensions of the Aghia Sophia Cathedral in Nicosia. I assume he must have visited Nicosia and Famagusta to see the Lusignan Cathedrals and the other medieval churches there. But if he did, for some reason they never made it into his ghost stories.

I was reminded of M.R.James and his brief stay in Cyprus by something I was once told by one of my postgraduate tutors, Professor Somerville, when I moved on from History to Archaeology. For, as a young postgraduate student himself, Somerville had spent a year in Cyprus in the early 1950s, working at the Nicosia Museum. It was before Independence, before the intercommunal fighting and before Partition. It was a time when you could travel anywhere there and Somerville did, and like M.R.James, by bicycle.

Cyprus and the Cypriots had made a huge impression on Somerville. It was his first year in the real world, I guess, and the defining year of his life. Whenever he was happy in all the years I knew him, he'd start to reminisce about Cyprus. And his memories were as sharp, clear and bright as the sea and sunlight of the island. Which, I suppose, is why the story I am going to tell you now is so unusual. For it was a uniquely disturbing anecdote from his wonderful year in the early 1950s. And one that he would probably never have told me had it not been for his first heart-attack at college which came out-of-the-blue and jolted him. I remember going to visit him in a cubby-hole room in hospital where he lay on his back recovering for a week and reflecting on his first and unexpected brush with death.

It was a different Somerville I found that afternoon on a grey, November Cambridge day. There were no jokes or wit, just a sombre thoughtfulness. I remember him smiling as though he was looking at me from a long way off, with an understanding I did not have. He gestured for me to sit down on the chair beside his bed and then unburdened himself, I think that's the best way of describing it, of a Cyprus story I'd never heard.

He described, or tried to, the afternoon heat of July to September in Nicosia, the way all life stopped, having no choice, the silence of the tired and deserted streets. For it was precisely these dead, afternoon hours when all was in limbo, that he would get on his bicycle and head off to the coolness of the great Lusignan Cathedral, Aghia Sophia, now the Selimiye Mosque with its two minarets added as a victorious after-thought to the great medieval cathedral. Riding past the closed shops with their metal shutters pulled down and padlocked, he could feel as though the town belonged to him alone. It made him feel privileged as well as happy.

Arriving at the mosque, he'd prop his bike against the stone wall of the washing area. At the huge wooden cathedral doors (for this could be nothing but a cathedral), he'd kick off his sandals and put them down in the empty space where the faithful would leave their shoes and then he'd walk into the silent, empty cathedral.

The Lusignan walls, once covered in paintings, were now a uniform expanse of whitewash. The high windows which once held stained-glass were now filled with tracery, allowing the breeze, if there had been one, to blow through. The only sound came from the pigeons on the roof, ruffling their feathers like the quiet rustling of silk on a stone floor. But the cathedral's stone floor with its few remaining flat, broken tombstones of knights and clerics, was now completely covered with faded but valuable Turkish rugs, laid down any-old-how and overlapping, adding a strangely homely touch to the otherwise austere and looming interior.    It was as if the cathedral had been domesticated and was just waiting for the van to arrive with the sofas.

But this was where Somerville would come for coolness in the dry, burning heat of the Nicosia Summer afternoons.  And the more often he went there, the more he began to feel the true solemnity of this space, as though the carpets and the whitewash had gone and he was back in the 15th century in the final years of Lusignan rule before the Venetians secured Cyprus through marriage and then lost it to the Ottomans in violence.

And it was on one of those afternoons when he'd just propped his bicycle against the wash-shed, that he was stopped in his tracks by a shadow against the wall near the cathedral door, for all the world like a short, stocky man sitting in the shade.  But the shadow disappeared as soon as he got close to it and there was nothing unusual about his quiet walk inside the cathedral. Just the blankness of the whitewashed walls and that gentle sound of the rustling of silk as the pigeons fluffed up their feathers on the windowsills high above him.

Which was why he was unprepared on his next visit, to see the same shadow by the door rise up from the bench as he approached, putting out its hand to stop him.  The man's strong arms were bare from the elbow, covered in the scars of old knife wounds, a fighting man on his feet now and blocking the path. But, as Somerville stood there uncertain and scared, the man or the shadow were gone.  There was nothing there but the blank stone wall and no bench for a man to sit on.

Hurrying inside the cathedral, Somerville realized his nerves were still on edge.  For when silently walking on the thick Turkish rugs, he could distinctly hear the same rustling of silk from the pigeons.  But this time the noise came from in front of him, not above, and there were no pigeons inside the cathedral. He stood for a few minutes listening to the rustling sound,

4

taking deep breaths to calm himself down as he sought some rational explanation for this trick of the acoustics. He couldn't find an answer, and he was relieved when he was brought back to reality by the sound of one of the shopkeepers from the hardware stores outside.

The man had obviously decided to re-open early for Somerville could hear the thump as a heavy sack was tossed down onto the pavement from the back of a lorry. Cycling home in the heat, he shook his head at his own stupidity. He had arrogantly thought he was immune to sunstroke and had laughed when his Greek-Cypriot landlady had insisted he should take a siesta "like all good people".

For the next week or so he was busy with his work at the Museum. They had a visit from London from the British Museum and Somerville was on-duty every day taking the visitors to Classical sites from Polis to Paphos to Salamis. It was only after a break of ten days that he had a free afternoon and could cycle back once more to the cathedral. He'd compromised with his landlady by wearing a sun hat, although this still didn't seem to satisfy her. A siesta was a siesta and, in her view, an almost medical requirement. For him, a floppy green bush-hat was a concession in itself and it made him feel more confident as he cycled through the backstreets towards the cathedral.

But the stocky man was there again by the door, his face in shadow, and Somerville could see what he hadn't seen before. That the man was wearing a tough leather breastplate over his rough cotton shirt and that there was an evil-looking dagger thrust in his belt. Not the distinctive dagger the Cretans still wore, but something long and thin and more lethal. A poniard they might have called it in the Middle-Ages. And once again the man stood up to bar his way, shaking his head as if to confirm that entry was forbidden. Only to fade away as Somerville approached, leaving nothing behind but what looked like a farthing coin under the bench where he had been sitting, had there been a bench there for him to sit on.

Somerville, ever the archaeologist, quickly picked up the coin and ducked into the cathedral. Where he was not alone. For when he turned around when he was half-way across the cathedral floor, he saw an old woman in black, whom he hadn't noticed when he entered, sitting just inside the cathedral door. At first, he thought she was knitting, but then he could see that she was telling a rosary made of pink glass beads, the kind a young girl would give as a present. But, on second sight, she too was gone and he was left with nothing but the persistent sound of the rustling of silk, like a silk dress trailing across a stone floor. Until that too disappeared, reality returning with the same shopkeeper tossing his heavy sack from his lorry. The only puzzling thing was that, when Somerville left the cathedral, he couldn't see which shop had re-opened.

He was happy, though, with his 'farthing'. For the next day at the Museum, Professor Loizides identified it as a sixain of James II, James the Bastard, as he was known, the last Lusignan king. Somerville donated it to the Museum and the small coin was duly catalogued with a note on the card describing it as a gift from C.H.Somerville Esq, found in the dust in front of the Selimiye Mosque. For the Classicists at the Museum, the 15th century Lusignan coin was more of a curiosity than anything else, but Somerville felt he'd done something of value.

The next time he went to the cathedral, he had to admit that he was nervous. The acoustics and the tricks of the light in the cathedral were unsettling. It was no longer somewhere he could feel at peace. He went back, he guessed, for the coolness and for the chance of finding something else in the dust outside. He was used to kicking up fragments of yellow and green sgraffito ware Lusignan pottery in the empty city of Famagusta, but to find a coin in Nicosia where people had walked for centuries was unusual. It was worth another try.

And he knew he'd made the right decision when he walked up to the cathedral doors and there was no shadow of a man to stop him. It was just a normal, hot afternoon in a sleepy, quiet city with "the good people" like his landlady all safely taking their siesta.

Inside the cathedral, he took off his bush-hat and tucked it in his

6

belt making that rustling sound as he did so. It seemed that any movement in the cathedral might be misconstrued by the acoustics. But turning around, he could see the old woman was again sitting by the door. This time she stopped telling her pink glass beads and looked at him, or past him at something further ahead. He couldn't see her face which was lost in the shadow of the black cotton shawl around her head, but the way her hands were frozen in her lap suggested fear.

And her fear communicated itself to him, for he could now hear clearly the rustling of silk and see that it came not from the pigeons but from a young girl, seventeen at most, slowly pacing the cathedral in a fine silk dress which trailed along the stone cathedral floor over the faces of the long-dead knights and clerics. And all around him there was sudden bright colour, as though a real world had rushed in to fill a vacuum. The walls were brightly painted in blues and reds, the colour poured down from the stained-glass windows and the vault of the choir was now Heaven, a brilliant bright blue, studded with golden stars.

Turning around in confusion, he lost sight of the girl until he suddenly heard the rustling behind him and felt the light touch of a thin hand on his shoulder. He heard the words "Pardonnez-moi" in a young girl's voice and wheeled round to look into her face, or into the void where her face should have been. He was about to gasp for breath when he heard the same deep thud of the heavy sack being tossed down on the ground outside. This time, however, there were screams, from the girl and from the old woman by the door, but both of them had disappeared by the time their screaming was done.

Somerville raised himself up in the hospital bed and reached out to take a sip from the glass of water on the small table beside him. We sat there in silence for a while staring out of the window at the grey, November sky, a world away from Nicosia in high-Summer and several worlds away from those events in its cathedral.

The historian in Somerville had made him write the story down, however improbable it might seem, however ridiculous it might make him look. He gave me a copy, but he admitted he didn't

7

have an answer for what had happened.

Years later, when that second manuscript of George Boustronios's Chronicle resurfaced in a monastery at Mt Athos, an explanation of a sort did appear. Somerville by then was dead, but I'd kept an interest in the period of James the Bastard as a hobby because of Somerville's strange story. This second manuscript contained additions to Boustronios's Chronicle and life of James the Bastard, additions written by one Petros Kouklianos, a priest from near Paphos. In the few extra paragraphs he'd added, Kouklianos touched on some more of the scandals of that turbulent period at the very end of Lusignan rule. In one paragraph, he briefly referred to a nobleman's daughter, married off at fourteen (as was the custom) to a much older man for reasons of family advantage. There were few places a nobleman's daughter might go with her maid and her bodyguard, but the cathedral was one of them. And it was there that she met a young priest/confessor with whom, in Kouklianos's polite language, the girl had "formed an attachment". The story ended when their secret was betrayed for money by her bodyguard. One day, he left his post at the cathedral door and her husband's retainers stormed in to drag the priest up one of the octagonal staircases to the roof, taking him out onto the flying buttress from where they tossed him like a heavy sack onto the pavement below. They sent the girl to a nunnery where she gave birth to a boy six months later. They killed the child and threw it down a dried-up well. Kouklianos doesn't record what happened to the mother.

"Dieu pardonne" is all one can say. I hope she is at rest.

# 2 THE COMRADES

I think we'll have trouble following that, said Abigail, smiling at us as we sat in that upstairs dining-room in Maiden Lane, eight former History students, now in our sixties and still meeting once a year for a reunion and to tell a ghost story or two. The after-effects of the story we'd just heard hung in the room like cigarette smoke and even the normally loquacious Harrington seemed unusually quiet, speaking only to order us another bottle of port.

A good story but a bit erudite for me, said Giles, but then I don't suppose any of you read my paper. It would be a bit down-market for you, a tabloid. Not that I blame you. But the one thing that working on the tabloids does teach you is how to tell a story, and quickly. You don't get the column inches of the broadsheets. You've got to hook the readers in the first sentence and keep re-hooking them in every paragraph till the brief roller-coaster is over.

The problem, though, like all journalism, is that there are some stories you can't tell. Not because they're not well-sourced or because you can't check them out, but simply because your readers would take one look at them and decide you had a screw

9

loose.

You don't mind if I smoke, do you?  We did but we were all too polite to say otherwise.  So Giles brought out a pack of Rothmans, tapped one out and lit up.

My first boss in Fleet Street got me onto Rothmans, he said.  In those days the office was just a fug of cigarette smoke, with a deeper cloud in the corner where our chief crime reporter sat with his pipe.  My boss, though, was Rothmans and a chain-smoker.  It was he that taught me pretty much all I know about journalism, and it was he who showed me that, once in a while, there comes along a story you just can't publish.  For your own sanity, I suppose.

My boss had been in on some of the big stories of the Fifties when he first started out in Fleet Street.  Sex scandals, spy scandals, the lot.  He had a track-record and we all looked up to him.  He had a sure grip, sound judgement and a confidence in his abilities that radiated out to the rest of us.  He was a real leader and it was a good paper, if not one that any of you, my friends, would have read.

I only once remember him ever looking flummoxed by anything.  It was when one of our best reporters took off to Barcelona unannounced with a staff photographer in tow.  The latter started phoning back to say something was wrong.  My boss got hold of our Madrid stringer and sent him up there to check it out.  The stringer got to Barcelona and had a few quiet drinks with the photographer on expenses, as stringers do.  The photographer said that he thought the reporter had gone mad.  The stringer then spent a day going around with the reporter gently teasing out what was going on.  It turned out that the reporter had got a tip-off, from an Archangel apparently, that Christ's Second Coming was due within the week.  It wasn't clear why Christ had chosen Barcelona, but an Archangel is a pretty good source.  Not surprisingly, that reporter never worked in Fleet Street again.

And he was one of my best reporters, said the Boss to me later, shaking his head sadly.  It was a week or two afterwards and I was standing with him in his office in those dead hours after midnight when the presses had started rolling. He brought out a bottle and two glasses from his desk and lit up another Rothmans. You think I'm tough, he said, but it always bloody scares me, the fragility of the human mind. And I bet that's not the sort of phrase you'd ever hear me say, he said laughing. Sit down, have a drink. I'll tell you about one of my greatest triumphs.

Have you ever heard of the Baxter suicide in the early Fifties? That's right, the up-and-coming Labour MP who filled his pockets with stones, like some sad wronged woman, and threw himself off Westminster Bridge early one morning "just as the sun was rising". There were long columns of speculation in the papers, but no-one ever knew what was behind it. Except me, of course, I got the whole story, neat and tidy and all cross-checked. It was a scoop that could have kick-started my career a lot earlier. But I couldn't publish it for the simple reason that my editor would have had me sectioned.

It was before your time, I guess. Baxter was one of those upper-class Englishmen with a glowing war record and a young wife who looked like a film star but who had a lot more going for her. She ran a Charity sorting out housing for ex-servicemen. She was a real power in her own right. He'd found Socialism while serving in the Army. He'd been with Tito's Partisans in Yugoslavia. Baxter and his wife were the great hopes of the Labour Party. He was already set to become a Minister and she looked ready to join him as an MP herself. I think his suicide put an end to her political ambitions. She just seemed to lose all heart in it. And that too was a tragedy. All-in-all the Labour Party might have turned out a lot stronger if he'd lived.

You can understand why every young journalist in Fleet Street went hurrying off to dig up the truth behind the Baxter suicide. All of us could see there had to be some pretty big story there and our editors were breathing down our necks for results. You know what it's like when there are a dozen or more of you from different papers all going hell-for-leather after the same story. However hard you try, you can't keep the others from getting a sniff of your leads, of getting some idea of what you're up to. I'd been through his war record, found some blokes who'd been with him in Yugoslavia. Baxter had worked for one of the secret mobs in their offices in Bari. By the time he went into Yugoslavia, it was by motor torpedo boat and he was passed like a package all the way to Tito's HQ to join the others already there. It wasn't like the early days. Parachuting on your own at night to land God knows where and to find God knows what. I'm not knocking him. It's just that he went there late in the day. It was all fairly organised by the time he went in.

I'd then tried all my Labour Party contacts, gone through them with a fine-tooth comb. From a couple of them, and from what I was picking up from the slipstreams of my rivals from other papers, it seemed as though we were probably looking at another spy scandal, Baxter and the Russians, which the Government was going to do its best to cover up, not wanting to admit what it had lost. That was the line I was working on when I managed to get close to an electrician doing some rewiring work on Baxter's house. He had a couple of kids and was a bit short of cash. He liked to place too many bets as well, I think. Anyway, we soon came to an arrangement. He'd bring me an envelope of letters and bills from the late Mr Baxter MP's writing desk each evening. I'd give them the once over, pay him and he'd put them back the next morning. Little by little, we got through the lot.

It didn't help much until, two nights running, my electrician friend's envelope contained two polite letters from a professional typist in Muswell Hill. It seemed she'd done some unspecified work for Baxter and not been paid. I don't know why his wife or the police hadn't followed it up. A stone they just didn't want to turn over perhaps, for fear of more scandal. Anyway, I put on my best shirt and tie and turned up at the Muswell Hill address claiming to be a solicitor's clerk from the law firm handling Baxter's estate. I was there to settle unpaid bills. The money wasn't much. I paid it and she was happy. It seemed he'd wanted a manuscript typed privately. She still had both the typescript and the original. He'd told her it was a work of fiction. He didn't want anyone to know about his amateur literary efforts until he'd decided if it was any good. So there I was on the bus back from Muswell Hill with a large brown envelope of Baxter's private thoughts which I'd duly paid for, above board, you might say. It was the strangest bloody document I've ever read.

Here you are, he said, unlocking the bottom drawer of his desk and tossing over a thick and aged envelope. Some weekend light reading for you. Don't show anyone else. Bring it back when you've finished and I'll tell you how I managed to check it out. Not that it did me any good.

I took the Boss's envelope home, turned on the three-bar heater in the sitting-room, made myself a large mug of coffee and read on through the deep dark hours until the first birds had started singing. The manuscript was written as a diary, with dates, and it ran for about nine months, ending a few days before his death. It wouldn't have been a great work of fiction, it was too repetitive, but it would have been good enough to pass muster as fiction with the copy-typist. Baxter must have delivered it to her as something to be going on with, and she'd assumed that they'd be more to come. I'll leave out a lot of the description and just give you the gist of it. He'd added a title in pencil, almost as an afterthought for the typist's benefit:

## THE HAUNTING

I can't say for certain when it began. But I've put down this date when I had to go up to Birmingham to give a speech. It was early afternoon when I got onto the train. It was a quiet time of day and I found a compartment to myself. And it stayed empty for the whole journey. A couple of times at different stops, someone on the platform reached out to open the door but for some reason they turned away at the last minute. I guess I was just lucky. My only complaint was the strong smell of Woodbines from whoever had been in the compartment on the way down. I tried opening the window, but the stink of Woodbines only seemed to get worse. It was only later that I realized what was happening...

I was having lunch with the Minister of Trade. We'd agreed to meet at 1pm in the House of Commons dining-room. His secretary had booked a table for us. I got there on the dot to find the Minister was already seated and having words with the head waiter. The Minister had picked up his linen napkin only to find an angry-looking dirty-red wine-stain on the white tablecloth. He showed it to me as I arrived, asking whether I too thought standards were slipping. There was something very strange about it. It wasn't from the sort of stemmed wineglass we used in the Commons. It was more like the red stains from cheap glasses I'd seen on rough wooden tables abroad when I was travelling before the War...

I was travelling to Paris for an international Socialist conference. As it happened, my birthday was going to be on the second day I was away. My wife had given me a wrapped birthday present to put in my suitcase. She always gives me a book for my birthday. I confess that I cheated and opened it when I was on the train from Calais to Paris. She'd written a card saying she hoped I'd like it. She'd seen it well-reviewed. It was apparently the best study so far of the damage done by colonialism in Africa. Only it wasn't. The book was, in fact, a very battered dirty copy of a 1930s Left Book Club title, one of those solid paperbacks with the bright-orange covers. It was scuffed and frayed as though it had been a long time in someone's pocket. It was when I saw the owner's name on the flyleaf that I realized what was happening to me...

By now, I admit that my nerves were on edge. I know it was beginning to affect my work. My wife knew that something was wrong, but I put it down to tiredness, which she accepted. She then started talking about how we should take a holiday, get away from London if just for a few days. She had a good deputy she could trust at the Charity. It wouldn't be a problem. At the end of the day, it was your health that was important. We were none of us going to live for ever. I'd agreed but without fixing a date. Instead, I'd taken up smoking again to try and steady my nerves and stay sane. I was smoking Rothmans which was why it was such a shock, when I finished a packet, to see an old cigarette-card of an actress tucked down inside, issued not by Rothmans but by the United Kingdom Tobacco

Company Ltd. No.26 from a series of 32 'Cinema Stars', Dolores Del Rio...

I didn't know where the next one would come from. I didn't know what places to avoid. All I wanted to do was hide but I didn't know where or from what. They were singling me out, that was certain. I could see the quiet smiles on their faces. But it wasn't a game to them, it was serious and justified retribution. What did they want me to do? I knew I could never make amends but there must be something I could do. We were all practical people. Surely, they could see that what I was doing now for Socialism was for the good? But perhaps I was wrong about the game. For we were spending the day with my wife's sister and her two small children. A boy of six and a girl of four. It was after lunch and the sunlight was streaming through the windows onto the Persian rug where the little girl was sitting with a toy workbox and pieces of felt. She'd been entrusted with a small pair of scissors with rounded ends which she was using to cut shapes from the material. She smiled and held one up. It was better cut than her others. A red star cut from felt, still with a few strands of cotton where it had been pulled from a soldier's cap...

I wasn't sleeping. I was chain-smoking. I looked terrible. Colleagues in the House would recommend doctors and specialists who'd helped members of their family or friends. One of the Party Whips had started to look at me out of the corner of his eye, as if he'd marked me down as a potential problem. Women, boys, worse? He didn't know but he'd seen that sort of thing before and it was his job to sniff these things out, nip them in the bud if he could. And, if not, then the Party interest would have to come first. I tried to keep my mind off it by working even harder, even longer hours. I'd be sitting there in the small office I shared with two other MPs long after they'd both gone home. The only people still there were the cleaners. One of them, an old Cypriot woman, would take a quiet peak at me round the door, just to make sure I was alright. Sometimes she'd pop in briefly and recommend some Greek folk remedy. One morning, I arrived to find she'd left me a small present wrapped in brown paper. A folk remedy? It was a cheap tin icon with a picture of the saint on printed paper. He was dressed like a Roman soldier, but his face had been scratched out with pencil...

I think I'd had about as much as I could take. It was like being bullied at school but here there were no holidays now to peg out for. Everywhere I went, they seemed to be waiting for me. I could see now that I'd never been strong. I just looked the part and that had got me by. Oh, I worked hard, and in a good cause, but everything about me was built on that one great lie. They knew it and they were not going to let me forget it. The end, of course, came in the most banal of ways. I stopped outside the Tube station on the way home to buy *The Evening News*. There was going to be some headline the Whips had been worried about. I hurried down to the Tube and it was only when I sat down on the train that I could see the newspaper-seller had made some mistake. Instead of *The Evening News*, he'd given me an old copy of *The Daily Worker*. It was crisp and white and had been lovingly ironed as though it was *The Times* delivered on a silver tray in an upper-class Victorian household. It was the very neatness of the folds and the pressing that were so terrifying. I could visualise the hands that would have picked it up and read it. This beautifully folded paper had a finality to it, like a judgement or a death sentence...

And that was where the manuscript ended. Being a good journalist, I checked the manuscript and the typescript for discrepancies, but the lady in Muswell Hill had done a good job. I had read all there was. I resealed the envelope and passed it back to the Boss through his secretary on the Monday morning. It wasn't till after midnight at the end of the week that he called me to come in for a night-cap.

He poured us each a drink and held up his hand when I was about to say something. I managed to check it out, he said, after a fashion and some years later. Put it this way, I met a man who had known Baxter before the War. What he told me made some sort of sense of this 'Haunting'.

My source was a strong man and I liked him and believed him. But he was an alcoholic between drinks and not someone my editor would have felt comfortable risking the paper's reputation on. And soon after I met him, the drink killed him. So that was that you might say. My Boss smiled, aware that he'd no right now to keep me on tenterhooks.

Most newspapers do charity work as well, you know. It's not just the politicians and their wives. My old paper back in the Fifties used to have a big thing for reformed alcoholics, particularly ex-servicemen. There were a lot of them on the street at that time. Not being able to find a place in Civvy Street. I was up in Glasgow at a home we were supporting. I met one of their residents, an old-time Scottish Commie who'd been a docker before the War. We were talking about this and that and he asked me whether I'd ever had a scoop. For some reason I mentioned Baxter as one that got away. You could say that, said the old docker, laughing loudly.

It turned out the docker had been in Spain in the International Brigades. He got there in the early days when it was all a bit rag-taggle. He was at the Front in a small group. Six Brits and a Greek Cypriot who'd joined them because he spoke English. They were looked after by a real soldier, a British Major who kept an eye on them from Brigade Headquarters.

They'd got to know each other quite well in the two weeks of makeshift training before they reached the Front. They'd even been allowed to fire off five or six rounds at tin-cans as target practice. Although most of the tin-cans survived.

In addition to the docker, there was a young lad from Battersea. He lived in one of those terraced houses down near the Power Station and had never left London in his life. His Dad had given him six packs of Woodbines as a parting gift. He was eking them out to remind himself of home. In complete contrast, there was a merchant-seaman who'd travelled the world and got drunk in every port. When there was no alcohol, he was fine. But show him a goatskin of red wine, or six bottles in a bodega, and you'd lost him for the rest of the day. There was a university lecturer who'd left his job to come to Spain. The

17

Party wanted to use his talents in the propaganda struggle, but he wanted to be at the Front. He always had a book in his pocket. He didn't say so himself, but the Major told them the lecturer had published an article in one of those thick monthlies, on Hegel and Marx, the Major said. There was also a real dopey lad who had a heart of gold and who loved animals. He was always looking after the mules. He used to carry a cigarette card in his wallet of some glamorous Spanish actress. He was always hoping he'd meet her when she turned up one day with the other celebrities visiting the Internationals. The Major had a look at the card and told them later that the actress was Mexican and in Hollywood. But he said it was better not to burst the lad's bubble. We all needed dreams to help us get by. There was also another dreamer, a political dreamer. A keen young bloke from Watford. He'd been a Party-member since before birth. He'd even sewed a red star on his beret. But you should have seen him when charging for an attack in the training, said the docker. Out to save World Socialism single-handed. Like a bloody whirlwind, he was. And then there was Panos, the Cypriot. His mother was a Greek from Rhodes. She had an Italian passport, he said, and she didn't know why he wanted to go to Spain. He was Baxter's No.2 on the machine gun. Oh yes, Baxter was there.

Last of all, there was the Major. The old docker got almost dewy-eyed when he talked of the Major. Always striding around with his shiny long boots and his swagger stick and his handsome young Spanish batman, a good-looking young man, all white teeth and hair oil. The Major was the son of an East End butcher, no better than the docker, but he'd got himself promoted from the ranks to be an Officer in the Great War, so he had what it took. And that was all that mattered to the docker or to the rest of them. They'd have followed the Major anywhere. In Spain, you see, they didn't care who you were or who you were pretending to be. They could forgive all that so long as you showed you had guts and judgement. You needed both to be of any real use there. The docker laughed as he described how the Major would order his batman to iron his newspaper for him, on the rare occasions he got one.

The Major knew what had happened, that Baxter had panicked and run when the Moors attacked, abandoning the machine-gun which would have soon jammed when the Cypriot tried to fire it on his own. They didn't have a hope then, against regular soldiers. The Major knew the docker was the only other one to get out alive. But neither of them had time to report it. They were both hit in the same artillery barrage the next day. The Major died instantly. The docker took six months to recover in hospital and could never go back to the Front. The Party weren't interested in his story. They didn't want a scandal. Cowardice wasn't the sort of story that would help them win wars.

Now you can see why I never got it published, said my Boss.

# 3 JOINING THE DANCE

The following year, it was Abigail's turn to host our reunion, eight former History students all now forty years adrift from our three years together at college. And this time we were in Abigail's small 1820s house in a side-street beside Richmond Green. She'd packed her husband and daughter off for the evening and was able to give us a guided tour of the ground-floor, for those who hadn't been there before. I particularly remember the tiny room she'd turned into her study. On one wall there were shelves of box-files. Some of my more interesting old casework, she said. On the other wall there was shelf upon shelf of cookery books, recipes from every country you could name.

How did you manage to grab this study for yourself, asked Harrington. Didn't your husband or your daughter want the space for themselves? Abigail smiled. It was my barrister's salary that bought us this house in the first place and I needed somewhere to work where I could sit up preparing my cases till two in the morning without disturbing the others. And yes, there's nothing like stopping to read a good cookery book to give you the strength to get that casework done.

The meal she served lived up to her reputation. A Sephardic chicken dish followed by pears stewed in Marsala. One of the best meals I'd ever eaten, let along one cooked by a Supreme Court Judge.

When we were all sitting in her living-room again with our coffees, Harrington piped up. Well, Abigail, that was delicious. I have no doubt the story you are about to tell us will be just as superb.

Oh, I'm not telling a story tonight, laughed Abigail. I am just the cook and bottle-washer. Rachel and I have already planned that she'll be the one with the entertainment. We turned to Rachel, some of us with slight disappointment, having been looking forward to some perfectly crafted plot from Abigail's brilliant mind.

I hope you'll all forgive me, said Rachel, I don't have Giles' journalist's gift for words or his story-telling skill. I've had to make a few notes, if that's alright. And she pulled a folded sheet of A4 from her handbag. I've always been better with pictures than words, so I've had to put down a few things to jog my memory and make sure I don't drift off-track. I'm going to tell you about something that happened to me thirty years ago. I don't know whether it would count as a ghost story but it's all I could think of that might interest you.

I really enjoyed reading History with you at college but, as you know, I changed direction when I graduated. I'd always been an amateur artist. (Giles and I both smiled, remembering the excellent watercolours Rachel had exhibited while still at college). I was never talented enough to be a professional, but I did want to work with my hands. After graduating, I was out of work for a year, just doing temping and other odd jobs, until I got a place on an Art Restoration scheme at a public Gallery. I was there five or six years and was very happy. I think I found my role as an art restorer. The research drew on my history training but I was working with my hands.

Things changed in my late twenties. My marriage broke up and I shan't bore those of you who don't know them with the details.

21

I was a bit wrecked and one of my friends said a new challenge would help me to get through it. So, I made the jump, left the Gallery and set up as a freelance restorer. The work wasn't well-paid or plentiful, but I did get a helpful six months as the assistant restorer on a project to restore the 15th century wood panel paintings of saints in a church in East Anglia. The paintings had been painted over at the Reformation and the saints had been lost under a new surface of severe Protestant texts, making the point, I suppose, that under Protestantism, the parishioners would be able to read and no longer needed pictures to help them get closer to God. I can't say I believed it myself. I don't think literacy levels had improved that much.

But I really enjoyed the work, using the x-ray images to decide what was underneath and then beginning the delicate process of trying to reveal the original painting without damaging it. And the work was a success. It went so well that we even got a long write-up with photos in one of the art magazines. I guess in those days I was more photogenic than my boss. His photo wasn't as prominent in the final article. It was me standing next to one of the restored panels with my name in the description. And it was that which got me my next job, in the Baltics.

For one of the newly independent States was looking for a restorer to do some work on one of its most famous religious paintings. It was a late 15th century Dance of Death by the Master of Hamburg. The painting, or series of paintings, had been taken to Moscow in the Soviet period and had been fully restored there. But it was thought that the paintings needed a closer look, a health-check you could say, and for understandable reasons this independent Baltic Republic didn't want anything to do with their old Russian masters. They'd latched onto me from the article they'd seen, even though this Dance of Death was painted on canvas and my published expertise was with wood panels. Perhaps they just missed that in the article. Anyway, I jumped at the chance and went. I was there for six months over one very magical Winter.

The paintings were in a beautiful, white-walled church in the old part of town. Walking to work from the small flat they found me was like walking through some old European fairy tale. Long icicles hanging from snow-covered rooves and the thick snow swept up into huge piles at the side of each pavement. In fact, the only downside for me were those pavements. I've been scared of ice since I was a child, when one of my friends slipped and broke her leg. Before I left England, a friend had bought me a pair of calf-length Swedish boots, thinking the Swedes would know about snow, and I used to progress slowly along the pavements sliding my feet in front of me, as if I were a trainee tight-rope walker setting out on her first trip across the Big Top. The locals used to glance at me and smile, but they seemed sympathetic and gave me the benefit of the doubt as a foreigner.

The church itself was freezing. There was heating but I used to keep my coat on when I was working and I was alright. It's always such a relief to be allowed to work on your own and to be your own boss. That makes up for so much. Obviously, it was still a newly independent country and you couldn't expect everything to be in place. For the first couple of weeks, the Institute I was working for couldn't get access to a working x-ray machine. I had to start just by observation which is not how we did it in East Anglia,

The Dance, as I say, was painted on a series of canvases, of which only the first few had survived. They showed devils leading mankind towards its inevitable end. A somewhat stately procession of emperors and kings, nobles and clergy, a text in Latin beneath each figure with a short dialogue between Death and each man or woman. Those paintings which hadn't survived would have taken us down through the social order to the peasant working on the land. But all we had were the upper classes.

What struck me immediately was the painting of a priest. It just didn't look right. It didn't seem to fit naturally into the composition and there was no Latin text beneath his feet. He seemed to have missed out on his own dialogue with Death. Unlike the other figures, he hadn't had the chance to express himself. And unlike the others, he lacked their patient resignation. In fact, his face was turned outwards towards me with a look of despair. It was particularly haunting in the afternoons when the natural light was fading and the church would come alive with the subdued shuffling sound as if the mice in the woodwork had decided it might be safe to come out for the night.

The second week I was there, I started to pore over the surface of the paintings with a magnifying-glass, to learn what I could about the visible surface of the brushwork while waiting for the x-ray machine to become available. To tell you the truth, I didn't learn a great deal, but that might have been due to my lack of expertise rather than anything else. The one breakthrough I made was on the unhappy priest. I could see with the magnifying-glass that there was a line of some later over-painting (18th century perhaps) round his wrists and leading to the hand of the smiling devil in front of him. The more I looked at it, the more I came to the conclusion that, beneath this over-painting, his hands were tied and that, unlike the others, he was being dragged along by the devils.

I put this to my project supervisor at the Institute at one of the weekly meetings I had with him each Friday. He was a middle-aged man, always wearing the same dark-grey suit and very old black shoes. He looked as though he'd spent long years in the Soviet system learning how to keep his head down. But he was very helpful and friendly, and I think he understood English much better than he would let on. He always claimed that Russian was his only foreign language and we'd be joined at our meetings by Lia, one of his assistants, who would act as interpreter. She was in her early twenties and all the men in the Institute went crazy over her long legs, her smile and her short, boyish blonde hair. All the men apart from my supervisor, I should say. The two of them clearly got on well but it was like being with a loving father and his daughter. I used to enjoy our Friday meetings.

I made my points about the priest, about the 18th century over-painting and what looked like the rope beneath it. The supervisor didn't dismiss it but, quite rightly, he decided that we should await the x-ray results before deciding what to do next. It took another week for the x-ray machine to become available. Until then, there wasn't much more I could do but pore over the surface of the paintings with a magnifying-glass before standing back to look at the whole composition of each painting from a distance. I never tired of doing that. The paintings were so gorgeous that I had to keep pinching myself to make sure it was real, this privileged job of mine. Only the mice would get on my nerves in the late afternoons as they started their shuffling. But on two or three evenings, Lia put her head round the door unannounced and took me off to tour the small bars and restaurants with her old student friends.

The x-rays when they came were a revelation. The one really interesting point was the priest. I had been right about the rope. It was later over-painting to hide the fact that he was being dragged along by a devil. But the real revelation, which I could never have got with the magnifying-glass, was that the priest too was a later addition. The x-rays clearly showed the grass and bushes of the green landscape on the original layer of paint. For some reason, he had been added on top of them as an afterthought. We would need to analyze the pigments to find when the priest had been added.

My supervisor was happy for that to go ahead and the results came back suggesting that the priest had been added in the late 16th century, around a hundred years after the Dance had been painted. The question was what we should do next. I set out my case for full restoration, removing the priest and returning the painting to its original late 15th century state. My supervisor could see the logic of that as my arguments were carefully translated for him by Lia at one of our Friday meetings, but it was not something I could expect him to decide himself. It would have to go to the Minister of Culture. He would discuss it with the Minister and arrange for all three of us to go and meet him, so I could present my arguments.

I remember vividly the brilliant blue cold bright morning when Lia picked me up at my flat to walk with me to the Ministry. As befits a Ministry of Culture, it was in a beautiful and large

19th century wooden house of the kind you can still see in photographs of Siberian cities like Krasnoyarsk, the kind that have lop-sided wooden fences around them. Here, though, they'd taken the old fences down and made an open space which in Summer would have been cleanly-swept cobbles. But now, in Winter the whole expanse was three feet deep in shovelled snow. All that was left was the flag-stoned path, thirty yards long, leading to the Institute's door, a path which I could see was covered in a horrific layer of sheet ice.

Lia saw me hesitate and laughed. We have a saying, she said, a proverb. When the ice is thick, you have to dance. I must have looked dumb-struck, dancing on ice having a somewhat different meaning in English.

Watch, said Lia, and she quickly hopped, skipped and danced her way to the Ministry door, swinging round to smile back at me. See, she called. She then repeated the performance, sliding the last few yards, bumping into me, hugging me tightly and spinning us both round to stop us falling. Come on, she said, now we'll do it together.

She slipped her arm through mine and led me out onto the icy path. I was terrified but I could feel her strength and confidence begin to surge through me as she held me firmly, pulling us out to dance our way the thirty yards to the door. When we stopped at the steps to the entrance, I was utterly drained but elated.

The meeting with the Minister was not so exciting. We sat at a long table in his office with views down towards the Baltic. I remember a line of those Soviet-style bottles of mineral water, the ones with strange-looking pond stuff floating in the bottom. I always did my best to be polite, but I always tried to avoid the mineral water if I could. And, if not, I'd just take a few sips from my glass, so as not to disturb what was at the bottom. I made my arguments in favour of verisimilitude with Lia heroically translating. But I think it would have just been a step too far for a newly independent State to risk 'ruining' one of their significant works of art. They'd be cautious about laying themselves open to Russian charges of ineptitude.

The Minister was very kind and complimentary about my work. Perhaps as an olive branch, he said we should have a word on the way out with his assistant who would arrange us a meeting with the Head of the National Archives. The latter had been briefed about the addition of the priest and was intrigued by it.

A week later, Lia and I found ourselves in a small room in the Old Library with another friendly but slightly older middle-aged man in another grey suit. He asked me to repeat what he'd already heard, just to be sure of it. He sat there nodding as Lia interpreted my account. When I'd finished, he took a long drink of his mineral water, bottom and all, and said he'd like to tell us a story. He didn't know if it was relevant to our discovery but that we might be interested to hear it nonetheless.

In short, the Master of Hamburg's Dance had only survived at all because of the brave actions of one man. In the Reformation when the Protestant iconoclasts (if that's the right word) were vandalising the former Catholic churches, tearing the religious art from their walls and destroying it, the mob here had been frustrated by the priest of the church where I was working. To stop the mob from entering, he had locked himself inside the church and poured molten lead into the locks. By the time they arrived, they couldn't get in and, with other churches to wreck, they moved on. After a few days, the mob's passion had subsided, as one usually finds with mobs. Friends of the priest tried to rouse him but, getting no answer from inside the church, they had to organize fifteen strong men with a stout oak beam to use as a battering-ram to smash in the church door. Inside, they found the triumphs of medieval art still intact and the Death unscarred in its place on the walls. The priest, however, was a broken man. He was sitting by the altar, his head in his hands, rocking backwards and forwards mumbling something about being dragged against his will into the dance.

And that's how he remained for the forty years until he died. He was well looked-after with a small room in a townhouse in the Old City, with board and lodging and care provided by its grateful townspeople who now valued the Art they had tried to destroy. But he never regained his sanity. He just kept

27

rambling about being dragged into the dance against his will. I have no explanation, said the Head of the National Archives, for who might have painted him into the Dance by the Master of Hamburg. Nor can I say when it was done. But you say the science points to the late 16th century.

Rachel paused and put down her page of notes. I must confess I have always been sad that I couldn't get them to agree to remove the priest from the Dance of Death. He was a brave man and he never deserved to belong there. I suppose all one can say is that the dead or the devils are neither grateful nor forgiving.

The only thing I should add is something that happened later in my time there. It's no secret to tell you that Lia and I became inseparable while I was there. I don't think I had ever been that happy before. It was certainly the turning-point in my life. She took me once to see her perform with a national dance troupe. Dancing was her great hobby. I remember when the line of young women came out onto the stage, all in long brightly coloured national dress and white fur hats, Lia the third in the line, looking for all the world like some perfect but benign Snow Queen from the fairy tales. What struck me was not the costumes nor even Lia's smile. It was the shuffling noise their feet made as they came out onto the stage when they were ready to begin their dance.

# 4 GHOSTS IN THE MACHINE

I don't have a ghost story to tell you, I'm afraid, said Harrington. Cathedrals and haunted medieval paintings are not really my sort of thing. I enjoyed the three years I spent studying History with you all at college but, since then, I've had my feet firmly on the ground in the real world, running flat out most of the time. If you want to stay at the top in Business, you have no other choice.

Is it true, interrupted Richard suppressing a smile, that you made your first killing a year after college when you bought a tanker of frozen orange pulp while it was sailing from Latin America to Europe, and that you sold it on for vast profit before it docked?

Come now, Richard, said Abigail, let Harrington get on with his story.

That's right, Richard, said Harrington. For once suppress your VSO background. We know you're a teacher and a Liberal Democrat Councilor, but it's firms like mine that bring in the money to yield the tax to fund the NHS.

Gentlemen! said Abigail.

Thank you, Abigail, I'll continue, said Harrington, straightening his tie.

As I say, this is not a ghost story, but it was terrifying while it lasted and we in the firm never got to the bottom of it. It was shortly after we moved into our new London offices. You probably read the coverage when we moved in early last year. It was very high-profile. The architect won an award for the design and we were shown to be in the front rank as regards providing facilities for our staff, in-house creches, clinics. We also got a lot of praise for our work to help the local community by creating a public park, a rose garden beside our building. Think how much that land is worth where we are in the City!

I read somewhere, said Richard, that the rose garden is on top of an old cemetery and that was why you couldn't build on it.

Quiet, Richard, we all chimed in. Let Harrington tell his story.

And it was not just the rose garden, said Harrington. We agreed to stop the development project for six months to allow London University to carry out a complete archaeological rescue dig before we started on the foundations. In effect, they were digging with our firm's money and everything they found has gone to the Museum of London.

Harrington paused to take a sip of his after-dinner malt whisky. Working on our HQ site, they found the corner of a Roman bathhouse with one good geometric mosaic as well as a Roman coin hoard which was probably buried there in the late 4th century, long after the bathhouse had fallen into disuse. And then, of course, there was the usual range of burials under the rose garden site. One of them, though was out of the ordinary. It was a mass grave of jumbled bones. They identified at least eight skeletons, all men, which they dated to 1600-1700, but the skeletons, as well as being jumbled were incomplete. They'd also died by violence. There were so many knife-cuts that one of the archaeologists described them as "butchered bones". Unidentified casualties from the English Civil War. The

Bishop of London led a small religious service when the bodies were re-interred.

But that's not what my story is about. I should say here that what I am going to tell you is not common knowledge and I'd be grateful if you would keep it within these four walls.

Even Abigail had to suppress a smile at this. We'd always liked Harrington and we'd known at college that you just had to aim off for his pomposity.

My story, said Harrington, is about cyber-crime. In fact, it's about one of the most sustained and determined attacks my firm has ever experienced. And not just my firm. It went far wider in the City than just us.

It started on a Sunday. I was Head of Research at the time. For us, Research is a loose term which covers a lot of territory; Due Diligence, Commercial Intelligence, Strategic Risk Assessment, all that and more. Anyway, it was our Cyber Security people who rang me up. The Board wanted me and some of the other Division Heads in immediately with no reasons given over the phone.

There were about a dozen of us around the President's long table, all wearing our casual clothes. We'd all dropped everything to get there. Jennifer, the Chief Finance Director, had her two-year old on her lap. Our creche doesn't open on Sundays. Those who'd already been briefed looked ashen and that helped brace the rest of us for what was to come. Jennifer's 2-year-old was the only one who looked cheerful as he sucked at his organic rusk. The President turned the meeting over straight away to the Head of the Cyber Team.

In short, said our Cyber expert, over the last three hours we've been subjected to a lightning storm of sophisticated, varied and fast-moving attacks. They are ongoing. At first, we thought it was a case of malfunctioning algorithms, but after the first few minutes we realized we had a much bigger problem. These were malware attacks and of a sustained intensity and range that neither I nor any of my team have ever seen. Whoever it is has been deploying the works against us. Trojan horses, root kits, key loggers, man-in-the-browser, botnet attacks, phishing and ransomware but without anyone asking for the ransom. We've been countering with the machine learning algorithms we have. Some of the attacks have used server-side polymorphism.

What does this all mean in layman's language, asked the President?

I can best describe these attacks, said our Cyber expert, as a huge tidal surge trying to smash through our dams to destroy us. Our counter measures are like having 30,000 small Dutch boys out there, each one of them with his finger in a hole in the dam. We are just about surviving.

And who have you spoken to outside, asked the President? Are we in this alone?

I've spoken to the National Cyber Security Agency (NACSA). They are giving us all the help they can, but they are being very tight-lipped about the extent of these attacks.

I think that's one for you, said the President, turning to me. Can you get that man in your Due Diligence team to talk to his old friends? It would be useful to know if our competitors are up against the wall as well. And who does the government think is attacking us, criminals or State actors?

The rest of the meeting was taken up with planning for what I might call a Doomsday Scenario. We agreed on the work we all had to do overnight to be ready to brief our clients and chief investors when, as seemed possible, the malware attackers released all their data and corrupted and distorted all their and our financial transactions. What on Earth would we be able to say to them?

But by nightfall, the Cyber Team were reporting a falling away in the attacks. It was as though the black hat attackers, whoever they were, had decided to leave us in peace. Indeed, nothing happened to us for the next few days. The one event, so to speak, was a Police raid on the office of a National Trust property North of Hampstead to confiscate their computers, following a tip-off from GCHQ. The Police went in mob-handed with armed officers and dog teams which proved to me that the malware attacks had been directed at significant infrastructure targets, not just us. The Police raid must have shocked or intrigued all the old age pensioners on their day out in that National Trust tea-room.

The range of the Sunday attacks was confirmed by my colleague in Due Diligence. He was ex Intelligence Service and recruited for his ability to plug into his old contacts when we needed it. He was a rather austere fellow. A man of few words with me. But people who'd worked closely with him said he did have a sense of humour. It was all a question of whether he trusted you and your ability to deliver, they said. Anyway, he earned his money on the Monday. The Sunday attacks had apparently hit all our main competitors in the City, as well as the Stock Exchange and other financial institutions. The Bank of England had also come under sustained attack, but its defences were more robust than any of ours.

And so there we were, licking our wounds, counting our blessings and very thankful we had not had to go into the Doomsday briefings for our clients and investors. It would have been the end of us if we had. No more in-house creches, clinics or Christmas bonuses. Nothing at all, in fact.

Which is why we felt it even harder when the full force of the second wave of malware attacks hit us on the Wednesday morning. And this time round, I confess that some of our little Dutch boys were blown back from the dam by the full force of the water. Our Investment and Lending arm was particularly badly hit. The malware began to trigger false transactions with massive sums being chalked up to client accounts. Personal financial data of key investors began to disappear from our screens and we had no idea where it had gone. The strange thing, which made it even worse, I guess, was that we didn't receive a single ransomware demand for payment. If we'd had a demand for £6,000,000 in Bitcoin, then we would have at least known that there was a way out if we'd had to take it. But we were being subjected to ruthless and determined attacks in complete silence.

The President was supportive in a grim-faced way and showed the right signs of leadership, but even he was getting fairly terse down the phone to the Head of the Cyber Team and to me and the Due Diligence Team. Things became worse mid-morning when the Cyber Team revealed that some of the attacks were being launched from the Chief Finance Director's personal lap-top and we had to suspend her and ask her to leave the building just to be on the safe side.

My Due Diligence guy was reporting that our competitors and some of the financial institutions were also in meltdown. The Stock Exchange was paralysed by rogue transactions. Small investors with a £2,000 portfolio of investments in a couple of FTSE 100 firms were now bidding to buy 30% of the shares of major Oil Companies, and their bids were being approved. The Stock Exchange had no choice but to cease all trading for the day. You probably remember that and the "software failure" it was ascribed to in the Media.

And this time round the Bank of England was also suffering. Four members of the Bank's Prudential Regulation Committee had resigned, run away more like it, by lunchtime. They didn't know what to do in these unexpected circumstances and they just couldn't take the pressure. Luckily for the Bank, there was a woman on the Committee who'd worked for a few years as a mental health nurse before she qualified as a Chartered Accountant and ended up in banking. She had more experience of the real world and had the grit to hold the rest of the Committee together.

The one positive thing my Due Diligence guy was picking up was that the attacks were confined to Britain and to London.

However, we could see the extreme level of the Wednesday attacks and the threat the City was under by the surge of support we were getting from NACSA. GCHQ had clearly pulled out all the stops and had also taken all the help they could from their foreign partners. Late on Wednesday evening our Cyber Team were delivered a fix by NACSA. We didn't know whether it came from GCHQ directly, from the Americans, from other partners or, indeed, from some reformed former black hat hacker sitting in his bedroom in Barnsley. Wherever it came from, it put an end to these sustained and determined malware attacks.

We were able to pick up the broken pieces, repair the damage, brief our clients and customers as necessary and breathe a great sigh of relief. We learnt afterwards, through my Due Diligence guy's contacts, that the City of London had only survived as an ongoing concern due to the vintage of the malware attacks. They were all based on malware that had been developed a year before and were thus fixable. The reason they nearly destroyed us was the determination and sheer ruthless way in which they were deployed. And the supreme manoeuvrability of those carrying out the attacks. GCHQ apparently described the attacks as "wildfire". They had never seen attacks carried out with such rigour and without any apparent aim other than to destroy. No ransom was ever requested and no perpetrator was ever identified. All in all, we were lucky to get through it.

So not a ghost story as such, said Harrington, more a tale of ghosts in the machine. But I should be very grateful if you wouldn't pass it on. We need to keep up the reputation of the City of London more than ever now, if Britain is going to continue to generate the income it needs to pay for our Health and Schools and other Social Services.

We sat there in silence for a while until Richard lent forward from the sofa where he was sitting.

Your new building, he said, it's in Upper Thames Street, isn't it? I was thinking of your dead bodies, your "butchered bones" in the rose garden.

Oh, come on, said Harrington, we are talking about malware not 17th century skeletons.

Well, said Richard, it's just that your rose garden is on the site of the old churchyard of All Hallows the Great, long since

35

demolished. And I was thinking of Cromwell's head.

Cromwell's head? said Abigail.

Yes, he was dug up at the Restoration when he and other Roundheads had their corpses hung, drawn and quartered and their skulls put up on display. It took a long time but eventually Cromwell's skull found its way home to his friends at his old Cambridge college, where it remains today safely buried, held securely and respected. I was thinking of this because All Hallows was one of the main churches used by the Fifth Monarchists.

I can see you never went to Professor Wilkinson's lectures when you were at college, said Richard, looking at Harrington's expression of bewilderment. I know Wilkinson was viewed as an eccentric but his lectures on the radical religious groups of the 1650s were a highlight for me. The Ranters, the Baptists, the Quakers, the Muggletonians, the Fifth Monarchists, some of whom survive today albeit in different forms.

I liked Professor Wilkinson, said Richard. At a time when everyone was starting to see history through modern eyes, 'The Diggers as Proto-Marxists', 'The Socio-economic Factors behind the English Civil War', Wilkinson stuck to the old belief that "the past was another country". If you wanted to understand the Ranters or the Fifth Monarchists, then you had to put yourself in their shoes and see things through their eyes, not ours.

And the Fifth Monarchists, of course, were the ones who took their millenarian radicalism to the most extreme. One of their leading figures, Major General Thomas Harrison, who had a house in Highgate, was hung, drawn and quartered alive at the Restoration, as a regicide. Which was why, on a Sunday in January 1661, 40 or 50 Fifth Monarchists, led by a wine-cooper called Thomas Venner, put on their helmets and breastplates and picked up their swords in a chapel in the City of London and stormed out to capture St Paul's Cathedral, to destroy the existing order and to pave the way for the Fifth Monarchy when Jesus would come down to rule on earth.

Under a banner with the motto, "The Quarters Upon the Gates" in memory of Harrison and the other Roundheads, the Fifth Monarchists fought off an attack by the Trained Bands (I suppose the Police you'd call it in modern language), before retiring North during the night to bivouac up in in Ken Wood. They stayed up there for a couple of days before storming back into the City of London on the Wednesday morning. And this time it was all-out war. Contemporary witnesses describe the Fifth Monarchists as well-armed, well-disciplined and manoeuvring around the City with great rapidity "like wildfire".

They first appeared in Threadneedle Street where they routed the Trained Bands on guard there. They then made their way via College Hill and Cheapside to Wood Street where they repulsed an attack by King Charles II's Life Guards. "It is Jesus who leads us," shouted Thomas Venner.

But under continued attacks by the Life Guards and Trained Bands, the Fifth Monarchists had to fall back. Small groups of them then held out for as long as they could in buildings in the City. About ten of them made their last stand in The Blue Anchor Inn near the Postern. The Life Guards had to climb up the neighbouring building and tear off the tiles from the Inn roof so they could fire down on them. The Fifth Monarchists fought to the death. They were offered quarter but refused it. The only ones who were taken alive were those who were too badly wounded to stand.

The survivors were tried and the majority, sixteen of them, sentenced to be hung, drawn and quartered. Only three sought for mercy. The rest were drawn on hurdles to Tyburn, which was just as well since they too badly wounded to stand. Venner's deputy, Roger Hodgkins, a button-seller, called down vengeance from Heaven on the Crown, the judges and the City of London as he was dragged away to be hung and quartered. Like Cromwell, their heads and quartered bodies were put up on display as a warning.

I just wonder, said Richard, whether it was like Cromwell's skull. Did the Fifth Monarchists' supporters manage to collect some of those butchered bones and inter them in their churchyard at All Hallows?  I know this is all just coincidence and I am not suggesting anything more than that.  But if you were a Fifth Monarchist now, who would you attack?  The Crown and the judges no longer preserve their same influence.  And you wouldn't go looking for a seat of power in our current government, would you?  But the City of London, the financial institutions and the multinational finance companies based there, well that might be something of interest to the Fifth Monarchists if they still wanted to overturn the existing order.

But where, in Hell's name, would the Fifth Monarchists have discovered malware, expostulated Harrison.

Perhaps in Hell, I said.  If you'd spent 350 years in Heaven, it must get pretty boring, just that ethereal music over the tannoy all day.  You'd speak to newcomers, find out what had been going on in the world, learn what you could.  And in Hell, too, I am sure there'd be a small, determined group of resisters who would club together despite the torture to share the latest knowledge in making their plans to escape.  And if anyone did have the sheer determination needed to escape from Hell then, from what Richard's been saying, I guess the Fifth Monarchists would be top of the list.

# 5 MR WESTGROVE

Our reunion dinner the following year found us in the small dining-room of a Derbyshire rectory. Stephen was the vicar there and he'd invited us all to stay for the weekend. We'd arrived in dribs and drabs from Friday night to Saturday morning, depending on how important we were or on how much we wanted to get away. We'd been treated to a guided tour of the plague village of Eyam and then of Little John's grave (for the Robin Hood enthusiasts), while the more adventurous amongst us had followed Stephen on a quick scramble on the Dales to end up on a high, scarred hillside where we'd walked over and admired a depression in the barren ground which could well have been the remains of an old Roman quarry. We'd already had more fresh air than most of us got in a month.

The Roman quarry had been the best part for me. Standing high-up on that bare hillside, imagining how very bleak it would be in the wind and rain, it was a rare chance to be where Nature was once again elemental, to be back in a world that had been home to our ancestors. A world of hillforts and trackways and clean open air. A place of hard living where few would have survived beyond their thirties.

Not a problem that we'd had to face that weekend. Stephen's wife, Claire, had cooked us a huge pot of cassoulet, followed by pear tart and cream. With the bottles of red wine all drunk, we felt quite smug and at peace with the world as we sat round the table with our coffees and Armagnac.

I imagine that you think because I'm a clergyman, said Stephen, that I'll have some special insight to offer you on the spiritual world, that it's a small step from administering to people's souls to their demons and that I must have travelled in a world where you have never been. Sadly, I must confess that I have never seen a ghost or a spirit or a demon. I was once asked to perform an exorcism but, luckily for me, it coincided with my move to another parish and I escaped having to perform a service that would have been difficult for me to carry out with conviction. It fell to my successor to make that leap back to the Middle Ages and I can't say I'm sorry that I missed it.

But that exorcism does take me back to the story I shall tell you. For although I do not believe in ghosts, I once knew a man who had met them, indeed had made a study of them. He was a man I much admired in a strange sort of way. I suppose you could say the exorcism was for him and, had I been forced to carry it out, I would have done so and would have put the best face on it that I could, for his sake and in his memory.

I was still single when I was first ordained and my dream was to be sent to an inner-city Mission, somewhere where I could roll up my sleeves and try to help where that help was truly needed. It was a shock, therefore, when they sent me to a parish in Surrey. It seemed an odd choice for them to make. You'd have thought they'd have sent someone with a family. But it was to a small stockbroker town I was sent, a town beneath the North Downs and still surrounded by green fields. A town for commuters, but where the locals could still remember when there had been a dairy farm by the church and when the cows were driven through the town twice a day on their way to the fields and back again. A practice that had been stopped because of complaints by the new commuter generation who objected to the halting of traffic and to the cowpats on the tarmac.

40

I threw myself at this respectable safe Home Counties parish as though it had been a deprived area in an inner city or a disaster zone in the Third World. But there were no immediate problems to tackle, no mountain that had to be climbed. It was more a question of a daily and weekly routine, punctuated every so often by the death of an elderly resident or the sickness of a child. I think they must have been puzzled in those first few months as I rushed around like some sort of latter-day crusader. But I am sure they just shook their heads and smiled and waited for the slow pace of their world to subsume me.

It was only after those first few months that I got to know Mr Westgrove. He was a milkman and much-liked not just for his cheerfulness but for his side-line. For what marked him out from his colleagues was not just that he was still unmarried in his late fifties, but the brass plaque fixed to the gatepost of his cottage. A plaque which was lovingly polished by Mr Westgrove himself and which read, 'W.H.Westgrove, HERBALIST, Pneumatoid Arthritis and Rheumatism cured, Mon & Thurs, 6.30-8.30pm.' I remember mentioning this to the town doctor who, surprisingly, spoke highly of Mr Westgrove.

Oh, Mr Westgrove is very useful to me, said the doctor. He is a good herbalist. There's no quackery or black magic about him. Everything he knows comes from Gerrard and Culpeper. He's a sympathetic listener and his cures do help people. He charges next to nothing and they love him for it. But he's also a good psychologist. He knows when to give the hypochondriacs some plain syrup to calm them. And he can also tell when his patients have something seriously wrong, which is when he'll pass them on to me, whatever their hang-ups about doctors and hospitals. Just as I'll pass them to you, Vicar, when there's nothing more that science can do. Mr Westgrove's a great help to me. He frees up my Surgery from the worriers with nothing wrong and from those with the minor ailments that he and Culpeper can cure. He's also very well-read, said the doctor, and a demon at Scrabble.

Which is how I got to know Mr Westgrove who invited me round one Friday evening to play Scrabble after I'd consulted him with an old knee injury from college rugby. He'd prescribed me chamomile flower oil and it worked, and he laughed when I'd looked so surprised.

Mr Westgrove was a very methodical man. Every Friday evening, he'd record the scores of our games in a special notebook and it was he who always won. He had all the herbalist's vocabulary from Culpeper which I'd never heard of, words such as lohoch and electuary. But the main reason was that he was just phenomenally well-read. Those were the days when small Public Libraries were heaving with books and when you could fill out a form and order what they didn't have from some central store. Mr Westgrove had been a regular at the library with his orders every Saturday morning and his knowledge was much broader and usually much deeper than mine.

He seemed never happier than when talking about herbalism. Culpeper is my Bible, he said, even if I don't share his belief that it's the individual planets which govern all plants. I'll just skip the bit on 'government', Venus, Mercury and the like, and move straight to where Culpeper describes the 'virtues' of a plant. And, like Culpeper, I follow Dr Reason and Dr Experience. I make notes of all the treatments I use and of the results. You have to be guided by reason and learn from experience. That applies to herbalism as much as to anything else in life.

His cottage garden was full of his useful plants. Even the damask roses, he explained, had their medicinal properties. His one regret with sticking to useful plants was that he'd never grown chrysanthemums, one of his late mother's favourites. He'd grow them when he retired, he said. Though it wasn't clear whether he meant as a milkman or a herbalist.

So the two of us muddled along quite well together with our Friday Scrabble sessions, drawn together by the fact that we didn't quite fit in that pleasant commuter town. Both of us were respected in the community but both of us were fish-out-of-water, single without family. And both of us had our baggage-train of learning to drag behind us, Mr Westgrove's perhaps more useful than mine.

And I would never have guessed there was another side to Mr Westgrove had I not mentioned, one Friday evening, that I'd heard a local rumour about a ghost that was said to haunt the lane out of town towards the dairy farm where he worked. He smiled as I described the place where the lane ran past the last houses and then crossed the stream before running uphill for a hundred yards through a sort of shaded hollow, high banks of earth on each side, tall trees growing on them, their branches reaching out to form a canopy over the road. An unusual and gloomy place where the trapped cold air hit your face with a sudden chill. On one side, there were rhododendrons clinging to the steep bank. On the other, there was a mass of huge, exposed tree roots, gnarled and worn and scarred, from the tall trees that covered the lane. More than once, I'd been told, cars at night had crashed into those huge bare roots, swerving, their drivers claimed, to avoid a woman in the road. Although my own view was that it was probably due to the alcohol, given that they were driving home from the Pub out past the fields.

Oh, the headless woman, snorted Mr Westgrove. And will you meet anyone who's actually seen her? No you won't. And I've always wondered what they are supposed to do with their heads, those headless ghosts. I mean, take this woman, has she got a head? Has she mislaid it somewhere? If she's got a head, what does she do with it? Carry it tucked under one arm, hold it up repeatedly like some footballer brandishing a trophy, or does she walk towards you holding it in her outstretched hands beseeching you to kiss its lips? The whole thing's just ridiculous.

I can see you don't believe in ghosts, I said.

On the contrary, said Mr Westgrove, I have seen hundreds of them. I have had a lifetime's experience recording each encounter and analysing them, which is why I feel so strongly when the ignorant prattle on about this so-called headless woman. Only the ignorant would ever assume that ghosts were terrifying or threatening. How many times have you met a mad axeman, Vicar? Why should ghosts be any different?

Seeing me sitting there speechless, Mr Westgrove smiled and went over to the sideboard. He opened the wooden doors and took out a pile of solid black ring-binders. My 'ledgers', he said.

Opening Volume One, he described for me his first meeting with ghosts. It was late one Sunday evening, he said. I was out in the Bluebell Woods, searching for figwort. The dog-walkers had all gone home and I had the woods to myself, or so I thought. I was working my way slowly through the trees when I became aware of them. A feeble grey crowd of wraiths, softly keening to themselves, desperate and dithering, wanting to approach me but too afraid to do so, as forlorn and empty as they had been in life, like a wet mist or a damp cloth on your face, beseeching me with their greyness, as if failure was at any time attractive. I could see they were harmless, so I walked right through them. They parted for me like a flock of sheep in a rain-soaked field. That's ghosts, I thought to myself.

Over the months that followed, Mr Westgrove took me through his 'ledgers'. He'd made a study of ghosts, was an expert in the field and was proud of it. He had a gift, it seemed, for noticing them, for observing what most of us could not see. With the passing of the years, he'd acquired quite a knowledge of them. He knew their ways and their limitations. They weren't all as timid and feeble as that first crowd he'd met in the wood. Some of them were like robins when you're digging in the garden. They'd come right up to you, glad of your company. Then, of course, there were the haughty ones, stand-offish and arrogant, expecting you to approach them, with the requisite awe and humility, as if they were film stars you might see in the street and go up to, ever so politely, for their autograph.

We're in the same line of business, he joked, the spiritual. But then this talent of mine to spot ghosts has never done me any good, not like my knowledge of herbs and simples. No, the ghosts are just a hobby. I record what I've seen in the same way some men stand on the platform at Clapham Junction Station trainspotting, writing down the numbers of railway carriages. I write down what I've seen but I don't suppose my ledgers would be of any use to anyone when I'm dead.

I asked him once what he'd learned from these ghosts. Nothing, he replied. They never speak. They are just there in the background, some of them whining. It seems very prosaic really, the world of ghosts. But then I've been reading Swedenborg recently. Do you know his first contact with the other world, with angels and the like, was when he saw a man sitting in the corner of a tavern dining-room? The man suddenly turned to Swedenborg and told him not to eat too much. The man turned out to be Christ, apparently, and it was Swedenborg's first brush with the unknown. You can't get much more matter of fact than that. Tell that to these people here with their melodramatic headless woman.

I must admit I tended not to press Mr Westgrove on his experiences with ghosts. I liked him and I got on with him and I enjoyed his company over Friday Scrabble. As I say, he was well-read and interesting. I guess all of us know friends who have a quirk of some sort. You just skirt round it. And it was not as though Mr Westgrove would raise it himself. He'd seen ghosts, he'd known them and, although he recorded his knowledge, I think he found them pretty boring. There was nothing about them to interest him as there was with herbalism. They weren't useful in any way.

And so it was not ghosts I thought of a year later when I first noted a change in Mr Westgrove. He was clearly not well. He seemed to be nervous and easily distracted. He still won every game at Scrabble but when he concentrated on reaching a high-score square, it would be with a word like 'fraught' or 'uncertain'. Gone were the days of the Culpeper vocabulary. I wondered at this but then Dr Reason told me that this was Scrabble not a Ouija board. Mr Westgrove was choosing the words. They weren't messages from some other world.

I raised my worries with the doctor. I remember waiting in his Surgery for the last patient to leave. It was a deliberately cheerful room with a sunlit oil-painting of an English holiday beach scene on one wall and brightly coloured copies of *The Huckleberry Hound Comic* and *Look and Learn* magazine on the coffee-table to help keep the children's minds off their illnesses or their treatment. The doctor nodded when I described Mr Westgrove's symptoms, but he said he'd examined him and that there was nothing wrong with his heart that he could see. He wondered whether it was anxiety, some external worry that was inducing these 'symptoms', but then Mr Westgrove had always been too practical. He was not someone who would worry himself into an early grave.

I must admit I was still worried and, when I got the chance, I had a quiet word with the manager of the Dairy. He agreed he'd noticed a change in Mr Westgrove. He was uncharacteristically jumpy. He'd take things the wrong way. He'd never snapped at his colleagues before. He'd arrive back at the Dairy in a cold sweat, grey in the face. They all wondered if he had heart problems.

I was wondering how I might raise my concerns as tactfully as I could when Mr Westgrove himself touched on his problems at one of our Friday evening sessions. He looked up from the Scrabble board and asked me, out of the blue, whether I had ever had doubts in my faith. Did I ever fear that I might have got it all wrong, that my beliefs had been misguided or false?

It was a rhetorical question because he carried on without waiting for me to reply. He was in his late fifties, he said, and he was wondering for the first time in his life whether he might have missed something in how he saw the world and understood it. He was wondering if there was something blindingly obvious that might have escaped him. You build up a body of knowledge, he said, based on your experience. The more you know, the more you understand. At least, that's how it had always seemed to him. But there were times, he added, when you could sense that something was coming, something which you would have to face on your own, as you did with all the big things in life.

I didn't know whether he was talking about his herbalism or his 'ledgers', his encounters with ghosts. In either case, I didn't know what to say. How can anyone in their mid-twenties talk about Life with a capital 'L' without sounding pompous? So I turned the question back on him by asking what Culpeper would have said.

Mr Westgrove looked at me sadly. I don't think Culpeper ever reached the point where Dr Experience outstripped Dr Reason, he said. I don't know how to explain it, he added. It's as though there is a great weight bearing down on me. The pressure leaves me short of breath and anxious. It's as though something malign is sucking the oxygen from my lungs, something evil that's determined to leave me lifeless.

I made all the sympathetic noises about overwork and stress and the need for a holiday. He'd never mentioned that he'd ever had one. He nodded and smiled but I could see that he wasn't really listening, that his mind was far away.

The following week I tried to find out what I could about the headless woman in the lane to the Dairy, in the gloomy stretch between the high banks which Mr Westgrove would have to pass twice a day. I spoke to a lot of the older people but all I got was the same gossip. A headless woman that haunted the hollowed lane, causing accidents through her malevolence. Some said that she'd been murdered there several centuries before, but no-one knew the detail or could explain how she'd lost her head. Just as no-one I spoke to had ever seen her, though they all claimed they knew someone who had.

I then tried the library to see if any folktale had been recorded. I should tell you that the assistant librarian there was a beautiful young woman with long brown hair. She had a gorgeous figure. 'Willowy' is the word, I guess. I remember her to this day.

Stephen glanced across at his wife, Claire, and grinned.

It's where Stephen and I first met, she said smiling. We have poor Mr Westgrove to thank for that. I and my colleagues tried to discover something about the headless woman, something that might help. The senior librarian remembered having seen a reference to her in a self-published pamphlet that had come out thirty or forty years before. The pamphlet, by an amateur local historian, long-since deceased, had referred to an earlier book on Surrey folklore. We found that book but there was no reference to the headless woman. We never tracked down a copy of the pamphlet. That's the problem with the self-published ones. They are a labour of love, vanity mostly, but when they do contain some nugget of interest, you can never find them. They don't make it into libraries and they don't survive.

The climax, when it came, was a few weeks later, continued Stephen. They found the milk-float abandoned at an angle in broad daylight on that stretch of lane between the high banks. Mr Westgrove was pressed up against the tree roots, as though he was trying to climb them to safety. The terrible expression on his face was one that I shall never forget. It reminded me of those texts we had to translate for our Classics A Levels. The life-destroying stare of the head of Medusa. The writhing snakes around her head.

The doctor examined him and made the only judgement he could. Mr Westgrove had died of a massive heart-attack. It was death by natural causes.

What can I say? My experience has all been with questions of the soul, the spirit within. The external spiritual world of ghosts and demons is beyond my ken. It's something I would have to leave to Swedenborg and Mr Westgrove. No ghost has ever approached me whining in the woods.

The doctor and I did take a look round Mr Westgrove's cottage before the house-clearance people went in. His only relative was a second cousin in Australia. The proceeds from the cottage and contents would be sent out to him there. There are two things I remember about Mr Westgrove's cottage. The first was the bonfire patch at the bottom of the back garden. He'd been burning things recently and I could see a few charred plastic scraps and the metal rings from Mr Westgrove's 'ledgers'.

The other thing was this. And Stephen went over to the bookcase and came back with a large, early 19th century leather-bound book. It's his copy of Culpeper, he said. He'd left it on his dining-room table with a note, bequeathing it to me as a gift "should anything happen to him", in memory of the Friday evenings he'd so much enjoyed.

We leafed through the Culpeper which was heavily annotated in neat pencil. In two or three places a passage had been sidelined in heavy ugly red crayon. There was one right at the beginning of the book marking out Amara Dulcis, also known as Mortal, Felon-wort and Bitter-sweet. Amongst its other properties, it was "excellently good to remove witchcraft in men and beasts."

The locals insisted I carry out a service of exorcism in the lane between the high banks, said Stephen. But I, or rather we, were moved to another parish and the exorcism was left to my successor.

No, I can't say that I believe in ghosts, said Stephen, but I often wonder what it was that Mr Westgrove saw.

# 6 THE GHOSTS WITHIN

I'm like Stephen, said Abigail. I can't say I really understand the world of external ghosts. I regret to say I've never seen a spirit or a demon. My life has been quite humdrum and normal. My experiences as a lawyer and as a judge have kept me rooted in the real world and in the problems we all make for ourselves. I've always seen sorting out those problems as my contribution. And, as for the Law, well I've never seen it as some free-standing and independent framework, some perfect model against which you compare the facts of the case and from which you devise some solution. To me, the Law has been more like a border to our ragged lives. It helps us to make sense of all the strangeness and error we fall into.

The Law is like a plain wooden frame around one of those 18th or 19th century samplers sewn by young girls. Many of those samplers can be charming and attractive, but they are always the work of an amateur. They are all very human, with their misspellings and their mistakes, which is why I love them so much. My first husband bought me my first sampler from an antique shop twenty years ago. It's early 19th century and has a wonderful, embroidered text. "Labour for learning before you grow old/ For learning is better than silver or gold." I have a collection of a dozen or more now, but that one is still my favourite.

All samplers are exercises in stitch-work, with the alphabet sewn in capital and small letters, the lines of numbers from 1 through 9 to zero, the names and ages of their creators. But some are quite beautiful with houses and trees, the Garden of Eden, a favourite pet. And all of them are set off by their plain wooden frames. Without the frame, they would appear tatty and crude. I've enjoyed my career in the Law. I've enjoyed being the plain and boring frame that helps order and set off the lives of all those clients or 'cases' that I've dealt with.

Christ, I'm getting pompous! It's time I started to talk of someone apart from myself and of issues far-removed from the legal profession, you'll be relieved to hear. As I say, I have no experience of ghosts or demons. All I can tell you is a story about the ghosts within.

When my first husband died five years ago, he'd already been ill for more than six years. Some of you will know that he suffered from frontotemporal dementia (FTD), a degenerative disease of the brain. I am not going to depress you now with the details of what it's like to see someone you love destroyed by such an illness. All I'll say is that, during his illness, there were sudden moments of absolute lucidity when he would return to us and when I'd catch a glimpse of the person I'd married. I remember once we were walking in the country, my husband completely silent as usual, when he suddenly raised his head to look at the amazing sky and he began to speak clearly and with precision for a few sentences about the cirrus clouds above us, their specific properties and their defining characteristics. And then the curtain came down again. The ghost of his former self was gone and I was back with the silence.

Sadly, my husband was not the first person I'd seen to die from FTD. My uncle suffered from the same disease and died in his early sixties. When I was a girl, I used to visit my aunt and uncle for a couple of weeks each Summer at their house with its beautiful garden in Sussex, which they'd bought when they came back from Washington, which turned out to be his last overseas posting in the Foreign Service.

My parents sent me down there to Sussex every year for the fresh air and I loved it. When I was small, I'd always wanted a pony, but ponies don't go with a life in West London. My aunt and uncle's neighbours had a farm and being allowed to ride the horses there was as close as I ever got to my dream.

My story, though, is from a time when my uncle was already very ill. He could still walk and get around the house and garden unaided, but it was as though his mind had left us for some other world for much of the time. Although there were still occasions when he could speak clearly and rationally and at length.

I remember the Summer when I was twelve years old. My aunt used to walk my uncle down to his greenhouse at the bottom of the garden in the morning and leave him there till lunch. She'd gone round the greenhouse and carefully removed anything that might do him harm. Where there had been several pairs of scissors hanging from nails in the wooden frame, she'd replaced them with small canvas bags filled with pieces of green garden-twine which she'd cut to different lengths. They served my uncle's purpose and he didn't seem to notice the difference. He could still go on with growing his flowers from seed and potting and re-potting them on.

His speciality were plants from the Himalayas and Western China. Himalayan gingers, blue poppies, Tibetan tree peonies. He'd sit me down on the deckchair in the greenhouse and talk me through the Latin names of the Roscoea and Meconopsis in his small pots, all waiting for the day when they would be big enough to be planted outside. He treated me as an adult and an equal which was probably why I liked him so much and enjoyed listening to him talk all morning in the greenhouse and more than forgave him his lapses into total silence.

It was perhaps because of his illness or because I was only a 12-year-old girl that he started to talk to me about his work in the

Foreign Service. I had the impression these were things he hadn't spoken about before and that it was almost as though he was talking aloud to himself, forgetting that he had an audience. Some of what he spoke about, I understood. A lot of it I remember. It was a different and memorable world he was painting.

Abby, he said to me one day, don't believe all the nonsense they'll tell you about ghouls and ghosts and monsters. Take it from me, the only ghosts you'll ever need to worry about are the ghosts within, the ones you carry around inside you. The ghosts of your mistakes and the ghosts of those things you should have done, but never did. Those are the only ghosts you need to watch out for. And it is always the latter that are the most terrifying and haunting.

For, despite our best efforts, we shall all of us make mistakes and those mistakes will have consequences. But you can't allow such mistakes to grind you down and torment you. If you've done your best and failed, that's just human and it will happen to nearly all of us. You can't undo those mistakes. The best you can do is to learn from them. You will carry them always as a ghost within but, believe me, they are not the most terrifying. If you are a half-decent human being, the kind that would only commit evil by accident, then the chances are that you will only ever be haunted by the things you haven't done. By those failures to act. By standing motionless when you should have taken one step forward.

I sat and listened and it was as though he was delivering a lecture. But, instead of an auditorium, there was just the greenhouse and this 12-year-old girl.

When we make mistakes, he said, remember that we are not alone, that there have been worse mistakes which, if we are lucky, we shall have had the good fortune to have learnt from. There are many times when we have been deceived by our enemies. You only have to think of The Trust or Das Englandspiel. We fail so often to read our enemy's playbook, never suspecting that most of them will repeat what's worked for them before. We, of course, go to great lengths to craft something new every time we take action, because we always overestimate our enemy's intelligence. They don't make the same mistake with us.

At this point, my aunt popped her head round the greenhouse door to walk us back for lunch, asking us if we'd had a good time re-potting. My uncle smiled and we went back up to the house for our cheese salad.

The next morning when his mind eventually switched from the blue poppies to the past, he returned to the subject of the ghosts within.

I had a friend and colleague once, he said, who worked with me when I was attached to Special Branch in Cyprus. It was during the EOKA Rebellion. I was based in Nicosia and my friend was down in Limassol. It was the time of 'The Murder Mile' when off-duty British soldiers were being assassinated in Ledra Street in Nicosia. It was often the same MO, a young man with a handgun walking quickly up and firing a few rounds before running off. We eventually caught Nikos Sampson. He's the gunman that everyone remembers, because of the part he later played in the 1974 Coup against Archbishop Makarios, but there were others.

My friend in Limassol got a walk-in, an informant, a 19-year-old Greek-Cypriot girl. It turned out her brother was one of the gunmen. They lived in Limassol and he carried out his attacks in Ledra Street at Saturday lunchtime, when everyone was out before the shops shut for the weekend. He'd be driven up to Nicosia the night before in a truck owned by an EOKA colleague on its way to deliver fresh fruit for the market.

The girl was sick of the bloodshed. She'd seen a photo in the papers of the wife and children of a British sergeant her brother had assassinated. She was also scared for her brother. She wanted him arrested and sent to prison where he'd be safe. She didn't want him to carry on till he was killed in a shoot-out. The problem for us, she said, was that we'd have to arrest him with the gun in his hand. The way it worked was that a boy on a bicycle would hand her brother the gun in a side-street moments before her brother turned into Ledra Street for his attack. The best she could do would be to warn us on the day of the attack.

The plan my friend agreed was simple. If her brother had left for Nicosia on a Friday night, then she would walk along a stretch of the promenade of the Limassol seafront between 0930-1030 on the Saturday morning. My friend would be sitting half-way back inside one of the sea-front Cafes from where he could see her pass. That would be enough for him to phone through to me in Nicosia.

But the first time she gave her signal, he missed her. He was there the whole time and fifteen minutes either side, but he just didn't see her. A British soldier was shot dead in Ledra Street around 1pm. It was my friend's fault. The girl had walked by, but with her sister and her sister's small daughter. For some reason he couldn't explain, my friend had been fixated on looking for a girl on her own. She was in tears when she met him as agreed a few days later. In tears and angry.

The next time she walked along the front, three weeks later, my friend saw her. He phoned me with the warning and her brother was arrested as he turned into Ledra Street with the gun in his hand. He served a few years in prison and was released with the rest at Independence.

My friend, though, was destroyed by his failure. It haunted him to death, eating away at his insides. He died an alcoholic. But I tell you, Abby, that is not the worst sort of ghost to carry around inside you.

At which point, my aunt again interrupted us and we filed up the garden for lunch.

It rained heavily that afternoon and my aunt decided to confine us to the house in case we caught our deaths in a chilly greenhouse. My uncle and I sat in his study, in silence for most of the time. At one point, though, he got up and took a small silver box from the mantelpiece. He told me that it was a 19th century 'gau', a Tibetan reliquary. The silver front was decorated with hand-punched letters in Tibetan script. He explained what each one meant, their holy properties, but I don't remember them now. There was a small glass window in the front, behind which was the model of a Goddess. I do remember that. It was Tara, the Goddess of Compassion who protects from fear. My uncle then took out a sheet of plain paper and laid it on his desk. Placing the gau face-down on the paper, he carefully prized open the metal back. The gau was full of what looked like brown and yellow dust, some of which spilled out onto the paper. A pilgrim would have acquired this gau at some special monastery or shrine, my uncle said. Dried flowers and plants from the holy site would have been carried back home in the gau by the pilgrim as a permanent link to the shrine.

The next morning, back in the greenhouse, my uncle showed me a small pot of what looked like grass. It was a special project which he was very proud of. He'd taken some of the dust from the gau and planted it. Over the years he'd tried to grow it on everything, on blotting paper and on every compost mix that he knew. He'd eventually managed to get this one small plant to germinate.

It looks like grass, I said.

That's probably what it is, my uncle replied. But it's grass from a Free Tibet, from a time when the Dalai Lama ruled Tibet from Lhasa, a time when lamas rode around the country carrying ritual phurbas, or daggers, which they would use to exorcise demons. I have a phurba in my study. It's a blunt blade for ritual or 'medicinal' use only and it's decorated with skulls and horses' heads and Naga dragons spitting snakes, all symbols of power. I'd show it to you but I think your aunt has hidden it, fearing I might use it do myself harm. He laughed and then added, I'm not mad, you know, Abby.

I asked my aunt about the phurba. She said she couldn't remember where it had got to but she said my uncle had always been fascinated by Tibet. It had started when he was a boy at Rugby School. In the 1920s, a Minister in the Tibetan government had decided that they ought to try and learn what was useful from Western science and technology. As part of that programme, they sent a dozen Tibetan boys to Rugby where your uncle became best friends with one of them. And then, of course, we were at the High Commission in New Delhi for four years, my aunt said, where Tibet was one of your uncle's responsibilities.

In my last few days there that Summer, my uncle emerged from one of his silences as we sat in his greenhouse and began to talk about his time in Delhi, in the years after Indian Independence.

I think I've told you, Abby, that the worst of the ghosts within are those that belong to the things you failed to do. They are far more haunting and terrible in my experience than the ghosts of your mistakes. They linger and grow. They become stronger each year. They were born with your failure to act and they will live with you and dog you till you die.

We were in Delhi during the Chinese invasion of Tibet in 1950 and that's when the ghosts inside me first appeared. When the Chinese army marched into Kham in eastern Tibet in October, the Tibetans fought back. But a regional governor defected to the Chinese, signed a treaty with them and the Tibetan resistance fell away. Sitting in the High Commission in Delhi, I was still getting reports from Kham, passed hand-to-hand along my loose network of contacts in Tibet. It often took a long time for those reports to make their journey, but I suspect I was getting the news from Kham as quickly as the Tibetan government in Lhasa.

The next steps were at the United Nations where El Salvador sponsored a motion by the Tibetan government protesting at the Chinese invasion. And that was the time we should have acted. The Chinese had a foothold in Eastern Tibet, but international pressure might still have pushed them back. We, the British, had a duty to help. We'd invaded Tibet ourselves in 1904. After that we became, if not Tibet's protecting power, then at least her guiding power in the first half of the 20th century, to the extent they needed a guide. We had a responsibility to speak up and to act. But what did we do? Nothing. We abstained at the UN vote.

I remember arguing with my boss at the High Commission. But he was old-school. It's not our job, he said. We just provide the facts. Policy we leave to the men in pin-stripe trousers, to the diplomats and the politicians.

I couldn't let it rest. I wrote letters to London. I wrote a paper for the High Commissioner, which my boss hated me for. More importantly, I lobbied every contact I had in the Indian government, but they didn't want to rock the boat with China, having bilateral problems of their own.

I should have done more, Abby. I failed to act. I should have resigned and gone public. I should have campaigned for Tibet. I knew what was happening in Kham and I felt a personal duty to the Tibetans even if my government did not. My boss told me I'd gone native. For him that was the worst abuse he could deliver.

The Tibetan resistance later formed an army, Chushi Gangdruk or 'Four Rivers, Six Mountains', the traditional name for Kham. But the Chinese continued to consolidate their grip. In 1959, Chushi Gangdruk had to help the Dalai Lama to flee into India, which was when the real war began. But Chushi Gangdruk were a medieval army that moved in thousands with their families, their horses and their yaks. They wouldn't take advice to split up into smaller groups and switch to guerrilla warfare. Once the Chinese had built roads and airstrips throughout Tibet, Chushi Gangdruk were straffed from the air, hunted down and destroyed. Some of them are still resisting from exile, based in Mustang and supported by the Americans, but they are restricted to small cross-border raids. The resistance now is mostly spiritual, as the Dalai Lama and his exiled government keep the ideas and the culture and the inspiration of Tibet alive.

I'm sorry if I'm boring you, Abby, he said, but this is very important. You must always act when you can. It's your duty as a human being. If you don't, then you'll be haunted and dragged down by the ghosts within. They will torment you till you die. You'll dream of them when you sleep and you'll wake to find them sitting by your bed. They are like a coldness that never leaves you, however close you draw to the fire. They are a reminder that everything you later do or say is irrelevant. They have caught you and they will never let you go. Whatever you do in life, Abby, remember this. Remember your uncle. Please.

He then released his tight grip on the arms of his chair and lapsed back into silence.

The next Summer I visited them, my uncle never spoke at all. He was still taken down to his greenhouse each morning, but he just sat there rocking himself backwards and forwards in his old wooden chair, clutching the small pot of Tibetan grass, now dried up and dead. I would sit with him and talk of ponies and riding and of how much I enjoyed talking to him about his plants and about Tibet and his experiences, but there wasn't a flicker of recognition.

I next went down there in the Winter for his funeral. When we were standing around his open grave, my aunt stepped forward with that little pot of dried grass, tipping the soil into his grave "to remind him of the things he had loved". I gasped so loudly that my mother looked down at me. I managed to turn my gasp into a sob and my mother smiled and squeezed my hand. I think that was the worst part for me, seeing that soil tipped onto his coffin, knowing that death would be no border to his ragged life and that his demons would follow him into the grave.

# 7 A SOUND OF SINGING

Our annual reunion the next year found us, unexpectedly, back in a private dining-room at Rules restaurant in Maiden Lane. In sad circumstances, for the first of our number had died, the first of us who'd arrived at that small college to study History over forty years before. Harrington, the richest of us all, had fallen suddenly ill and had died within six months from a brain tumour. Like everything about him, Harrington's will was exuberant, loud and larger than life. He'd left a small fortune to the university to set up a Chair in Business Studies to be named after him, and to our old college to establish a number of scholarships in Economics and in Business Studies for UK and foreign students. Nothing for History. He'd put his money where his mouth had been, in his 'real world'.

He also left a strange bequest of £30,000 to Abigail, "because she's the most reliable of you lot." Under the terms of the bequest, she was to use the money to book and pay for dinner at Rules in a private room for our annual reunions, "for as long as we lasted, or until the money ran out." He'd signed off the bequest, "Cheers!"

We'd done justice to him in his honour by dining and drinking well, and we now sat with our coffees and port ready for our traditional pair of ghost stories to round off the evening.

I imagine Harrington would have said there's too much bloody history in the story I'm about to tell you, said Richard. Out of respect to him, I'll try and keep the history part short and move on quickly to the 'real world', although it won't be Harrington's world. But he might have enjoyed this all the same.

As you know, I did try to be an academic. I stuck with the college after graduation and signed up for a PhD in Byzantine history. Initially, it was going to be on some aspect of the monophysite and Melchite schism in the 6th and 7th Centuries, but I soon got distracted and started looking at Byzantium's links to the world beyond its borders. As when the Empress Theodora sent her priest Julianos south from Egypt to convert the African kings of Nubia, creating that lost outpost of Byzantine culture in Africa which survived for 700 years cut off from the Empire by the Arab invasion of Egypt. An African Byzantine world epitomised by the beauty of those wall-paintings from their sand-buried cathedral at Faras. God, The Virgin and the saints surrounded by Greek inscriptions, their hands resting in protection on the shoulders of the Nubian kings and dignitaries. Saints and kings all dressed alike in the ornate and jewelled robes of the Byzantine Court. Perhaps the fabulous forgotten world of Prester John.

But, sadly, after a year I had to accept that Academia was probably not for me. I think the problem with Byzantine history was that I soon got sick of the brutality of the Imperial family. All those blindings of deposed emperors, the murders of siblings. It seemed more Ottoman that Greek.

What I was better suited to, of course, was aid work, mainly in Africa. It's that which kept me happily occupied for over thirty years before I came back and switched to teaching. Like a fair number of people of my generation in the Aid world, I got into it through the side door, by answering a small advert in *The Guardian* seeking English-language teachers for secondary schools in the Sudan. You turned up at the Sudanese Embassy Cultural Office in London and, as far as I could see, if you had a degree of any shape or form you were accepted and taken on for a year for a salary of about £1,500 pa. I could never work out where the Sudanese Government got the funds for that salary, although there was a rumour that the whole scheme was Saudi funded.

So with twenty others and after a false-start in London for a few days when our plane was cancelled (at that time, they'd only fly when full), we found ourselves in the Arrivals Hall at Khartoum in front of a dusty and non-working carousel, our luggage tipped out in a pile on the ground. It was my first introduction to the world I would love.

After a couple of weeks in Khartoum and a geographical lottery of job-allocations, I was on an old turbo-prop aircraft flying North to Nubia. The plane was flown by a British expat veteran of The Battle of Britain, complete with a handlebar moustache. He clearly loved flying and I imagine Sudan Airways Internal was the last company on earth which would still employ him at his age.

When the plane landed and I bounced the few miles across the desert to the small town in the back of a Toyota pick-up truck, that was the last of the technological world for me for the next year. The world which had been waiting for me there was one of peace and of silence, where time for most people was still measured in seasons.

I think it was the silence that had the most profound effect on me at first. The town had a marketplace and a few hundred yards of tarmacked roads, but they quickly petered out into the desert. When flying in from Khartoum, you could see that Nubia in those days was really just the thin line of the Nile with a narrow green strip of cultivation each side. The rest was just the desert. And the desert belonged to silence. It couldn't fail but to heighten your senses.

As did the intense heat, the brilliant blue of the sky, the star-studded blackness each night. There were no half-measures. What mattered there were the simple things. Well-water in a chipped enamel bowl, the shade of a mud-brick wall, the warmth of a blanket at night. So much of my former life had become simply irrelevant.

Where I was lucky was in having landed by chance in the Sudan at the start of a working life in Africa. The Sudanese were interested and friendly and curiously tolerant of a young foreigner who had no discernible skills beyond the ability to speak English. And their own wealth was something I could only begin to unlock as I learnt more Arabic, writing words in a notebook as I heard them, learning just enough to get by. Enough to sit and talk to a farmer about his crops, about how he was planting a windbreak of trees so it would be ready for the future when his son would run the farm.

If I don't talk much about my work as a teacher in the Sudan, it's because I don't think it was of much value for the Sudanese. I had no idea what I was supposed to be doing and I made it up as I went along. I remember searching through the school storeroom at the beginning of the year to see what books there were to use. After a quick count and bearing in mind that there were fifty or more boys in each class, it came down to a toss-up between two battered twenty-year-old editions of *Edited Versions of the Classics Produced for African Schools*. It was either Jane Austen's *Sense and Sensibility* or *Moby Dick*. I opted for the latter, even though the biggest fish the boys had seen was a foot long and came from the Nile. I didn't think they would be able to relate to Jane Austen's concerns. I think the most useful thing I did in the whole year was to hand my two copies of English-Arabic dictionaries to the two brightest boys when I left. Most of the others, I just tried to keep amused. I am sorry to say that nearly all the education came my way.

And I learnt a lot there which helped me in my later work with Aid and Development. I remember travelling in the East of the Sudan during the school holidays and meeting a man who'd been in politics in Khartoum. He pulled up his jellabiya to show me the knife scars on his stomach to prove it. Sick of the infighting, he'd switched to work for the Co-operative Movement. His job was to sort out problems, to get things done. One of the examples he gave was how the Government, flush with foreign funding, had built a huge dam in one of the regions. The only downside was that the water catchment area was the only cultivatable land in the area. He'd worked out a compromise with a system of walls to keep some of that land above water for farming. I learnt a lot in the Sudan.

But using that knowledge would be for the future. This story is about my time in that small Sudanese town and about the heightening of senses. For if you live in a place where you feel Time has stopped, then Past and Present will tend to lose their meanings. And as your senses become heightened, you begin to be aware that the past is all around you, pressing in on the present whenever it can. Not threatening or intimidating, but slow and calm and as natural as the flow of the great river, without which Nubia would be only sand.

It began with the most obvious places, like the graveyard in the dunes out of town where bleached bones stuck up from shallow graves in the sand, with scraps of shroud forced up and in view, free again to blow with the breeze.

And then there were those things left abandoned in the desert itself. The Egyptian temple in the sands across the river, two lines of stone with hieroglyphs showing as clean and precise as when first cut. Or the traction engine, perfect and un-rusted, still standing where it had been abandoned fifty years before, memorial to some uncompleted project to build an artificial lake and canal way out in the desert to increase the cultivatable land.

And the much smaller things, like the hurricane-lamp, its glass all gone, lying broken in the rubbish on the dunes. And, in the centre of town, those two metal rings fixed into the ground on a patch of weed-covered wasteland. Each ring marked 'Slazenger'. The last vestiges of a tennis-court and all that remained of the Colonial District Commissioner's Residence. And I swore sometimes that I could even hear the ripple of laughter and English voices from some long-forgotten tennis afternoon.

But then, of course, there were the living ghosts. The way the sand was whipped up by the wind to form shapes that hung in air, like men running forwards, their arms outstretched, as if desperate to greet you. And the story the local people told of a Russian woman who'd come to work as an engineer, but who'd married a Sudanese husband and now lived in purdah in a village up-river. A living ghost whom no-one saw.

But it was the sounds that began to haunt me. For it was my sense of hearing that became most acute, as though I could listen in on wavelengths that I'd never imagined had existed. And whether it was the wind in the graveyard, or the old man at the school who came out each evening to lay the dust by sweeping an old water-can across the yard, I began to hear an undercurrent beneath their sounds. It was a sad sound of quiet singing which I could hear hidden in the wind or lost in the soft splash of the water-drops hitting the ground.

And I came to look forward to this undercurrent of sound which became a hallmark of my time in Nubia. For I took it to be some softly murmured Byzantine liturgy from the cathedrals and churches of those Nubian kings, as though 700 years of history had not been lost and as if their music, which we could only imagine, was still playing as this undercurrent to our lives.

I heard it beneath the Sufi chant at a festival and beneath the plaintive Sudanese pop music from the cassettes in the truck-drivers cabs, the endless chorus of "Ya Habibi" (My Love). I heard it when travelling, sitting high on a hill above the town at Sinkat while waiting 36 hours for the next train. Sitting there next to a small memorial cairn to Douglas Newbold "Who loved these hills and these people," listening to the sing-song cry of the small boy in the town below, selling twigs for teeth-cleaning at five-pence a time.

I heard it beneath the roar of the Third Cataract, that crashing rush of water which was itself a hymn to transience. I heard it beneath the ululation of the women, whether in fear in the landing-craft crossing the Nile when the water slapped over the sides, or in pleasure at the wedding ceremony when their Pigeon Dance began. It was the one time I saw the women unveil their heads, uncovering their black oiled hair glistening as they danced, swaying from side to side with their arms outstretched, the tension amongst the young men crackling through the crowd like swift-running flames.

And I came to love that undercurrent of sound which I would listen out for, wondering whether I was the only one there who knew it for what it was, this long-lost liturgy of the Nubian Byzantine Church. I could imagine it sung in their last years at Faras when the Cathedral walls were almost engulfed by the rising sand. When the congregation were forced to brick up the windows and tunnel down to the main door so they could enter to pray, in fear of the pressure of sand against the walls. A congregation determined to persevere, as befits a lost outpost of Byzantine culture, as heroic as the last Palaeologus emperor seizing his sword and running out into the front-line as the Turks breached the walls at Byzantium.

For someone who's spent most of his life doing practical work, Richard laughed, I confess I have always been an incurable romantic.

And I would have left the Sudan with my romance intact if it hadn't been for a bad bout of illness. I used to catch dysentery there almost every other week and I lost two stone in my time there. But I remember once it was worse than usual and I'd been off-work for a day or two. The morning I was on my feet again, it was a Friday, my one free day, and I walked down to the river at dawn. I was still pale from the dysentery. Tall and thin, I could probably have passed for a ghost myself, sitting there beneath the palm trees in the grey light of dawn, staring out at the empty river. I was hollowed out by the illness and I suspect my senses were raised as never before, or since.

Which is when I saw them, a succession of dhows sailing down-stream, sailing North towards Egypt. Dhows as I'd seen so many times before. Except that these flew the white flags marked with the double-armed yellow cross of the Byzantine Christian kings of Nubia. The dhows were filled with people, women and children mostly, and I could see they were Southerners. They were captured slaves from the South being sent to Egypt by the Nubian kings. It was the annual tribute the kings paid to the Arabs of Egypt, a tribute paid for hundreds of years to buy off the Arabs and prolong Christian Nubia's freedom.

And I heard the sound that came from the dhows, just a murmur of song, kept quiet so as not to provoke. This was the undercurrent of sound in all that I'd heard. Not a Byzantine liturgy or a lament for a lost Byzantine Nubian world.

# 8 THE FINAL PAGE

Lance looked around the table at us, gave us one of his knowing smiles and began.

I suppose Joseph Stalin must hold the record for the production of ghosts, he said. I mean, there are others like Hitler and Ghengis Khan who have set industrial scale slaughter in motion, but it can only be Stalin who really stacked up the numbers all on his own, sitting in his office each night signing off the lists to be shot, deciding on the target quotas for killings which would be sent out to each Republic and region of the Soviet Union. How many were executed in those two years of Terror in the late 1930s? 800,000, wasn't it? That's a lot of ghosts. It makes Robespierre look very second-rate.

I once saw an exhibition of photographs, he continued, black-and-white mugshots taken from the KGB files at the time. Men and women of all ages and backgrounds, pulled off the street and shot within days to fill the quotas and ensure the policy of liquidation was a success. I remember one was a young hairdresser in Moscow. She'd once done the hair of the wife of the Japanese Embassy Second Secretary. The file said she was convicted without trial charged with espionage for Japan. Her photo shows pure innocence and incomprehension. And then there was the photo of an elderly civil servant. He'd been an Army Officer in WWI. He just looked very tired and puzzled.

There's something about any individual who can calmly sign an order to kill. And you have to wonder, don't you? Are God and the world asleep? How do these people get to live out their natural lives? You'd think at the very least they would choke to death on a fishbone. Sadly, though, the laws of chance seem to act independently from any sense of natural justice. Some poor child who's never harmed anyone will get the fish-bone.

This is all pretty grim, Lance, I said. Is it leading anywhere? Are we going to get a ghost story?

My apologies, said Lance, I was just trying to get myself in the right frame of mind for the macabre. Can I say, though, before I start that I've always been grateful that you invite me to these reunions. It can't be often that Abigail, a Supreme Court Judge, sits down for a fine meal with someone who's done time. Three times I've been in prison. Twelve years in all. The last time was the worst. You just get sick of it. It's the boredom, the pettiness of it all. I don't suppose any of you have been excited to find an Agatha Christie on the weekly book trolley. I shared a cell with a London Cypriot once and I tried to get him to teach me Greek, but his Greek was just dialect he'd learnt from his grandmother. I think the family, second generation, spoke English at home. "Pame spiti" seemed to be the main ingredient. "Let's go home." Not an option he or I had at the time. I never got to learn Greek. I didn't learn much in prison, except patience.

What I do have in common with you all is that I really enjoyed studying History at college, particularly the Russian history paper. And I enjoyed finding out what I was capable of. I never knew I could learn a foreign language before. It had never occurred to me or to my Secondary School teachers, but at college I started Russian-language classes and surprised myself by how well I did. The Russian language lessons certainly helped me with the Russian history paper which was my only First.

But for a scholarship boy like me, from a school that had never sent anyone to Cambridge before, the three years at college were mainly my chance to see how the other half lived. I guess at best you thought I was a wide-boy. I certainly turned bad soon after graduation. But then you could say I was just following in the family tradition. My Dad had a small swallow tattooed on each hand.

My Dad had never given up. He died in prison, of old age. I think it was the memory of that which set me thinking about retirement when I was still in my early fifties. I didn't want to end up the same way as my dad. So I started to think about one last job, big enough to fund me for the rest of my life. I'd decided that this big job would be the final page to my career of crime and, God knows, it was about time my career of crime began to pay. I think I could have earnt more as a Tube driver than I ever did as a criminal. But, as I say, I was following in the family tradition.

My dream was to 'earn' enough from one last job for me to buy a flat somewhere within walking distance of a great library. A flat in one of those white, modern Brunswick Square blocks would have suited me down to the ground. I've always kept my Reader's Card for the British Library, renewing it when I got out of prison. A Brunswick Square flat would have been in nice easy reach of the British Library. And I've always liked those white futuristic blocks with their balconies and wide plate-glass windows.

And, if I'd had to go on the run abroad somewhere, then I'd have had a choice. I learnt Spanish after I left college, mainly because I lived with a Spanish girl for a few years in London. On the run, I wouldn't have wanted the Costa Del Sol, too much like Little England in the sun. No, I'd have probably opted for Buenos Aires, somewhere in walking distance of Borges' great library.

I've always thought I should do some proper research, you see. I thought I'd like to write a book about a Civil War. I wasn't fussed which. Russian, Spanish or English would have done equally well. The true horror of war and conflict is too often disguised, ameliorated you could say, by the notion that you're fighting some alien 'other'. With a Civil War, there's no such obfuscation. You're killing your own kith and kin. I've always wanted to study a Civil War properly. I've always thought Civil Wars are the best judge of a nation's character. Yes, some serious research is what I had in mind when I'd done my last big job.

I think it's the planning part of crime that I've always enjoyed the best. Having been born with a brain, I thought I might as well use it. Getting stuck into the complex planning, the targeting, that was always my forte and I'd built up quite a reputation in the right sort of circles. It's why I never found it difficult to find good people willing to come in with me when they knew I was onto a new job. For this last one, though, I decided to keep it simple and just work as a pair. That made it an easy choice for me. I'd worked off-and-on with Trevor for years and his dad worked with mine. It was the perfect team for what I had in mind.

What neither I nor Trevor had, of course, was the capital. I don't know how much you know about London crime. You'd be surprised how much it resembles the business world nowadays. If Harrington was here, I'm sure he'd recognise the scene I'm about to paint for you. A smart office in the West End with front-of-office staff that looked as though they'd walked straight out of a modelling agency and who sounded as though they'd been to Cheltenham Ladies College. Probably had, some of them. Once you were into the inner sanctum, there were three middle aged men in Saville Row suits ready to weigh up your business proposal.

On the other side of the long conference table sat me and Trevor. Trevor was in his cleanest jeans and best black leather jacket. I was in a suit. The one I'm wearing now. Trevor left the talking to me and I made the pitch. I was asking for £20,000 in cash as my 'start-up funds'. Once the job was done, they'd get £200,000 back from me and Trevor. They didn't ask or even want to know the details of the job we were planning. They just needed reassurance there would be no violence, which they correctly identified as a greater risk. But they knew my track-record and Trevor's. We were what Dixon of Dock Green would have called 'honest criminals'.

So we walked out of their office and past the Cheltenham ladies with £20,000 in used tens in a couple of expanding black briefcases. All very proper, we must have looked. Our backers trusted us and, if the job didn't succeed, well they could probably live with a few such failures and still reap a handsome tax-free return on their investments year-on-year. On the rare occasion that a team tried to do a runner after a successful job and not pay, then these investors could always hire outside contractors, with power-tools and sawn-off shotguns, to make an example of the offenders. But they knew they could trust us. We'd always been a class act, me and Trevor.

And what was this job, you ask, this job which was to fund my early retirement and historical research into Civil Wars? It was a bank branch in central London, at the bottom of Marsham Street, down near where it runs into Herrick Street. At that time, there was a nondescript-looking bank branch on the corner there. What made it special for me was that I'd heard a few years before on the grapevine that this innocent-looking branch office had a basement where they stored the bullion for all branches of that bank in South-East England. It was that which made it a target worth planning for.

Always being a touch old-fashioned, "retro" they'd call me now, I decided that we'd tunnel into it. I spent a few days pacing out distances between the bank and neighbouring buildings. Quite frankly, there was no real risk of anyone getting suspicious. You can get away with a great deal as long as you're dressed smartly. The only risk was that they'd pore over the CCTV after the job was finished, when they would identify me as suspicious. So for that I wore light disguise. In my case, that simply meant growing a beard and wearing a pair of glasses with plain glass. I could simply return to being clean-shaven when I began my new life in Brunswick Square or Buenos Aires.

A hundred yards from where I judged the bank-vault to be, there was a small, block-like brick-built shop. It had been built when they put up the estate of flats. There were several of these shops, all the same size, all with the same brickwork as the surrounding blocks of flats. This one was one of those shoe-repair and key-cutting businesses, run out of a single room. I started to get my keys cut there and had all four pairs of my shoes repaired. I got chatting to the Afghan owner about his children and about his son and daughter and about his ambition to get them both into college. His plan was to give up the lease on this shop and take on another somewhere in London where the State Secondary schools had a better reputation. He wanted to give his children the chance they'd need.

To cut a long story short, I nodded vigorously, said I'd just come into an inheritance, that I wanted to settle down having spent twenty years doing small jobs in Africa and that I could offer him £12,000 to buy the remaining three months of his six-month lease. The deal was done and I handed over £12,000 from our expanding briefcases.

There we were, with our own shop for three months. It was a bit like *The Red-Headed League*, but if a plan's worked once, then why not repeat it? Neither Trevor nor I knew anything about shoe-repairs but, luckily, locks had always been one of Trevor's specialities. So he took over the key-cutting and we were able to make it look as though we were a going concern. Although we did close a good few hours earlier each day than the Afghan, to give us more time for our real work.

The only problem for me was that I started to have minor health problems. I'd always been fine up till then, but I seemed to be developing tinnitus. There was always this scraping noise in my eardrums. It was proof, had I needed it, that I'd been right to look for this one last job. It was high-time I found the money I needed to buy a flat and settle down to some useful research before it was too late. None of us are going to live for ever, as poor Harrington has just proved.

We quickly got into a routine. Mid-afternoon we'd shut up the shop and pull down the blinds. Behind the shop-room, there was a tiny kitchen and a storeroom. The kitchen was six feet closer to the bank vault, so that's where we decided to dig. We kept it simple, doing most of the work by hand. Power-tools might be OK for contractor hit-men, but when you're trying not to disturb the neighbours, then working by hand is better. It took us one whole night to break our way through the kitchen floor and make a hole wide enough to start digging. Then there was the loose rubble base the shop was built on. That took another night.

The two main problems we faced were dumping the spoil and the risk of nosey or angry neighbours. On the first, we just filled up the storeroom. That kept us going for about six or seven days. When it got too much for the storeroom, then we had to close the shop. We spoke to our customers and put up a sign saying that we were closed for refurbishment but that we'd be reopening shortly. The advantage of closing was that we could work through the day and had prefect cover for the noise we were making. The downside was that the refurbishment seemed to be going on for too long when there was no sign of rubbish being taken out or of paint and cement sacks and new fittings being taken in.

We'd probably have been alright if it hadn't been for Mrs Armitage. She was a cantankerous old widow who lived on the ground-floor of the closest block. She'd come in and had some keys cut and come back and complained that they didn't work smoothly. Trevor had gone round to her flat and later told me there was nothing wrong with the keys he'd cut. She was just one of those lonely old people who liked to make a fuss, he said. Once we'd shut the shop, I'd spot her trying to peer in every time she passed by. I'd marked Mrs Armitage down as our likely Nemesis.

Mrs Armitage aside, we just pushed on as best we could with the digging. For me, the tinnitus was the real problem. The work I was doing with my spade underground didn't help. Any noise in the confined space of the tunnel would be amplified and make the sound in my ear-drums worse. I'd even hear the same scraping sounds whenever I woke during the night. The bloody noise was haunting me. I was beginning to worry that the tunnelling was getting to me, that sooner or later I'd just lose it.

It was funny because the tunnel itself was fine and Trevor didn't seem to have a problem. We'd stripped all the wood from the shelves in the shop and storeroom to make struts and supports. It was just the noise in my ears which was insufferable.

I had to admit, though, that the digging was slow-going. We'd kept it up for twelve days, but we didn't seem to be getting much nearer to the bank. We'd nearly used up all the spare space to dump the soil and Mrs Armitage had been round once banging on the door, shouting about the noise.

We can't keep this up, said Trevor.

Let's give it three more days, I said.

Trevor nodded and that was the end of our discussion. We'd never been ones for long conferences, Trevor and me. We'd worked together for years, as I said. We didn't need words. We were on the same wavelength, or so I thought.

We just kept digging. We'd take it in one-hour shifts, one digging, the other taking out the dirt. I think the digging was worse, never knowing how far you could risk carrying on before you needed to stop and laboriously wedge in some more struts. The temptation was always to cut corners and push on as far as you could. Being tired didn't help.

I remember I was digging on our fourteenth day. My arms ached, I was gasping for breath in the confined, damp, stinking tunnel and all I could hear was the wretched scraping and scraping in my ears, deafening me. The tinnitus was just getting worse and worse. We'd given ourselves one more day, but I didn't know if I'd even be able to last out that long. And it was at that point, as I gripped the pick head for the millionth time and rammed it into the wall of soil, that I broke through into emptiness. But it wasn't a bank vault and I wasn't alone.

For a filthy hand reached through the hole and then a head and a body. It was a man, covered in dirt, tears of joy running down his face, shouting at me in Russian, 'Bolshoi spasiba', "Thank you, Thank you.' And then he was through the hole. He dropped the pick in his hand, gave me a broad grin and then bear-hugged me, shouting and laughing, clapping my back.

And then there was a sickening thump in the tunnels behind both of us and everything went black.

Trevor would never have managed to dig me out on his own but, as he was trying to, the Police kicked in the door of the shop, Mrs Armitage hopping from foot-to-foot behind them. Just as they were about to try the door, they'd heard the roar of the tunnel collapsing and they'd barged in. They were in time to help Trevor pull me out. And so it was that Mrs Armitage, whom the Police had finally listened to, proved to be my salvation rather than my Nemesis.

That was my final job and it was curtains for my planned retirement. It would be neither Brunswick Square nor Buenos Aires. Instead, it was a seven-year sentence in an Open Prison. As I say, we'd never used violence in our careers, Trevor and me, and I think the judge was quite sorry for us. He probably gave us some extra marks for effort. All that digging.

There was a bit more technology when I went to prison this time. Once a week I'd get a one-hour computer affairs lesson when we were allowed onto the internet. It was supposed to equip us for employment outside. I managed to do a bit of research for a few minutes each lesson when the teacher was talking to one of the others. At that time, I wasn't interested in Civil Wars but in the man in the tunnel, grinning at me and slapping me on the back.

All I could find out in those internet sessions was about the old Millbank Prison which, in the 19th century, covered most of the ground where the Tate Gallery and those red-brick Millbank Estate flats stand now. The North wall of the prison would have run along where my bank branch stood. The Prison started life as a model Penitentiary, but in the 1840s it became just a holding prison for convicts awaiting transportation. And in

1870 it became a military prison. It finally closed for business in the mid-1880s and was then pulled down. You can still see the red prison bricks because they were used to build the ground-floor walls of the Millbank Estate flats.

That was all I could learn in prison. When I was let out after four years of my seven-year sentence, the first thing I did was to send a large bunch of flowers to Mrs Armitage. I signed the card 'From an Admirer.' I then went to the British Library to find my Russian tunnelling friend.

I found out that two members of the Russian terrorist group 'Narodnaya Volva', 'People's Will', had been arrested in London in Autumn 1880. They'd been part of a group of four sent to London to assassinate the Russian Ambassador. One of the Ambassador's previous posts had been Governor of Kiev where he'd overseen the executions of Narodnaya Volya members. The terrorist team in London were picked up during the planning stage, penetrated it is assumed by the Okhrana, the Tsar's Secret Police. Two of the terrorists managed to slip the net. The other two were jailed. Because they were terrorists, it was decided it would be safer to put them in the Millbank Military Prison.

Which was where the two started planning their escape. Security wasn't as good as it would be in a high-security prison nowadays. One of them spoke good English and he managed to get a few words with other prisoners when they were in the exercise yard. He learnt that there was a storeroom up against the North wall and that, inside the storeroom, there was a second room down some steps at the back. It was disused and the floor was just stamped earth.

I don't know how but they managed to break out of their cells one night, carrying the jug of water from each cell and the few scraps of food they'd managed to save up. They headed straight for the storeroom, picked up the tools they needed and began to dig. Looked at logically, their plan was impossible. But desperate men don't stop at logic.

The brilliant part of their plan was that the guards assumed they'd made it over the huge walls somehow. Why would anyone break out of their cells to remain hidden away in prison? So while the manhunt continued outside, they just kept digging as hard as they could. They were lucky not to be disturbed by any visits to the storeroom. Luck always plays its part. None of us can survive without it. But on the third day, their tunnel collapsed. One of them managed to fight his way out through the falling earth but he could do nothing for his friend who was further in. He ran for the guards for help, but they took one look at the collapsed tunnel and decided it would be better just to leave it. The dead Russian was left where he was buried when the tunnel collapsed.

That's what I found out in the British Library, said Lance. The internet is great for instant facts about something you know little about, but it's still the great libraries that will help you dig deeper, so to speak.

I've always thought I was very lucky to get out of our tunnel alive. That job did indeed turn out to be the final page of my career. I was lucky when I got out to be offered a role on a course for ex-offenders, lecturing to school-children. 'Crime Doesn't Pay', that sort of thing. It helped set me on a different course. I get by now buying and selling small antiques, pre-Revolutionary Russian silver if I can get it, but anything will do. I rent a stall a couple of times a week at the London antique markets. I never got that flat in Brunswick Square, but I'm alright. I tried to get Trevor to help me with the antiques, but he never could go straight. He's back inside now. I suppose I was lucky in having the gift of the gab. It allowed me to do these talks for schoolchildren. I tell them about the tunnel and its collapse, but I don't mention the Russian in the tunnel. They'd think I was mad and I don't want to lose the money I get for the talks.

My 'tinnitus' was cured as soon as I was pulled from the tunnel. I've always wondered why Trevor could never hear the scraping noises. Perhaps my love of Russian history and the fact that I can speak Russian made me more susceptible.

The one thing more I ought to tell you is what the Russian was saying as he bear-hugged me, just before the tunnel came down. He was screaming with joy, shouting at me, "Skolka zeem, Skolka lyet!" Loosely translated, it means "It's been a Hell of a long time!"

# 9 THE CONSUL FROM TUNIS

It's interesting how so many of our stories seem to belong to our first few years after college, I said. Perhaps it was the excitement of finding ourselves suddenly launched into the real world after all those years in the rarefied atmosphere of Academia. Perhaps it was just because we were younger then. The colours always seem brighter and sharper when you're young, the experiences more heightened. We were also probably a lot more trusting back then, less sceptical. I wonder if that's what made us more susceptible to ghosts and strange phenomena. I wonder if I'd even recognise a ghost if I met one now.

But that's enough about aging, enough gloom and despondency. I shall tell you a story about when I myself was young and susceptible. It was in my first year after college, before I'd decided to switch to Archaeology and go back for a PhD. Like most of us, I needed to work to pay the rent, I wanted to travel, but I had no idea of what I would or could do in the long term. So I did what a lot of people did back then. I invested my last £200 in a one-week crash course in Teaching English as a Foreign Language. The course was worthless. How could it not be for just £200? But my investment bought me a certificate I could show to prospective employers and my week's training did at least teach me the jargon, enough perhaps to convince prospective students that I knew what I was doing.

And it got me a job, on an initial six-month contract, at a Language Institute in a small quiet town on the Mediterranean coast in southern Spain. The director was very kind. He seemed immensely impressed by my university, even if he hadn't heard of my college. The university name alone was kudos for him and his Institute. It was more than enough to get me in the door and to give me the benefit of the doubt.

I settled in fairly quickly. Whatever the work, there's something continental and civilised about working 8-12 in the morning and 6-8 in the evening. I managed to get most of my marking done between noon and 2pm, have a quick lunch and still have several hours off for siesta. For in those days, the siesta was still a set part of life in such towns. The whole place shut down. It was almost as though you could hear the inhabitants' quiet breathing. I could imagine my director lying on his bed on a white cotton coverlet, no doubt in silk pyjamas, his cigarette carefully stubbed out in an ashtray on the bedside table, beside a half-filled glass and a carafe of water. And it was a simple step from that one scene to picture the whole town at rest on their beds, not so much sleeping as dormant, peaceful and out of this world, as if awaiting some act of magic to restore them.

Not being middle-aged myself, I only lasted a couple of afternoons of that before I had to take to wandering through the deserted streets after lunch, preferring to be part of life, however hushed and stilled that life might be.

I'd walk up to the small park on the hill, the gravelled paths all leading to the centrepiece, a circular stone basin now dried-up and dusty, with a statue in the middle of some solid-looking nymph, respectably dressed, who once would have poured water from her jug. But the fountain was turned off and there was no trickle of noise to disturb the parched parterres and the empty wooden benches.

Down in the town, everything seemed just as restrained. The

81

shops were shuttered and there was no breeze to disturb the tattered bull-fight posters which were peeling from the stone walls. 'Stasis' is what I think one would have called it.

But on my second or third afternoon, I did eventually stumble across some vestiges of life. And it was in an unlikely place, in one of those 19th century covered arcades of small shops. On the corner as you went in, there was an 'Ultramarinos', one of those old-fashioned looking stores selling coffee and spices, things which were once seen as exotic products from 'Overseas' in the days when the world for most people was still very small.

Inside the arcade everything was just as antique. The dusty stone floor had clearly been made to look like marble and it would have shined when it was clean and new. On either side there was a row of small, glass-fronted shops, their windows with much-worn gilt wooden frames. In their prime, they would have given the illusion of luxury. But now they just looked sad, like a Duchess after the Revolution, trying determinedly to cling on to a sense of privilege and aristocracy while being ignored by everyone around her.

In pride of place on one side was an old stationery shop, so old and unsuccessful that some of its merchandise from past decades had now found a new role as decorations. It was one of those places where time had stood still. On one side wall of the window there were battered picture-frames crammed full of old postcards of Spanish beauties from long before the First World War. Guerrero, La Belle Otero, La Tortajada, actresses in long, low-cut dresses wearing improbably large hats made of feathers. While the wall on the other side of the window had been completely papered with small chromolithograph cards depicting heroic scenes from the First World War, cards given away free by a Barcelona chocolate company and collected presumably by some former-owner's now long-dead son.

Opposite the stationery shop there was the one oasis of life in the whole siesta'd town, a small plain coffee shop with four or five tables inside and a couple of tiny metal tables for two outside on the dusty stone floor of the arcade. It was owned, as I discovered, by Mahfoud, a retired wrestler. He was originally from the Spanish Sahara and he appeared to cater for the waifs-and-strays from North Africa who'd found themselves living and working in this town. All men, they either had nowhere particular to go during siesta or they preferred to sit out the few hours gossiping or falling into silence at Mahfoud's before they'd return to their jobs or to their families, if they had one.

I soon made it a habit to kill an hour or more each afternoon, sitting at one of the two outdoor tables with a small Spanish-English dictionary and a copy of a second-hand Spanish comic book I'd picked up on the market. Mahfoud would come over and comment encouragingly on my attempts to learn Spanish and he'd then chat for a bit between customers, mostly with sign-language. I learnt he'd been a wrestler the day he produced an old photograph from his wallet showing him at the height of his career when he'd been in the Spanish national team. He took me inside to show me the framed posters from his bouts on the walls, his Arab clientele all nodding approvingly.

It became a very pleasant routine, my afternoons at Mahfoud's I gradually began to build up a little basic Spanish with the help of the speech-bubbles in the comics. I even learnt some words of Arab greetings from Mahfoud and his clients, greetings which, however stilted, meant so much to all of us when I used them. I suppose it was proof that I was making an effort, that I was trying to climb over the wall between us.

It was the second week of my visits there that I first saw him. A tall, thin, well-dressed figure carrying a cane in his hand, ambling without purpose along the arcade, pausing to look into the shopwindows, smiling or leaning forwards on his cane to peer in at an object more closely. Grey-haired with a military bearing, what struck me first about him was that all his clothes were tailor-made. From his tan-coloured frock coat to his white trousers with straps under the instep, and with the silver pommel on his walking cane, he had gentleman written all over him. And it was odd, as he walked slowly along the arcade that neither Mahfoud nor the others in the coffee shop so much as glanced at him. The gentleman with the cane had clearly become as much of a fixture in their lives as the dusty stationery shop and the 'Ultramarinos' store on the corner.

The odd thing was that he only seemed to appear once a week each Friday. All the same, he was a diversion of sorts in that quiet town and I'd look out for his arrival on Fridays and was happy when, on his fourth appearance, he briefly turned to me in passing and nodded. It was as if he'd let his guard down and I felt that we'd struck up an acquaintance. Although I imagined that, if he were some Spanish grandee, we might still have to wait until we'd been formally introduced.

So it came as an unexpected surprise the following week when he wandered across to my table and asked in polite and impeccable English if he might join me. I got up to shake his hand and quickly offered to get him a coffee as we sat down. He smiled and shook his head, thanking me with a slight wave of his hand.

But if you don't mind, he said, I would rather like to smoke one of these. And he took a plain and much-used silver cigarette case from his pocket, opening it to reveal a few hand-rolled Havana cigarillos and some loose matches. Putting a cigarillo between his lips, he took out a match and leant down to light it by striking it on the sole of his shoe. Settled back in the chair, he drew on the cigarillo and smiled.

It's my one weakness, he said. A nasty habit I picked up when I moved here to live with my daughter, when I retired. My daughter's quite strict with me, so I have to limit myself to one when I'm out on a Friday afternoon. It's my one luxury of the week.

We sat there in silence for a few minutes, while he enjoyed his cigarillo and while I sipped at my long-cold coffee. When he'd finished his cigarillo and stubbed it out on the ground, I ventured to ask him how he'd known I was English. By the cut of your jib, he replied, smiling at me. It takes one to know one. He then gathered up his cane and rose to leave, shaking hands and thanking me for our conversation. As I watched him walk off along the arcade, I wondered what conversation he was referring to.

The following Friday I was amused to see that he didn't dawdle to peer into the shop windows but walked straight up to my table, shook hands and sat down. Once again, he refused my offer of coffee and took out his silver cigarette case. But this time, before the ritual of lighting up, he reached across and shook my hand again. The name's Colonel Partington, he said. Formerly Her Majesty's Consul in Tunis. I introduced myself in turn and he said he was very glad to have met me. We then sat in silence for ten minutes while he smoked his cigarillo.

With the Colonel seeming to be a man of few words, I tried to get the conversation going by explaining what I was doing in southern Spain, describing my work as a teacher at the Institute.

He nodded at me and said that he envied me. I can't say I care much for retirement, he said. It's a kind of Limbo and certainly not something I would have chosen. I have always been an active man, you see. First in the Army and then, for more than thirty years, in the Consular Service. I have never been happy unless up and doing. And now look at me. I'm like a ship high-and-dry. He then slapped his thigh and laughed. What a load of poppycock I'm talking! But I must be off. My daughter will be expecting me. My apologies for boring you. So good to have had this chat.

I watched him as he strode away. There seemed to be more of a spring in his step this time. An eccentric Englishman, I thought, retired and at a loose end, happy to have a few words with a compatriot.

Over the next couple of Fridays, I began to realize just how reticent the Colonel was. He would never volunteer anything, seeming happy just to sit and smoke and listen to the sound of my voice. But when I did manage to get him talking, prompting him with some question that interested him, then he would talk freely and at length about his past and his career. For me, who had never been outside Europe at the time, it was fascinating to hear his stories of another world.

He'd been in Spain before, he said, during the War. But it wasn't clear to me which War he meant. Asked if he spoke

Spanish, he said just a few words. He'd had an interpreter with him all the time during the War, a young Spanish boy who did all his translation for him. And now, in retirement, well, the truth was he'd lost the desire to learn new things. Don't look at me like that, he laughed. You'll probably end up the same way. Give it forty years.

But it was Tunis that really got him talking. He said he'd been Consul there for three decades, something I found hard to credit. I knew friends who'd gone into the Foreign Office and they were not planning on spending more than three years in any one place. It was part of the attraction of the job. But perhaps things were different in Colonel Partington's day? Or perhaps this English eccentric was just a fantasist, making it all up?

But, if he was making it all up, he clearly had a vivid imagination. He described the two-storey Arab townhouse they'd lived in. It was built round an inner courtyard. The ground-floor was for the kitchens, the servants and the storerooms. On the first floor was the Consul's office, their living quarters and a wide verandah with a view of the harbour and the sea. Many was the day he would stand up there with his telescope trying to identify the colours on a Western ship approaching the port. It was a red-letter day when a ship flying the Union Jack came into Tunis.

And yes, he did say 'they'. His wife and children would sometimes work their way into his reminiscences. His wife, it seemed, had often been sickly in Tunis. The heat there, he said, could wear down the best of people. It had got to her nerves, he said sadly. After they'd lived there several years, she suddenly took against sitting up on the verandah. They'd be up there during siesta, his wife on a chaise longue, when she'd start and scream and point to the low parapet that marked the edge of the verandah. Lucy, Lucy, she would shout. She was convinced their small daughter Lucy, their first child, was about to topple over the parapet and fall into the street below. It was just the heat. For Lucy had been dead for five years by then, said the Colonel sadly. She had died of fever aged two in their first year in Tunis. She lies in the Protestant cemetery, the Colonel added, with her mother beside her now.

But the references to his family were few and far between. He was a professional man, devoted to his job, and it was the job that came first. Mostly he talked about the French. It seemed the French were his arch rivals in Tunis. Both Britain and France were keen to secure the overland trade routes to Central Africa. For that, they needed the help and the permission of the Bey of Tunis. That was my goal, said Partington, to secure dominance of those trade routes for Britain. That was the strategic reason why I was there, and it was for that that I worked so hard on the successive Beys and their advisers. Mine was a constant competition to wrong-foot and outwit the French. I should think my machinations against the French in Tunis probably took up two-thirds or more of my despatches back to London.

Trade in what, I asked? I suppose I was thinking of rare metals used in the nuclear and other high-tech industries.

Ivory, gold dust and ostrich feathers, replied the Colonel.

And is there money in ostrich feathers, I asked?

The Colonel looked incredulous. Ladies' hats, for God's sake, he replied. It's worth a fortune, the trade in ostrich feathers.

I confess that, at that point, I was beginning to doubt the Colonel's sanity. I was wondering if madman should be added to fantasist in my efforts to describe him.

It was probably just as well for our friendship that work kept me away for a couple of Fridays. I had to run a series of mock exams to prepare the Institute's students for the real external exams they would have to take at the end of the term. So for two weeks I and my students worked through the siestas, testing and retesting their knowledge and their exam technique.

When I next had a chance to go back to the Café on the first Monday afternoon I was free, I asked after 'the Englishman'.

Mahfoud shook his head, adding that I was the only Englishman he knew. But he said he was glad to see me back and he brought me my usual coffee and small carafe of water without asking.

When the Colonel reappeared on Friday, I asked him about all the despatches he'd sent to London during the long years he'd been in Tunis. It must have been difficult keeping up a dialogue with your bosses at such a distance , I said, but I guessed that telegrams and the telephone would have helped.

The Colonel looked thoughtful for a moment and then shook his head. It's not for a government servant to criticise his superiors, he said sternly. You forget I'd been in the Army. My job was to obey and to get on with the orders I'd been given.

I could only assume from his reply that there had been many occasions when his despatches had gone unanswered. And I began to feel quite sorry for him, in a way. There he had been, a thoroughly professional and dutiful man, putting his work for his government before all else, determined to secure the best he could for his country. Yet, all the time, without the slightest inkling of how he might have been regarded by his superiors in London, without any proof, in fact, that they were reading, let alone considering, his lengthy despatches, or indeed valuing all his work in Tunis.

As the weeks went by, I found it was safer to keep the Colonel away from France and French "designs in North Africa", as he termed it. It only annoyed him and seemed to ruin his Friday afternoon smoke. Instead, I tried to steer him to what interested me, to life in Tunis and to local customs, to a vibrant and colourful world I had never known. He talked of his audiences with the Beys, whom I presumed still held some honorary position even after French rule and then Independence. He talked of his local staff and of his "dragoman", the young son of an Armenian trader who spoke six languages, Arabic and English included. It was this dragoman who went everywhere with the Colonel, explaining to him as best he could the world they were living in.

They are a very superstitious people, the Arabs, the Colonel said to me one afternoon. They are always seeing ghosts and djinns, imagining them, rather. In fact, they are liable to see ghosts around every corner. The locals said the ghosts were souls lost in Limbo, some such nonsense. I had a real problem once with the servants, he added. For some reason they took against going into one of our ground-floor storerooms. It was a dark, dry place which was useful to keep terracotta jars of oil, sacks of dried beans and vegetables, chopped wood for the Winter. Oh yes, it can get very cold in an old Arab house in Tunis.

Anyway, they became scared to go in there, mumbling something about djinns. I asked my dragoman what it was all about. He said they claimed to see the ghost of a lady in there, a Faranji, a European. They wouldn't go near the storeroom. Luckily, my doorman and gatekeeper was a big Sudanese fellow. He went into the storeroom brandishing a large kitchen knife, saying no ghosts would scare him. When he came out alive, the others calmed down a bit. The dragoman arranged for a Sufi Dervish to come by the house and chant prayers in the storeroom. That seemed to do the trick. We didn't have any problems after that. It's funny, really, my late wife had had that storeroom cleared out at one point. She'd fitted it up with calico awnings and a day-bed with a small Arab side-table for her water jug. She used to sit out the worst of the siesta there, after she'd got too scared up on the verandah where she was always imagining she was seeing our late daughter tumbling over the parapet. After my wife's death, we'd turned her siesta room back into a storeroom. As I say, I always preferred the verandah myself.

At the mention of his wife, I asked where they'd gone for their annual holidays, assuming that they took them. How often did they get back to England? It's funny you should mention that, the Colonel replied. We were there ten years before we got our first leave. I remember writing a letter to the Department. They came back quite quickly approving three-month's leave. We spent the Summer in Italy. It was a relief to my wife to get away from the heat, though I was champing at the bit to get back by the end. As I say, I've always been an active sort of fellow, never happier than when I'm doing something.

One afternoon, once we'd known each other a good few months, I ventured to ask the Colonel about why he'd left, about why he'd taken retirement. He looked uneasy and fiddled with his cigarillo case before replying.

I didn't decide to go, he said. I always wonder if it was because I'd stuck my neck out a bit too far the year before. I'd written to the Department suggesting, just suggesting, mind you, that perhaps I could be up for a knighthood, what with my thirty years of service and my time in the Army before that. I never got a reply, but I did wonder whether I'd annoyed them with that.

And was that why you left, I asked?

No, said the Colonel, somewhat shiftily. It was that bloody incident with the French Consul. Excuse my French, he laughed.

The Colonel would not be drawn on this 'incident' but it seemed it was that which cost him his job.

I can't complain, he said. They asked me to leave and gave me a couple of months to get my affairs in order. My youngest daughter was by then married to a fine chap in the Service. He's the Vice Consul here. They very kindly gave me a berth for my retirement. I had nothing back in England and there was nowhere there I could have called home. Which is why you find me here, enjoying your company, annoying you with my cigar smoke each Friday. It's a habit I couldn't get out of, you see. Friday, the holy day, was the one day in Tunis no-one bothered me. I'd go for a stroll, take the air for a bit. Which is why you find me here on a Friday. I couldn't break the habit.

Asked what he did now during the rest of the week, he said he was reading about the Peninsular War. A lot of these fellows who write these books have got it completely wrong, you know, he said, slapping his thigh for emphasis.

I suppose I could have allowed this all to drift on for ever. The Colonel was clearly enjoying our Friday afternoon chats, as I was. It wasn't as though he was doing anyone any harm. On the contrary, you might argue that this was his punishment and that I should allow it to continue. Because for all his strengths, his devotion to duty and his selflessness, the faults were there for all but him to see. His complete inability to doubt or question his superiors, even when it was apparent to an outsider that there must have been times when they dismissed him as an eccentric and even occasions when they held him in contempt. And then, of course, there was his treatment of his poor wife and children. Oh, he undoubtedly loved them, would have done anything for them. It was just that he failed to see what they needed. If it had been pointed out to him, carefully by a friend, that his devotion to duty might have been in itself a form of selfishness, then I'm sure he might have acted differently. It's just that it never was pointed out to him, and his wife went to an early grave as a result. He had no notion of the sacrifices that he and his family had made.

I suppose we are all cautious about playing God. What swung me, though, the tipping point, you could say, was that even then, in the arcade, the Colonel appeared to have absolutely no idea of what had happened to him. To leave him to continue in that Limbo would, I felt then, have been like walking past a dead body on the road. Whoever it was, it was your responsibility to see it decently buried.

So, with the impetuousness of youth, I decided to take the matter into my own hands, to put him out of a misery he wasn't aware he was in. What I would need was something to shock him out of his current state. I should have to play the devil's advocate and find a catalyst to make the explosion happen. It turned out to be easier than I thought.

I steered the conversation one afternoon to the French, to their designs in Africa. That alone was enough to make the Colonel's blood boil. I then suggested quite mildly, as if I thought it was a wholly reasonable thing, that perhaps France was right to have become a Republic. It was perhaps the fact that they were a

Republic which explained their success in Foreign Policy and more generally. In fact, you could argue that the British Monarchy had outlived its usefulness…

At this point, there was a sudden crash and I felt a searing pain in my left hand which had been resting on the metal table. The Colonel, who had brought his cane down on my hand in an outburst of utter fury, was gone. It wasn't that he'd stormed off in a huff. His chair was still upright beside the table. It was just that he had, from one moment to the next, disappeared. And the only signs of his passing were the smashed glass and water carafe lying on the ground and the bright red weal across the back of my left hand.

The noise brought Mahfoud running out of the shop, shaking his head and looking puzzled. He called for his son to come and sweep up the glass. Seeing my hand, he led me through the shop and into the back-kitchen to his wife, whom I had never seen before. She put my hand under the cold tap and then bound it up with a clean white cloth, tut tutting in Arabic, advising me, I guessed, to be more careful.

I must admit I was surprised that Mahfoud never once mentioned this 'accident' when I went back to his coffee shop each weekday as usual. I was also surprised that neither he nor the others there seemed to have found it strange that I should have spent so many afternoons mumbling quietly to myself, the sole customer at the outside tables. I suppose it just didn't matter to them. After all, I was a foreigner and I'd been mumbling in a language they couldn't understand.

As for Colonel Partington, I never saw him again. And, of course, I switched from History to Archaeology. I probably would never have learnt any more about him if it hadn't been for the Internet and Wikipedia over the last few years. It's a godsend when you want to discover a few basic facts about something you know nothing about.

Partington can be found in the footnotes to the histories of North Africa. His army service in the Peninsular War against Napoleon is there, as is his thirty years as Consul in Tunis trying unsuccessfully to thwart French designs on Africa. In fact, his whole life is there, condensed to a few paragraphs. There's even a mention of the 'incident' that finally cost him his job. He'd allegedly struck the French Consul with his cane. I could imagine him doing it. After thirty years of his relentless but ultimately frustrated efforts to block French designs, he had to watch powerlessly as his own Government gave in and acquiesced to French aims in Tunis. It must have seemed like the end of the road for the Colonel, not realising, of course, that another long road was about to begin.

# 10 THE GHOSTWRITER

Do I believe in ghosts, said Giles? Well, I've never seen one. Until I do, all I can say is that I'm prepared to give them the benefit of the doubt. As a good journalist, that's all I can do. Until then, the only stories I can tell you are of other people's ghosts.

We had met again in that same London restaurant for our annual reunion dinner and were now sitting with our coffees and port in front of us, ready to hear the now traditional ghost story which we took it in turns to tell.

This story is from the late Sixties, said Giles. I was laid off from the paper for six months, internal politics I suppose you could call it. I'd spent several months working on an expose of a corrupt businessman. He was a donor to one of the big political parties. I had it from two cast-iron sources that his money was built on property deals which involved acquiring assets cheaply through intimidation. My story made the Front Page and was replayed by most of the other papers and media. The only problem was that soon after we'd gone public, one of my sources died, falling "accidentally" from a high building. My second source then outed himself in the Press to deny having any knowledge of the businessman or his business deals.

The businessman then took us to Court where, without sources to back up our claims, we were hammered. We had to pay enormous damages. Our paper's owner was a businessman himself and didn't like losing. He told the editor to get rid of me.

In short, the editor told me that he'd have no choice but to "rest" me for a while. If I kept my head down for six months, the owner and the world would forget me and the editor could then bring me quietly back. I remember him shrugging his shoulders and saying to me that there were times in life when the bad guys won. You just had to get on with it. He was a decent man, the editor. He even looked out for me financially. He put a word in for me with a publisher who was looking for a ghostwriter to help produce a film star's autobiography. Which is how I got the job for six months working with Gloria Worth, the Hollywood star, on her life story.

I dug out the basic facts from the newspaper archives before I went to see her. A brunette from Doncaster, Gloria Wrigglesworth got her first break in the Theatre during WWII when she was in ENSA in Egypt. She changed her stage-name to Worth, inspired by the 'Je Reviens' Worth perfume which had been her idea of everything glamorous when she was a teenager. After the War, she was talent-spotted for Hollywood and never looked back, at least for twenty years. She was the beautiful heroine of a dozen blockbusters with as many high-profile romances before she married the Argentinian racing-driver Juan Despadi in the early Fifties. At which point she became Madame Despadi in private life, the shining star of that glamorous marriage, one or both of them photographed in nearly every Society magazine for a decade. A marriage made in Heaven etc.

Everything seemed to go wrong for her after Despadi was killed at a Formula One race in the late Fifties. She carried on working for a year or two before pulling out half-way through a production of 'Anthony and Cleopatra'. The film project collapsed, the finance went down the toilet and the businessmen of Hollywood never forgave her. She disappeared from the

Society pages completely. Her only subsequent appearance was when old file photographs were dug out and reprinted at the time of her marriage in 1962 to Ronald Durkheim, the reclusive multi-millionaire. The two would reportedly live at his mansion in 35 acres of grounds in Sussex, but there were no Press releases or inspired leaks to the gossip columnists to flesh out the story. And, without those leaks, the story died.

And now, seven years later, I was being paid to ghost-write her autobiography. I confess I had no idea what I would find when I met her or why on earth she now wanted an autobiography at all. But on a warm, Spring day I stepped out of a taxi in front of imposing Victorian Lodge gates and rang the bell on the stone pillar.

Nothing happened. There was no Intercom, just a bell which I rang again. Patience being a virtue for investigative journalists, I lit a cigarette, leant against the pillar and prepared to wait. After what seemed like ten minutes, I saw this old man trudging slowly along the drive towards the Gates. I stubbed out my second cigarette and got ready to be civil to the staff.

He was about seventy years-old, thin and well-kept. His clothes might be dull, just grey corduroys and a grey cardigan over a white shirt, but there were gold cuff-links in the shirt and everything he was wearing was well-made.

I am sorry for the delay, he said, as he unlocked the gate for me. It's our butler's day off and I didn't want to bother the cook. She's making our lunch. Durkheim, he said, holding out his hand, Ronald Durkheim. I am very pleased to meet you.

What surprised me as we walked together up the long drive, and he chatted amiably on, was that he seemed to have done his research on me. He commented approvingly on various stories I had covered and was sympathetic about the most recent expose and the subsequent Court case. In an echo of my editor's words, he shook his head sadly and said these things were sent to try us, but that the good won out in the end. That was his experience anyway.

When we reached the front of the Georgian house, he paused and smiled. My wife won't be ready yet, he said. Come on, I'll show you the garden for an hour. And he led me round the side of the house onto a huge, paved terrace and down steps to a wide lawn and then, through an archway in a high hedge on one side, to a whole of series of enclosed spaces. Walled rose gardens, water gardens, hot-houses, temperate houses, pineapple beds and alpine rockeries. It was like being taken around Kew Gardens as a child. This was clearly his world, and it was enormous. Anyone in their right mind would be happy to be a recluse here.

This is just some of it, he said, as he led me back up to the house over forty-five minutes later. I hope I'll have time to show you more in future. But now we've just time for a drink before lunch. My wife should be in the library.

In what was a new experience for me, this kindly multi-millionaire took my coat and went off to hang it up in a Cloakroom before returning to lead me into a huge, book-panelled room, sunlight pouring in from four sets of French windows onto the rich reds and blues of Turkish rugs. And standing in front of one set of French windows, her back towards us, was a Hollywood star in what looked like a black Chanel dress, the sort of haute couture you might see on Aubrey Hepburn.

For the first thing that struck me as she turned round was that she was still very much a Hollywood star. Tall and slim and with a face that any camera might fall in love with. There was nothing 'retired' or 'withdrawn' or 'reclusive' about Mrs Durkheim. She looked just as Gloria Worth had done in the days when she'd be arriving at some Hollywood Premier. Everything about her said professional. But, for all that, there was something detached in the way she smiled and shook my hand and hustled her husband into fixing us drinks. I couldn't help feeling she was just going through the motions. Whatever the purpose was of the autobiography, it wasn't to promote a comeback.

And over lunch, it was her husband and I who did most of the talking. She sat there nodding at what we said, smiling at our jokes, but without any apparent desire to join in. She was there but not there, if you know what I mean. There was nothing about her you could latch onto. Not even her voice. There was no trace of her original Northern accent. Nor was there any hint of the Americanisms you might have expected her to have picked up in Hollywood. She spoke with a bland, washed-out neutral Home Counties middle-class English accent. It was as perfect as a Radio newsreader, but it was as though you were listening to the broadcast on another continent and the news being read was several years old. I remember when the cook came in to ask her Mistress if she might serve our coffees in the lounge, it was left at last to Mr Durkheim to respond.

I must admit I was beginning to dread my first working session with Gloria Worth. My technique as a journalist has always been to let the other person talk and it was difficult to see how that would work with her. But the time came when her husband duly left the lounge, wishing us every success with the book, and she led me off into a large room she described as her study. There was a small Georgian writing desk by one wall. But the room was dominated by two long silver-coloured satin sofas facing each other across a long mahogany coffee-table on which were laid out several piles of buff-coloured folders and expensive photograph albums each bound in matching red leather. Seating ourselves either side of the coffee-table, she began.

I've prepared all this to help you get started, she said. Perhaps the best thing would be for me to leave you for a couple of hours to look through them. We could then have a chat about how best to take this forward. And with that, she smoothed her dress over her thighs, stood up and was gone.

When she'd left, I took off my jacket, made myself comfortable and settled down to do what I'd been told. Whatever "this" was, it was going to be a strange sort of project.

The buff folders were easy to skim through. In date order, they started with playbills for her appearances, Press cuttings on her performances and longer reviews and profiles from the magazines. After the first few years, there were also Press releases from her agent and from her Hollywood Studios, mini-CVs with only the details they wanted to publicise left in. There wasn't a great deal in the buff folders that was going to help me, beyond giving me a structure for her career. I duly took out my notebook and jotted down the key points, passing over in silence most of the Studio publicity hand-outs.

I then moved on to the photograph albums. They seem to have been prepared, with no expense spared, all at the same time, just after her final aborted film, 'Anthony and Cleopatra'. It seemed as though she'd just dumped whole bundles of photographs, perhaps in envelopes for each year, on one of London's most prestigious book-binding firms. The result was this set of distinguished-looking red leather albums, with the spines ornately tooled in gold. The odd thing was that none of the photos were captioned. She'd obviously never had the time or inclination to record her life or her friends. But for some reason, she'd eventually decided all these photos should be gathered together and put in order. As a memorial?

There were a couple of albums of her early life, her family and friends in Doncaster. Cheap snapshots of her as a smiling baby. In a lot of photographs in her teens, she was in or near water. Swimming seemed to have been her favourite hobby. She was either at the Lido or, in Summer, out by the river.

However, as soon as she became an actress, the albums were dominated by Press photos of her roles. There were more photos of her on stage or on camera than there were in private life. Perhaps there were more envelopes of private photos which had never been passed to the London bookbinder?

The one album that stood out was the third in the series. It was during the War when she'd been in Egypt, in Alexandria apparently. What was most striking was that the contents, so different to the photos of the other albums, had clearly been collected with love. It was like a child's scrapbook with every small piece of ephemera being treasured and given its place. It seemed to be a love-song to Alexandria. There were bus-tickets and cinema programmes, cigarette packets and dance cards, all carefully pressed flat and mounted. Several pages were devoted to paper napkins from Cafes and Restaurants. Maison Baudrot, Pastroudis, Delices, Tornazakis, Gambrinus, Cap D'Or, Restaurant Stella. These were all things she'd pocketed and kept carefully clean, souvenirs perhaps of a fabulous new world she'd feared she would one day lose.

Absorbed in the ephemera of the sadly long-dead world of a cosmopolitan Alexandria, I didn't notice how time had passed, nor that Gloria Worth had quietly re-entered the room. She had closed the door softly behind her and was standing in front of it, her back leaning against the wood, a slight smile on her face.

I hope you've found some of the folders and albums useful, she said. We had better go and join my husband for tea. We'll leave our chat about the book until next time. I could tell you about some of the people in the photos, if that would help.

On the train back to London, I took out my notebook and read through everything I'd scribbled down. Flicking through the Alexandrian album was the only time in the whole day when I felt I might be ghostwriting the autobiography of a real woman, a living creature of flesh and blood.

Our arrangement was that I should visit her in Sussex once a week to interview her. In the meantime, I was supposed to follow up my other lines of research. She'd given me carte blanche to talk to any of her friends and colleagues and said that I should tell them to ring her if they wanted. She'd tell them that I had her permission.

That first week, however, I had precious little to go on, precious little to follow up. I did pay for a boozy lunch with our paper's film critic to try and get a better feel for what had made Gloria Worth so famous and so marketable. What the public liked about her, he explained, was that all her characters on screen were impetuous. They acted on impulse and it made for great drama. The women she played were a force of nature, not calculating or shrewd. There was an intense 'honesty' to her impetuousness which people admired. They could see that she was one of them. The only difference was that she was up on the screen and playing out the role of Lady Macbeth or Joan of Arc or Cleopatra. But then Cleopatra was the film she flunked, he said. So perhaps not Cleopatra. My point though, he added, leaning across the table for emphasis, is that whatever role she played, she was impetuous, fiery. People like that. Maybe it's because we can't live our own lives like that. In the real world, we have to compromise.

Standing once more outside the Victorian iron gates waiting for the butler this time to trudge up the drive, I found it hard to reconcile the impetuousness of her film characters with the detached and almost ethereal figure in the black Chanel dress whom I had met. I remembered how I'd looked up suddenly the week before and seen her standing just inside the door. I knew she was leaning against it but I just couldn't imagine that there was the slightest pressure from her shoulder-blades on the wood.

I was tugged out of this philosophising by the pleasant but uncommunicative butler who led me up to the front of the house where Durkheim was waiting for me.

You find me again in my gardening clothes, he said, smiling and shaking my hand. You won't be surprised to hear she's still not ready. Come on, I'll show you some more of the garden.

Taking a different direction from the lawn this time, we went through a red-brick arch and past two lawn tennis courts, immaculately kept but looking too pristine to be played on.

Tennis was always very popular when I had weekend house-parties in the old days, said Durkheim, seeing me looking at the smooth manicured grass courts. I keep them in good order, but we don't use them much ourselves.

Another high red-brick wall, another arch and we entered a wide, stone-paved area with a Roman-style arcade along two sides. In one of the arcades there were what looked like dressing-rooms. The centrepiece of this whole paved area was an almost Olympic sized swimming pool. The pool had shining blue ceramic tiles with painted gold dolphins and orange suns as decorations. Once again, it was immaculately clean. But there was no water in the pool. It was like a film-set, all-built and ready, just waiting for the cast and the technicians to arrive, waiting for the water to flood in and for the Director to shout 'Action'.

We don't use the pool much either, said Durkheim. But then, of course, it was always a summer thing.

Leaving the empty pool behind, we went through an old wooden door in another red-brick wall, this time 18th century, and entered the Kitchen Gardens, beyond which were a line of greenhouses and glass-frames.

All the fruit and vegetables you'll have for lunch come from here, said Durkheim proudly. Which reminds me that time is getting on.

After what was to become a set weekly routine over the following months of a quick drink, a long lunch a trois, with Mrs Durkheim smiling but saying little, and then a brief interlude for coffee in the lounge, I found myself back again in her study, alone with the subject of the book I was writing.

And, unlike the first afternoon, Mrs Durkheim did stay and talk. And, although I say it myself, it required all my skill at gentle and unobtrusive prompting to get her to talk. We began with the first photograph album of her childhood and her life in Doncaster before the War. She seemed more comfortable speaking about photographs than trying to articulate thoughts without these visual aids. Perhaps like all actors, she needed a cue or a prop. Whatever it was, the photographs did help to get her talking.

Yes, she'd been mad about swimming. Yes, the teenage boy in the photos was her first boyfriend. John he was called. In the Summer they'd go swimming in the river at Spotbrough. The river was more than twelve feet deep there and you could swim underwater. She was always a much stronger swimmer than John. He never could swim underwater. He'd read some newspaper story about someone getting tangled in riverweed and drowning. He was also hopeless at duck-diving, so he couldn't get underwater anyway. She would duck-dive down, swim underwater and grab him by the legs to pull him under. You should have heard him shout.

Poor John, I couldn't help thinking to myself. He had to put up with a lot for love.

I was happy then, she said. And she grinned as she looked at the old black-and-white snapshot of this long-legged girl in her one-piece swimming costume, a towel in her hands, shaking her wet hair by the river, a photo presumably taken by John.

But it was when we moved on to the Alexandria album that she suddenly became truly alive. It was as if a ghost had woken up, with blood coursing once again through her veins. She started to fidget in her seat and then moved round to sit next to me, so she could more easily pore over the pages and point out for me what she thought was the most interesting.

I joined the RAF for my war service, she said. They trained me as a typist and, after a boring year on bases in the UK, I was posted out to Egypt. You can't imagine what it was like to go from Doncaster to that brilliant sunlight and that bright blue sky. I was still on a base but this base was on the edge of Alexandria and I was in a wonderful new world. We'd get leave and, however short that leave was the invitations would come flooding in. Everywhere I went was exciting and glamorous. Iced coffees and Egyptian cigarettes at all those smart Cafes, car-trips to Lake Mareotis, dances at The Sporting Club. I was much in demand.

Don't name names in the book, she said, but there was a New Zealand Captain I spent a lot of time with. He was in the Long Range Desert Group. Whenever he was back, he'd find some way of smuggling me off base for a whirlwind of parties before his leave was over. It was a magical time. I felt as though I'd come alive, she laughed.

That was before you began acting, I said.

Yes, it was when I was on the base. There was this noticeboard by the canteen where they'd pin up things about Clubs or Sports. One day there was a notice about a play being put on by one of the English lecturers at the university in Alexandria. There'd be a "star" from ENSA in the lead role, but they were looking for some amateurs to fill the minor parts. It was a 1920s Country House farce and I got the role of The Fourth Flapper, or something like that. Anyway, I enjoyed it, I seemed to have a flair for it and it got me noticed by all those putting on plays in Alexandria. The RAF saw it as a contribution to the War Effort, keeping up morale etc. So, where they could, they'd give me time off to rehearse and act. I'd always look forward to those afternoons when the lorry would turn up at the gates with the ENSA crowd to whisk me off for rehearsals. There again, it was another world for me. That's when I became Gloria Worth. Wrigglesworth didn't have quite the same ring to it on the playbills.

Turning the pages of the album, I stopped at one of the small snapshots. It showed Gloria Worth and a young British soldier sitting together stiffly on a small bench in front of some cardboard scenery, as if they were the loving couple on some early cigarette card.

But that's John, I said, from Doncaster.

Yes, she said, looking at the photo. He'd joined the Army and, by a miracle, ended up at an airfield outside Alexandria, although he was doing secret work.

We don't look very happy in the photo, do we? I suppose the problem was that my life had changed since we'd last met in Doncaster. We did go out once for an afternoon in Alexandria when we both got leave the same day. I felt as though I owed it to him. But I didn't have anything to say. I remember it was a pretty grim afternoon. We had that photo taken at one of those small Armenian photo-stores.

We then went to one of the Egyptian markets. I needed to buy some black silk for a dress for a play I was going to be in. It was hot and dusty and neither of us were enjoying ourselves much as we trailed round the piles of cloths and cotton piled up any-old-how on the ground. Eventually I found some black silk that looked as if it might work. I'd haggled the price down as far as I could and was reaching for my purse when John started fiddling with the silk. He told me he could tell by the feel of it that it was parachute silk, one of the many parachutes that had been siphoned out of British Forces Stores and found their way onto the black market. He told me I couldn't buy it. It was wrong. Buying black market stuff wouldn't help the War Effort. Parachutes were like gold dust to the RAF.

So we stood there and argued in that hot, dusty Bazaar with the seller looking at us as though we were a boring married couple having a row over the household budget. In the end I just bought it. It may have been a parachute once, I said, but now it's just a length of black silk and I need it for part I had to play. That was my War Work. That was how I helped the War Effort. John just scowled and went silent, but I got my silk.

To try and cheer him up, I suggested we go to Pastroudis for iced coffee and cakes. But poor John just wasn't comfortable there either. It was all Officers, white tablecloths and shining cutlery. Poor John knocked over his drink he was so nervous. It wasn't a great afternoon. We ended up killing the last hour before we had to go back in one of those Department Stores. We went there just to be somewhere with the electric fans. It was one of those places where the Greek and Italian shopgirls follow you around always being too helpful. Until they decide, after ten minutes, that you're not going to buy anything, that you are no richer than they are. And then they just go back to the counter, dismissing you with a contemptuous glance. As I say, it wasn't a successful afternoon. I remember we ended up shaking hands when we parted. I'm not sure how that photo got in the album. I guess it was just in with all the other stuff I sent when I had the albums made.

And was that the last you saw of him, I asked?

No, she said sadly. I was going out with the New Zealander, as I told you. John kept pestering me for another date. He came to one of the plays I was in and spent the evening hanging around back-stage. It became a joke amongst the other actors. I told him about the New Zealand Captain but that only seemed to make him more persistent. John said he wanted to show me his secret work, assuming that it would somehow impress me, win me back, if I am not being too melodramatic.

He just wouldn't give up. It was getting embarrassing. Eventually I agreed to visit him on his airfield and see his great secret work. I thought it would be a way of bringing the whole thing to an end. I could tell him it was over and that he should find himself someone better.

We agreed a date at his base one evening. I got an Officer-friend to drop me off there, saying I was going to say goodbye to a friend who was flying out that night. Lucky fellow, said my Officer.

There was a guard at the gate who nodded me through and there was John waiting to escort me to the hangar where he worked. It seemed that the airfield was run jointly with the Americans. They were always managing to smuggle their girlfriends in overnight. The guard on the gate was obviously a friend of John's, but then the perimeter fence didn't look as though it would be difficult to get through.

John's hangar was a Stores hangar full of the equipment waiting to be packed into canisters and dropped to the Resistance in Greece and the Balkans. John's work may have been secret, but he was just a Stores Assistant.

I could see, though, why it was popular with the Americans and their girlfriends. Along with the trestle tables covered in weapons and ammunition and kit, there were piles of silk parachutes on the ground waiting to be folded. I imagine that a pile of silk parachutes could be just as comfortable as the cotton sheets in a luxury hotel.

John proudly gave me a guided tour. The explosives, the rifles, the pistols, the ammunition, the wireless sets and chargers, all of which, he explained, had to be logged in to a large ledger on a desk at one end of the hangar. The rest of the kit such as the

106

food and the clothes and the items for the parachutists' personal packs (the commando knives, the emergency rations, the silk maps etc), they were less fussy about. Which is presumably why parachute silk ended up for sale on the Market.

He then showed me the long, metal canisters. Weapons and wireless sets and other breakables would be dropped in canisters with parachutes. The less precious items like the food and clothes would be released from the plane in canisters without parachutes, silk being expensive in wartime. Boots were just tied together in bundles of forty and dropped out of the plane as they were. Yes, he said, it could be dangerous for those on the receiving end at a drop. He explained to me in great detail how the canisters were marked up with chalk when they'd been filled, to show which needed parachutes. John was in his element as a Stores Assistant and so proud of his role in this secret world.

After what seemed like a very long time, with me nodding politely at his every explanation and description, he moved on to make his pitch. Marriage was what he wanted. I shan't bore you, she said, with the professions of love, the pleading, the desperation. I just told him straight it was over. We weren't children in Doncaster anymore. Life had moved on and I had a different future ahead of me. I was sorry but that was all I could say.

After an hour of emotion with John ending in tears, I walked out on him, out of the hangar and off the base. The guard, John's friend, nodded at me conspiratorially as I left. I had to walk about a mile along a dusty road with my shoes in my hand till I was passed by the first lorry on its way back to Alexandria. I flagged it down and jumped in. I never saw John again.

He stopped bothering you, I asked?

No, he disappeared, she said. He deserted, went AWOL. No-one ever saw him again. There was a Court Martial hearing in absentia. They found that on the night he'd disappeared, a Browning pistol and a clip of ammunition had also gone missing. The base gate-guard gave them a description of me and they soon found the Officer who'd dropped me off there and even the lorry-driver who'd rescued me on the Alexandria road. I was hauled in for cross-questioning. Once they'd heard from me what had happened that night, they came to the conclusion that poor John had probably just walked off into the desert with the pistol to kill himself.

The Court came down on me like a ton of bricks, but the punishment wasn't as strong as their words. I got off with a month confined to barracks which meant I missed two plays. But it was a turning-point for me in a way. Once I was allowed back into the world, I lobbied my ENSA friends for a transfer to them. Acting became my full-time profession and I didn't look back.

You didn't marry the New Zealand Captain, I asked?

Sadly, he was killed on a patrol in Libya, she said. My life then changed in more ways than one.

She leaned forward to shut the album and suggested it was time we joined her husband for tea.

On the train back to London later that afternoon I kept my notebook shut. Instead, I just stared out of the window as the landscape poured past, musing at how this silent ghost of our first meeting had suddenly come alive in her descriptions of wartime Alexandria.

Over the next couple of months, we continued with the weekly interviews but I couldn't get her to return to the life and liveliness she'd shown when talking about Alexandria. She would sit formally on her side of the coffee-table, smiling and nodding at my questions, helping me with explanations but not, as far as I could see, in any way revealing herself. I might just as well have been a journalist turning up for a one-off interview at the Studios, sent there by a magazine to get two pages of inane copy about her latest film.

There were even times when she would fail to appear at all. I would spend a pleasant hour walking round the grounds with

Durkheim before lunch, wondering how long it would take her to put on her make-up for the act she was about to perform, only to find out when we got back to the house that she had developed a sudden headache and wouldn't be able to join us. Durkheim would apologise and always insisted that I stay to have lunch with him before I went back.

And so I got to know quite a lot about Ronald Durkheim, even though it was not his autobiography I was writing. This was his first marriage and I guessed it was his first experience of love. He was obviously besotted and was prepared to put up with anything to keep the marriage alive. Even the rich learn patience when they fall in love.

He was one of those people who, if not forever cheerful, was at least always prepared to make the best of things. He was a hard-working, straightforward man who had had one brilliant idea early on in his business career and who had capitalised on it. He'd seized his chance and run with it, was how this rather un-athletic man described it.

He once showed me in one of his greenhouses the fruit of some tropical plant, the name of which I don't remember. It looked like an exotic artichoke and Durkheim peeled back the overlapping layers of fruit which surrounded the kernel. Watertight, you see, he said, but all so simple. I saw it once in the Botanical Gardens. That's where I got the idea for my first big success, my milk cartons made of wax-covered cardboard. They were cheap but more than durable enough to serve their purpose. They closed in the same way as the plant and they revolutionised the art of food packaging. Naturally I made sure I had the patent. If it wasn't for that, I shouldn't own this house and these greenhouses. I shouldn't be lucky enough to find myself married to Gloria.

Come on, he said, I'll show you my other pride-and-joy. He led me over to a large, square greenhouse, built in the Victorian style with a white-painted timber frame and shining clean glass panels. From a distance, with the sunlight on the glass, it had looked like some futuristic temple. Closing the door behind us, he led me through a small lobby to the inner door of the greenhouse. Inside the air was tropical. Condensation ran down the glass walls of the greenhouse and it took me a few moments to adjust to the heat of this new-found world. A flag-stoned path ran around the edge with a three-seat wooden bench on each side. The greenhouse itself was given over to one huge, square shallow pond on which rested the most enormous waterlilies. Some of the leaves were six feet across. Victoria amazonica, he said. The leaves are so strong that a small child could sit on one.

We stood there in silence looking at the huge round leaves, resting flat on the surface, and at the white flowers between them. This is where I come to think, and to forget, he smiled. I am not a Catholic, as you can guess by my name. Watching these lilies is the nearest I shall ever get to absolution. The sight of them tends to wipe everything clean.

You and your wife must spend many happy hours sitting here, I said, pointing to one of the benches beside the pond.

No, I am afraid Gloria can't abide this place, he said. I don't think it's so much the lilies as the water. She seems to hate it. That's why, of course, we don't have water in the swimming-pool.

But your wife loves swimming, I said. I've seen photographs of her when she was a girl by the river. And all those pictures from her Hollywood days of her climbing out of swimming-pools.

Not now, he said sadly. I suppose all of us change.

And he walked with me back to the house for our lunch a deux before the butler phoned for a taxi to take me back to the station.

Finding myself baulked by the interviews, or lack of them, with Gloria Worth, I tried to put more energy into finding and interviewing her old friend and contacts. It became pretty clear quite quickly that there were more contacts than friends. She was not a person who seemed to make friends. As one former ENSA actress from Alexandria put it, what emotional energy

110

Gloria has she saves for her acting and for her lovers and husbands. There's not enough to go round for friends.

I asked the actress about the New Zealand Captain, whom she hadn't heard about, and Poor John, the Doncaster boyfriend.

The one who walked off into the desert and shot himself, she said? I didn't know he'd been a boyfriend. I thought he was just some star-struck fan. We do get them, she smiled, or used to at any rate. The scandal was a nuisance for Gloria for a while. She lost a good role. But then she fell on her feet when she joined ENSA full-time. She was grabbed by one of the British Institutes in Cairo who were putting on 'Macbeth'. Playing Lady Macbeth was her first real triumph. She'd wangled a black silk dress from somewhere and looked a million. And her acting was superb. You felt the character had been written just for her. She lived and breathed the role. In the short-term, it got her a romance with a Serbian prince. More importantly it was the 'Macbeth' that finally got her talent-spotted for Hollywood. She left for the US in 1945, dropping the prince at the same time. What's the use of a prince who has no country, she said to me?

I must admit that I got to like that former ENSA actress. We had several lunches together. Convent-educated, she had found a lucrative niche later in life playing Cockney character roles on TV. And she was very good at it. The public loved her and viewing figures always rose on the nights she was on. Her fans sincerely believed she was genuine.

But that's what acting's all about, she laughed. Why look so shocked? If Cockneys are what brings in a wage, then it's a Cockney I shall be. Although it's just as well my old nuns aren't still around to see me. They didn't hold with 'lying' and they always said I'd come to no good.

At our third lunch, in a small Italian restaurant in Soho, I put to her the problems I was having getting Gloria Worth to talk and I confessed that I had no real idea why she wanted an autobiography at all.

She looked at me and laughed. Men, she said, God help us! I don't know about the autobiography, but I gave you the clue to get her talking. Gloria saves her emotion for her acting and for her lovers and her husbands. If this autobiography ends up as just a list of her great films, then who will buy it? Why don't you cut to the chase and ask her about Despadi? From what I've heard, from people who knew them when they were married, I don't think anyone ever got as close to her as that Argentinian racing-driver husband of hers. A far cry from her current husband, I should imagine.

And so, when I was next granted an interview with Mrs Durkheim, I picked up the relevant photo album and turned to the photos of Despadi.

It was now early Summer, a warm day in June, and we were sitting on the terrace in wicker-work chairs beneath a green-and-white striped awning, with a low bamboo table between us on which were a selection of the photo albums. I remember she was wearing a white cotton shirt and a knee-length white linen skirt with three thin lines of coloured piping around the hem, red, orange and green. It was the only colour she was wearing. She stood up and reached down to pick up the albums and place them on the ground. She then moved the bamboo table in front of us and pulled her chair across beside mine. She took the Despadi photo album from me and placed it on the low table in front of us. She leant forwards, flicking the hair from her face before starting to leaf through the photographs from her marriage to Despadi.

I was wondering when you'd come to this, she said, continuing to turn over the pages of the album. You must understand that Hollywood is a very superficial place. Everything there, the emotions, the rows, the scenes, the romances, they could all come from the cheapest of B movies. The longer you live there and work there, you begin to feel you have left the real world and real people for ever. Everything there is golden and shining but it is all paper-thin. It's like one of my husband's cardboard milk cartons, which I am sure he will have told you about. His packaging contains milk. It serves a purpose. It's

112

useful. All that Hollywood contains is money, for those that are lucky enough to get it. No life and no soul. All hollow.

Which is why it was such a relief, such a joy, to meet Juan, she said. A real person who did things, who took real risks and was happy to do so. It was as though a man of flesh and blood had walked into a cardboard city.

What was he there for, I asked?

It was the Winter, outside the racing season. He'd been invited to be the technical adviser on a Grand Prix film my Studio was shooting. I wasn't in the film, but we met at a Studio party. It was one of the luckiest days of my life. We just clicked. We were married in a month. It was the first time for both of us. I suddenly found myself where my mother had always wanted me to be. "Settled" is how she'd have described it.

And we were very happy, she said, turning over some of the pages to look at the photographs of the two of them smiling together, pictures from all over the world, wherever she was filming or he was racing. We worked very hard to be together, she said, whenever we could manage it.

And for the next hour or more, she leant over the album, holding the hair back from her face with one hand while carefully turning over the pages and pointing out to me the places, the people and the occasions. I'd never seen her so absorbed. It was like watching a small child crouch down to peer into a rock-pool, transfixed by a whole new world. But, in her case, this was just memories, pictures of the past she must have pored over so many times before. I'd expected to see her become nostalgic or even sad. Instead, she seemed first-and-foremost to be curious. It was as though she was somehow puzzled at how happy she had been during that marriage, as though it was something she hadn't realized at the time, however much she had just told me she had been.

Can I ask you a personal question, I said at last?

She looked up and nodded.

I am just a simple journalist, a hack. I have never moved in your glamorous world, let alone lived and worked there. I have never even been particularly ambitious. What I am going to say will probably just seem stupid, but I have to ask.

She was still looking at me but this time half-smiling. I had the impression she knew what I was about to say. It even crossed my mind for a fraction of a second that the whole afternoon on that sun-lit terrace had been designed by her to get me to ask this very question.

Didn't you and your husband ever think of retiring, I asked? You had enough money to do anything, to live anywhere you wanted. Why didn't he give up Formula One and you Hollywood?

She shut the album slowly, stretched out her long legs, leant back in her chair and closed her eyes. As the seconds of silence ticked by, a slight breeze rustled the poplars at the far side of the lawn. I noticed that her hands suddenly gripped tightly on the arms of the chair. Her knuckles were as white as her blouse and skirt. I assumed she was steeling herself to reply. It was as if she was holding herself in like an alcoholic determined to put off the next drink, her whole body now taut with this effort of will.

After what seemed several minutes but was probably less than one, she opened her eyes again, released the grip on her chair and turned her head to face me.

He did want to retire, she said slowly. He wanted to give up Formula One for the very reasons you've mentioned. He said that we should buy a ranch in Argentina, he'd become a cattle rancher. He explained that this wouldn't be like being a farmer in England. In Argentina we would be landowners and could live in style and wealth. We'd have a house in Buenos Aires as well. He wasn't suggesting I should shut myself away on the Pampas.

But you didn't retire, I said.

No, she said softly, I persuaded him to race one more Season, so that we could have more time to think it over. I was the one who persuaded him to carry on racing. If it wasn't for me, he would have given up before the race that killed him. Perhaps his instinct had told him that it was time to call it a day. But he didn't. He listened to me. I suppose you could say that it was me that led to his death. You could say that I was the one that killed him.

When she'd waved away all my attempts to insist that this wasn't true, we sat in silence until the butler appeared from nowhere, as if by magic, with a new tray of cold drinks.

When he'd gone, she looked at me again, but without any expression on her face.

Well, that's a confession you've extracted from me, she said. That's what you investigative journalists do, isn't it, dig out secrets?

She then smiled and laughed. Don't worry, she said, I don't hold it against anyone for doing their job or for wanting to be good at it. She leant across with her glass of iced water and clinked it against mine.

Later that evening, when the train was pulling into London and I had been staring out of the window at the half-lit countryside and towns for the whole journey, I had to admit that I still had no idea why Gloria Worth wanted an autobiography or who this person was that I was supposed to be writing about.

As for her 'confession', what had she actually confessed to? Forcing myself to stay level-headed and unemotional, putting the image of her to one side, all I could say was that a racing-driver had chosen to carry on racing too long. Wasn't that all there was to it, however much she might feel she had made him continue against his will when his instinct told him it was time to stop? What I did have to accept, however reluctantly, was that Despadi's life was not the thing that had been most important to her.

115

The next week I was there it was the butler who came out to meet me at the gate.

I am sorry, Sir, he said, Mrs Durkheim will not be ready to see you until lunch and Mr Durkheim had to go to London yesterday on business. He asked me, if he didn't get back this morning, that I should make sure you had a drink on the terrace while you were waiting for Mrs Durkheim.

So I sat beneath the awning looking at the poplars blowing in the breeze and at the hedges and walls on either side of the lawn which led to all those different secret worlds of rose gardens and hot-houses and of swimming pools and immaculately-kept tennis courts which were never used.

When the butler returned with my drink, I stopped him and asked about the gardens.

I've never seen the gardeners here, I said. You must need an army of them to keep these gardens in order.

The butler put the empty tray down on the table and smiled.

Ah yes, there were a lot of gardeners when I was first here, he said, before Mr Durkheim got married. And ground-staff too for the swimming pool and the tennis courts, not to mention the hot-houses. They require an awful lot of work.

But who does the work now, I asked?

Well, I help Mr Durkheim with the tall hedges, he said. He's not so good on a high ladder as he used to be.

But who does everything else?

Mr Durkheim does it, said the butler. He has one of those sit-on lawnmowers for the grass and, of course, the hot-houses are all run by electricity and they all have sprinkler systems. It's not like the old days when the greenhouse boys had to be up at 6am to stoke the boilers.

But it still must take him for ever, I said. I am amazed he has

116

the time, given his business.

Oh, he's sold off much of his business, I believe. And he delegates much of what's left to his managers. They've been with him for years and he trusts them.

And this is all since he got married, I asked?

Yes. To be honest, Sir, Mrs Durkheim is not comfortable around a lot of people she doesn't know well. She feels happier now that it's just my wife, Cook that is, and me.

But what's she afraid of, I asked?

I really couldn't say, Sir. That's just the way she likes thing run. All employers have different ways of doing things.

I mean the grounds look pretty secure, I continued. There's the high perimeter wall and the gates are always kept locked.

Yes, Mrs Durkheim insists on that, said the butler. And, of course, she also insisted that broken glass be cemented along the top of the brick wall. So we should be safe from intruders. Not that we've ever had any in these parts, to be honest.

Perhaps thinking that he'd said too much about his employers, the butler nodded at me as he picked up the empty tray again and headed back to the house.

Mr Durkheim didn't make it back in time for lunch, so Gloria Worth and I were served a light lunch of salads in our wickerwork chairs on the terrace.

It's more fun like this, she said. It reminds me of picnics by the river outside Doncaster. Although it was just sandwiches wrapped in grease-proof paper and a couple of bottles of Tizer in those days.

Do you regret giving it all up, I asked, suddenly changing the subject?

What, the Tizer, she smiled? I suppose you mean Hollywood,

the glamour, 'Gloria Worth'?   No, I can't say that I do.

But you lead a very quiet life here, I said, a rather restricted life, if I'm allowed to say so.

You must say what you feel, she said.   It's important we are open with each other.  If we aren't, then how can you ever hope to get under my skin enough to ghost my autobiography? That's what we're here for, isn't it?

Yes, I said.   Although I can't say I was much convinced by my own reply.

We paused for the butler to clear our plates and return with a tray of strawberries, along with cream, should I want it, in a small Georgian silver jug.   There was a slight breeze in the poplars as we waited.

I am going to have those cut down, she said, when the butler had gone.   The noise gets on my nerves.   I'm sorry, she said, let's get back to business.

Could I ask again, I said, why you gave up your career after the 'Cleopatra' film?

Not "after" but "during", she laughed.   That's what caused all the problems with the Studio.   It was the fact that they lost a lot of money because of me.   At the end of the day, they can always find another Star.   It may take a little time but it's not as though there aren't hundreds in the queue just waiting for the chance. No, it was the fact that I'd lost them a small fortune in investment that I had to go.   Not that I wanted to stay, that is.

But why, I repeated?

Let me tell you about it, she smiled.   But here comes coffee, let's have that first.

When the butler had retreated and I'd stirred a spoonful of brown sugar into my black coffee, she began to describe what would become her second 'confession'.

The Studio decided we'd film 'Cleopatra' in Yugoslavia, she said. There was no logic to it. After all, most of the scenes were supposed to take place in Cleopatra's Summer Palace on Lake Mareotis, a place (Mareotis that is) I had known quite well. But the Yugoslav Government had broken with the Soviet Union and they found themselves rather short of cash. One of their Ministers, I believe, a former Communist partisan, as they all were, got in touch with one of the American OSS Officers he'd known in Yugoslavia during the War. The OSS Officer was by then a New York lawyer. He, in turn, put the Yugoslavs in touch with the Studio. My Studio bosses decided, never having been there, that Lake Ohrid might do just as well as Lake Mareotis and would be a lot cheaper, especially since the Yugoslavs were in a position to supply us with cheap labour for constructing the sets. Which is why we all ended up on the Yugoslav shore of Lake Ohrid.

Don't smile, she said. Stranger things have been tried by Hollywood to save money, or to increase profit rather. Cleopatra's 'Summer Palace' was a series of huge cardboard panels propped up against the walls of a military bunker complex. It's amazing what can be achieved with camera-angles and well-painted cardboard scenery. But then sets are like actors, I guess. We all look different once we've got our make-up on.

The problem was the shoreline, she continued. A thin beach rising up into a slope of pine trees was not exactly how I remembered Lake Mareotis! They solved it by using more cardboard screening and by doing interior shots on a mocked-up beach with sand and palm trees behind us. The lake itself was fine, of course. It was blue and lit up by the summer sun, just as our cinema-goers might have imagined Lake Mareotis to have been.

I used to go swimming in Lake Ohrid each morning before the filming began. It was idyllic. The Yugoslavs insisted on providing a bodyguard which made the Studio very happy, being able to cut costs on 'Security'. Anyway, my bodyguard, Stevo, sat on the shore while I swam long lengths, doing the occasional duck-dive for old time's sake, making sure I stayed in sight so as not to upset him.

Which was when the trouble began, she said.

"The trouble"? I asked.

Yes, she said. We always have problems, even in an out-of-the-way place as Yugoslavia was then. There are always people trying to sneak onto the set. Photographers from newspapers. You'll know some of them well, I imagine. And then there are the real nutters who get fixated on an actress or actor. Most of them are harmless, if annoying. But there are some who aren't which is why the Studio have to provide Security or, in this case, why I had to put up with Stevo.

The trouble was that, on several mornings in a row, I could have sworn that someone was swimming behind me. I stopped and trod water for a while but there was no-one there. On the third or fourth morning, I even asked Stevo about it when I got back to the beach. He swore there'd been no-one. I could see by his eyes he was being honest. He'd have lost everything, whatever 'everything' was, if he hadn't done his job properly.

So I continued to swim each morning in Lake Ohrid and I continued to hear this swimmer behind me. It was someone swimming confidently with strong strokes, a man I guessed.

But weren't you worried, I asked?

How could I be worried, she said? There was nothing there. Stevo saw no-one and, as I say, I trusted him. He was being honest. To tell you the truth, I actually came to quite enjoy the sound of this invisible swimmer. It was probably just a trick of the waves, but I liked to imagine it was Juan, my husband, swimming behind me to protect me. I just wished that one morning he'd have swum faster and joined me.

What went wrong, I asked?

You are a good journalist, she said. I suppose you must have a nose for the real truth in your job. If you didn't, then people like me could pull the wool over your eyes. That would be no good for the reading public. No good at all.

Those wretched poplars, she said, pausing and looking down the garden. When the breeze gets into them, they remind me of the sound of that swimmer. I think that's why I am going to have them cut down.

So what went wrong, I asked again?

What went wrong, she said, looking suddenly bitter and angry, was that the swimmer wasn't Juan. You see there was one morning when I heard the sound of the swimmer behind me get louder. And then, all at once, he was alongside me grinning with that stupid grin of his. Smiling like some small boy who's learnt some new tricks.

Who, I said?

John, she replied. Poor Bloody John from Doncaster. Except now he could really swim and so strongly.

I saw her shudder as she said it.

I shouted at him to Get Lost, she said. But he just carried on swimming around me, showing off with his duck-dives, bursting out of the water in front of me. But what was really terrible was that he never said a word. He just kept swimming round and round, laughing at me, grinning his stupid grin.

Four or five minutes he'd be there in the Lake each morning. And then he'd just disappear, as he'd done in Alexandria. I didn't know where he'd come from or where he'd gone. I didn't know how he'd slipped through the Security. Stevo certainly never saw him.

The first time it happened, I found Stevo hopping about on the shore with his pistol in his hand as I came out of the water. He'd heard me shouting at someone and wanted to know what the threat was that he hadn't seen.

Every time I went swimming, there John would be, swimming alongside me, invisible to the rest of the world. To be honest, it got on my nerves so much that I gave up swimming. And then I'd start looking for him back on dry land. I'd catch a glimpse of him in the distance on the set, dressed like any other Yugoslav workman in ex-Army trousers with a wrench in his hand. Any set is crawling with odd-job men. It has to be.

The whole thing just got on my nerves. Eventually I just chucked it all in and left.

She leant forward to reach for her glass of water and I saw that the cotton shirt on her thin back was drenched in sweat. I'd never even seen her perspire before.

And that's why you retired from Hollywood, I said? A hanger-on from your past turning up years later in Yugoslavia?

You'll have to admit, she snapped, it was in very strange circumstances.

She took another sip from her drink, pulling herself together and smiling. I suppose you must think I'm mad, she said. There you are then, you have it. The secret of Gloria Worth. You've done your job and you can write the book. Everyone will know the truth about Gloria Worth.

But I'm only going to write what you want me to, I said. I'm your ghostwriter, not your biographer. I am here to help you.

I know you are, she said, reaching across and patting me on the knee. Why else would I be telling you my secrets? I know you are my ghostwriter and I am very grateful. I always feel much calmer for having talked to you. It's like my husband and his waterlilies. He always comes back so much more at peace with himself when he's been down to that hot house of his.

You'll have to forgive me, she said, resting her hand on my arm. I'm just nervy this afternoon. I think it's the breeze in those wretched trees. I do feel tired, she said. I think we've probably done all we can for today.

The butler arrived on cue with iced tea on his silver salver and I asked him to ring for a taxi for me while we drank our tea.

On the train home I had no idea that that was the last time I would ever see Gloria Worth, nor that I would never hear from her again. Instead, the following week I received a letter from her publisher, thanking me profusely on her behalf for the work I had done, enclosing a very generous cheque but regretting that Mrs Durkheim had decided not to proceed with an autobiography. I should imagine he was livid at losing a best-seller, but there was little he could do.

As I say, I never heard from her again. I did get a very nice hand-written letter from Ronald Durkheim saying how much he'd enjoyed talking to me and wishing me well. He could see that I was a true professional and that I would go far in my career. He wanted me to know that my visits had done his wife a great deal of good. He was glad that she'd felt able to tell me so much. He was sure it had helped. She certainly seemed much easier in her mind.

I kept his letter but, for the life of me, found it difficult to determine what it was she had actually told me.

The one thing I did do was go and see the woman who'd been Gloria Worth's Personal Assistant throughout most of her film career and who had been with her in Yugoslavia. I had already fixed the meeting before I was stood down by the publisher, so I saw little point in cancelling.

We sat one morning drinking coffee in her small house in Fulham. She now worked as a Production Assistant for a TV documentary company.

The one thing that came across most clearly was her account of what had happened at Lake Ohrid. It was not "terrible", as Gloria Worth had told me. It was "terrifying", at least for Gloria Worth. She'd come back from the Lake in the mornings shaking with fear. There were times when Stevo practically had to carry her. No-one had ever seen Gloria Worth like that. Even when she stopped going swimming, she'd jump out of her skin

123

at the sight of some Yugoslav odd-job man on the set. Every electrician and soundman seemed to be her enemy and a threat to her. As far as her Personal Assistant was concerned, it had been a complete mental breakdown. She was sympathetic but she wasn't surprised that Gloria had never worked again. She wouldn't be the first actor who had suddenly snapped. It was such a shame the racing-driver husband had been killed. He might have kept Gloria Worth on the rails.

The cheque from the publisher would fund my modest lifestyle for several months or more, so I had a chat with my editor and found that he was planning to reinstate me in the Autumn, with a different job-title to get it past the owner, should the owner ever enquire. With my new-found wealth I rented a cottage in Cornwall for a while, a short walk from the sea. Luckily, there were no mystery swimmers to upset my morning routine.

Sitting down there in a deckchair in the garden, I had plenty of time to think back over what Gloria Worth had told me, but I couldn't make sense of her 'confessions' or her fears. I had no real notion of what she had been trying to achieve with her aborted autobiography or with her ghostwriter. Perhaps as the former Personal Assistant had suggested, Gloria Worth had just suffered a breakdown for reasons no-one could fathom.

As a journalist, I am used to dealing with layers of truth. I don't expect people to reveal the whole truth. Only Time will do that. Did I believe her 'confessions', her description of her breakdown in Yugoslavia? All I knew was that there must have been more to Lake Ohrid than some stupid grinning boy. As I said at the start, I am willing to give ghosts the benefit of the doubt, having no direct experience of them myself. If Gloria Worth was convinced she'd seen a ghost from her former life in Lake Ohrid, then I am happy to believe her. All I would say, as a journalist, is that my hunch would be that Poor John had done much more than just swim round her. Whatever he'd done or tried to do, she had come away terrified.

When my holiday ended and I went back to the paper, the Durkheims slipped into the past. I remember reading of Ronald Durkheim's death, falling from a ladder trying to clip his hedges.    Reading between the lines, Gloria Worth had eventually insisted that even the butler and cook should go. How Durkheim managed on his own, I have no idea. He too suffered a lot for love. I suppose it was his very dullness that had appealed to her after her breakdown.

Gloria Worth herself was found dead there a few years later. The one member of staff she had left, a nurse she'd employed from one of the best agencies, found Gloria lying face-down in the swimming pool one morning with a broken neck. She used to sleepwalk and had most likely tripped and fallen in during the night. Not the first Hollywood Star to come to grief.

I put the Durkheims out of my mind. I'd liked him a lot and had been half in love with her, but I had recognised the limits to my world and known that I would never belong in theirs. It was interesting to meet them, but that was it. And if I failed to understand her or what she wanted, well there are limits to what we ever really know about other people.

And that would have been it had it not been for our crime correspondent tossing a short Reuters piece on my desk one morning ten years after Gloria Worth had died. Although my colleague covered Crime, he was a bit of a military freak. He was a member of a gun club and could tell whether a pistol was loaded just by picking it up. He was also keen on everything to do with World War Two history.

Here's a strange one, he said. This might amuse you in an odd sort of way.

Marine archaeologists in Yugoslavia had been diving on a known crash-site in Lake Ohrid. A British Halifax bomber had been shot down in World War Two on its way to drop supplies to an SOE mission with the Chetniks in Eastern Serbia. The plane had been found some years before but the canisters it had been carrying still kept turning up from time to time when the archaeologists carried out a new dive.

The one they'd just found was odd. All that was in it was a Browning pistol, one clip of ammunition and a Commando knife.  That and a man's skeleton with the bits of metal associated with it.  Belt buckles and other stuff and, bizarrely, a handful of NAAFI tokens for use in Egypt, each stamped "One Cup of Tea".

As for a dog-tag, Service-issue dog-tags in those days had been made of fake leather and would dissolve eventually in water, which is why a lot of soldiers and particularly sailors would get their own unofficial dog-tags knocked up in the nearest market. This skeleton had an unofficial dog-tag with his name, rank and number engraved on the back of an old brass token from some smart Greek Alexandrian Café.  There was a hole punched in it so it could be worn round the neck.

I read the name and could suddenly visualise the scene.  I have no idea what Poor John had threatened her with, or what hold he had over her.  All I know is that, in the hangar that night, he had stood between her and her ambition.  She'd acted on impulse, picked up a Commando knife from the trestle table and killed him.  He himself had shown her how to mark up the canisters which were ready for despatch.  She hadn't cared whether his body would end up lost on a mountainside in Albania, Greece or wherever.  All she'd known was that she had to get rid of him.  She'd just never imagined that he would one day come back.

# 11 THE RAGGED GIRL

I suppose you will say this is cheating, began Rachel, as she took some sheets of typewritten paper from her handbag and smoothed them flat on the white tablecloth in front of her. I know we are meant to tell our own ghost stories at these reunions, but you saw the problem I had with my last one. I had to make notes for that. But then at least that was about something which I had experienced myself. There's really no excuse for this.

We looked at her and smiled, wondering what it was she was going to offer us and remembering that her first ghost story had been one of the best we had heard. She had always been far too modest about her own abilities.

You see, my partner, Kathy, is a writer, continued Rachel. When I told her it would be my turn to tell one of the ghost stories this year, she put me out of my misery and gave me this. It's the first ghost story she's ever written and she was keen to try it out in front of experts. Sink or swim, she said to me. She's best-known as a playwright but has turned her hand to most things. She's even worked as a ghostwriter when money was short, so she shares that with Giles. But, as I say, this is her first ghost story. If you are happy with me cheating, I'll begin.

We smiled again and nodded and Rachel started to read her partner's story which was entitled 'The Ragged Girl'.

Nearly thirty years ago now, I had a two-month contract one Winter to facilitate a theatre workshop on scriptwriting. It was a small avant-garde theatre in one of the old university towns, student productions mostly. My job was to help the young writers develop their ideas and turn them into workable scripts. We'd then bring in the actors and prepare for a one-night performance of their short plays "to showcase their talent", as it said in the prospectus. Some of them were quite good, those would-be writers. It was fun working with them. It wasn't particularly well-paid, but I stayed rent-free with a friend who was a Theology lecturer at the university. Thanks to her generosity, I finished the two month's work with some savings. She's ordained now, but this story took place before anything like that was possible. It was another world.

I settled into my new routine there quite quickly. The workshop hours were fairly relaxed and flexible if needs be. It was only four days a week and each free Wednesday I would spend in the University Library working on my next project. I've always described myself as a 'Freelance Writer' rather than a 'Writer'. The Freelance part is the key to it if you want to earn a living. And if you want to earn a living then, in my experience, you have to make sure you've always got your next project on the go while you work on the first one. My next project then was to produce a popular account, a potboiler really, of the London Pleasure Gardens in 18th century London. No original source research. Just a brief, lightly handled and entertaining run through the subject for the general reader. It was the sort of work my agent had been good at pushing my way and, like the workshop, it would help to pay for the time spent writing the plays I loved.

It was a very pleasant two months. The theatre was in the centre of the old town, hidden away behind 18th century buildings. It even had a side entrance, which I would always use, which came out onto a quiet passageway beside a small church and churchyard. The passageway was lined with very individual-looking two-storey houses, one of which was, and had been for more than a century, a second-hand and antiquarian bookshop. I'd pop out of the theatre at lunchtime and sit wrapped up well on the low churchyard wall to eat a sandwich if the weather was dry. If it was raining, I'd idle away a half hour talking to the bookshop owner, or rather his wife. She said her husband preferred to work in the office room behind the desk. Sadly, I think his work probably began with a sherry each morning soon after the 10.30 opening and, I guess, he never looked back for the rest of the day. But I was happy to support her by entering into her fiction and we'd stand there at lunchtime chatting about the rarity of Warwick Wroth and the other great writers on the Pleasure Gardens.

By the time I left the theatre on my own in the evenings, after the workshop participants had all gone, the bookshop would be closed with its window in darkness and there was nothing but the old-fashioned streetlamps to cast silvered rays onto the dark-grey glistening wet paving stones that ran along beside the churchyard wall. It was thirty yards of magic, a throwback to a fictional Dickensian world. The sort of place where you felt anything might happen. All it demanded was that you should not be surprised.

But nothing did happen to break the routine of my first few weeks in that university town. The only change, imperceptible at the time, was that I was entering deeper into each aspect of that routine.

My research for the Pleasure Gardens book was taking me further into the world of entertainment in 18th century London. Some entry tickets might have been more expensive than others, particularly on the grand occasions, but there wasn't really a gradation of pleasure in the Gardens. High Society and Low would go to Vauxhall, to Ranelagh and to Marylebone Gardens. And while the satirists and the lampooning poets would try to belittle the "trade dressed up as class" who might go to Bagnigge Wells or to Hampstead, the accompanying engravings showed the same dresses, hats and hairstyles at each

Garden, Wells or Spa. Everyone it seemed would somehow dress up to drink the chalybeate waters or nibble the over-priced bread-and-butter with slices of ham so thin as to be translucent which were on offer. And, if there were prostitutes and pickpockets who worked their trades in the darkest tree-lined walks at Vauxhall, it didn't detract from the Gardens as an innocent pleasure-ground for all. The fun may have been over-priced but at least you got something for your money. It wasn't like the three-card trick on the city streets where you never found the lady and lost your money each time.

In the second-hand bookshop, too, I was penetrating deeper into its unique strange world. The first time I made it to the backroom was when the owner's wife had a cold and wasn't really up to chatting. I loaded her with sympathy and then left her to the whisky and hot lemon on her desk. At first sight in the backroom, I thought the owners were taking a chance by leaving a whole wall of 18th century and early 19th century books with fine leather bindings unattended and easy for a book-thief to slip into his pocket unnoticed. It was only when I saw the titles and started to take some of the books down that I realized why they were safe unguarded.

The backroom was a graveyard of sermons, no doubt privately printed at the authors' expense, many of them lavishly bound with still-bright gold-tooled lettering on the spines. The bindings were works of art. It was just the contents which Time and Taste had made worthless. Standing there on my own I could visualize those Anglican clergymen from parishes all over England, at a time when to be a clergyman meant wealth and status, all of them self-publishing their *Collected Sermons* at the Press of their old university, the triumph of their provincial lives, lived for better or worse, and now come home like salmon to spawn. Beautiful leather-bound books, gorgeous to smell, but now abandoned there like so many forgotten tombstones.

We'll have problems shifting those, smiled the owner's wife blowing her nose and sipping her hot lemon when I was back in the front room. But it would seem like sacrilege to throw them out, she added.

Back in the theatre that afternoon, we were working on the first draft of one of the more promising writers. Unlike the clergymen in the backroom of the bookshop, she had literary talent. The problem would be how to channel her ideas in a way that wouldn't dent her confidence. She was writing powerfully and, it seemed, from personal experience. But the script was a long way from being accessible for an audience. What she'd produced was a sort of modern Revenge Tragedy complete with ghost and retribution. Nowadays I and the other students would have come straight out and asked her what terrifying experience it was all based on. Back then, however, people were more reticent, polite I suppose. So we just carried on with me trying to tease out the key strands from her script and get beneath the surface to help her produce something more clearly-drawn which an audience could follow. It was a good draft and it would be worth the effort to turn it into something great.

I guess it was the hours spent on this modern 'Revenge Tragedy' that 'facilitated' what was to follow. For there was nothing different about the passageway as I left the theatre on my own and stepped out onto the wet paving stones. The old-fashioned streetlamps shone, silvering the stones of the churchyard wall. It was a homely and reassuring setting, more *The Pickwick Papers* than *The White Devil*.

Which is why it was such a shock to see her standing there. A small thin child in a ragged white night-gown, her hands and arms stretched out towards me, beseeching but silent. And it was the silence that was the most terrifying. There was no sound from the houses or from the distant streets. I was alone in a vacuum with something I didn't understand. Because I knew at once this child was not normal. This was no refugee beggar. The country she had come from was not one you and I could visit. It only existed as a final destination.

When she finally disappeared, I realized that I had my back flat to the wall of one of the houses. It was as if I'd been trying to press myself back into the bricks for safety, for a sanctuary, for anywhere that would get me away from that little ragged girl.

What's the matter, said my friend as I stumbled through her front-door?

I'm sorry, Sally, but I just need a drink, please.

With the whisky in my hand, I explained what had happened.

But you're such a rational person, Kathy. How could this happen to you? You don't believe in God, let alone ghosts.

Seeing me look such a wreck, Sally then did what I should have done in her shoes. She deployed every last rational explanation from a trick of the poor light to a child playing a joke. When that failed, she filled me with spaghetti carbonara and half a bottle of red wine and then sent me off for a hot bath and bed. Things would be better in the morning.

They were, but mostly because I deliberately chose not to leave the theatre by the side entrance in the evenings.

As the days passed, I became ever more disgusted with myself and my cowardice. I thought of the young writer in my workshop trying honestly to turn whatever terrifying experience she had suffered into Art. And here was I, supposedly an established and successful playwright, hiding from experience when it happened to me.

So I steeled myself and walked out of the side entrance into the evening darkness. And life did not disappoint. It was just that my knees went weak as I saw her. I started silently to recite Protestant hymns not sung since childhood, stirring lyrics about hobgoblins and fiends. Sally would have been proud of me. The hymns at least allowed me to stay standing and keep away from the wall. It was just me and the little ragged girl in that silent vacuum. She with her hands and arms out towards me, beseeching me, terrifying in her silence. It was as though she expected me to know what she wanted.

She disappeared when a cat jumped over the churchyard wall,

saw her and quickly realized its mistake. I had never seen a cat clear a brick wall so fast.

Back at home, it was Sally who was the rational one again. There has to be some reason for it, she said. Perhaps you should do some research when you're in the University Library. They have a newspaper archive there, you know. There might be something.

And that was my mistake, I guess. I wasted a lot of time by starting with records rather than people. I started with the burial records, but it was pointless. We forget the horror of infant mortality in previous centuries. Little dead girls were sadly two a penny in that churchyard. I then tried the newspaper archives but couldn't find any sensational stories about hauntings in the passageway. So I turned to the people inside the church, the long list of clergymen who'd worked out their lives there. I was looking for anything, however inconsequential, that might single one out. For what it was worth, I made a note of the names, their dates and any odd thing that had struck me about them.

That evening I was sitting at the kitchen table with the list in front of me as Sally was cooking.

What's this, I asked, pointing to one of the 18th century names? After 'Reverend Grailes' in the record, someone had scrawled 'Soul Sleeper'. Was it his nickname?

More a term of abuse at that time, said Sally. The 'Soul Sleepers' or 'Christian Mortalists' were more common in the 17th century than the 18th. They believed the soul sleeps between death and resurrection. One of those issues which mean so much to the keepers of doctrine, but which hardly affect the rest of us. There are still some Mortalists around today. Not one of the mainstream heresies. But if you're interested in the Reverend Grailes, I'll do some digging with my colleagues.

While she was doing her digging, I went to check the Parish Records on Grailes, just in case. He did have a daughter who'd

133

died at the age of five, but then so did many people in the late 1780s. His wife had died in childbirth a couple of years later. Unusually for a clergyman with a good positon, the Reverend Grailes had not remarried. In fact, he died not long after his wife.

My routine in that old university town returned to its normal pace, with the workshop at the theatre, the research on the Pleasure Gardens at the Library and my chats with the bookshop owner's wife. The only added element was my meetings with the ragged girl. For buoyed up by Sally's rational approach to life's mysteries, I would stand there and watch trembling as the ragged girl held out her arms towards me in the evenings. The silence became less terrifying with Time, but I confess I was still terrified that the ragged girl might make some sudden movement and attack me. I remembered the poor cat's reaction. But the more she just stood there, beseeching me, I sensed she had changed from a danger to a puzzle. And I felt it was my responsibility to help her, if I could only suppress my fear.

What Sally's helpful colleagues found for her was a memoir written by one of the Reverend Grailes' Anglican Church superiors. Grailes, long dead by the time the book was written, had a walk-on part as a curiosity. His belief in Mortalism had been the first thing to set him apart. And it would have destroyed his career and any hope of advancement if he hadn't heeded the kindly advice of the book's author who took Grailes aside and pointed out gently the facts of life. Namely, that while the Anglican Church was happy for its young men to have hobbies, it would draw the line at hobbyhorses. At which point, Grailes took the hint and quietly dropped his adherence, in public at least, to Mortalism.

Instead, he developed an interest in attacking what he saw as the last vestiges of Paganism. He preached against the Maypole, the Mummers, the placing of grave goods and other folk practises. He was somewhat strident but it wasn't heresy and his career did not suffer because of it. And like those other clergymen in the backroom of the bookshop, he too had fancied himself as an author and had published his sermons on Paganism in a slim pamphlet, no doubt at his own expense. I called up a copy from the Library Rare Books room. Grailes came across as a fun-denying bigot. You wouldn't have bumped into him at the Pleasure Gardens. And you certainly wouldn't have wanted to talk to him on these issues. But I accepted that two hundred years is a long time and that I would find most people from that period rather strange if I met them. There didn't seem to be anything in the pamphlet to link the Reverend Grailes to the ragged girl.

But then, as I say, records aren't much good without people. It was only when I mentioned Grailes to the bookshop owner's wife that I made progress. The books in the backroom were in alphabetical order, she said.

Which is where I found two pamphlets bound together. The first I had already read. The second was also what we would now call a Vanity Press production. Grailes had published it at his own expense and was presumably livid when the publisher misprinted the author's name as 'Grayles' which is why I hadn't found it in the library.

The second pamphlet was entitled, 'Sacrilege on God's Ground – A Prohibition Against the Use of Grave Goods'. It was a diatribe against the burial of anything with the deceased. Not even a Prayer Book or Bible. It was Grailes' "unshakeable conviction" that all Christians should meet their Maker armed with nothing more than their inviolable faith. You could almost hear the scratching of his quill pen as it cut into the paper of his manuscript. He was almost Victorian in his certitude and his moral outrage. He was clearly a man ahead of his Time. The language of this strident pamphlet was direct and simple and firm to the point of bluntness. It was as if the argument had become personal. It was as if the belief of a lifetime had encountered an obstruction, in the shape of one very small human being. The stridency, the annoyance, of the pamphlet suggested he was admonishing some wayward child. As I say, the world was different then. Small boys were beaten when they'd done wrong.

More interesting than the text were the hand-written notes on the flyleaf. For this was clearly Grailes' own copy. The notes appeared to be a brief diary of key events in the last few years of his life, jotted down in a staccato, almost shorthand fashion. By each date, there was the word "Appearance", sometimes underlined. Occasionally he'd added the words, "It refused to go away". You could sense the anguish in each short entry. It must have been doubly troubling for a 'Soul Sleeper' to encounter a soul that wouldn't sleep

The notes on the flyleaf seemed to make sense of a strange passage in the memoir by his superior which I'd read earlier. It referred to Grailes' singular practise late in life of holding a one-man memorial service each year at his daughter's grave on the anniversary of her death. It involved the sprinkling of Holy Water and the incantation of unidentified Latin verses. It seemed an odd way of communicating with a 5-year-old girl but his superior saw in it proof of paternal affection. The problem was that this 'Annual Service' became Quarterly and then Monthly. By the time he died, Grailes was in the churchyard almost every day. Even his charitable and forgiving superior had to admit that it was behaviour verging on madness.

I bought the bound pamphlets for their knock-down price and spent the next few evenings re-reading them and discussing them with Sally.

I then went back to the bookshop and confessed my true interest in Grailes to the owner's wife. I told her of the ragged girl, the ghost and all. Rather than make polite comments while trying to usher me out of the shop as a harmless lunatic, she just nodded and said that she would have to get her husband. It took her several minutes of gentle knocking at the door behind the desk to raise him.

Her husband, turned out, as expected, to be a dishevelled man in his late 50s or early 60s, bearded and with hair longer than you would have expected in a man of his age. It was clear that he had withdrawn some years ago voluntarily from life, his alcoholism having been a form of early retirement. If he were single, he'd have stunk but she had kept him in order as regards bathing. I noticed he was wearing a pyjama jacket beneath his jumper.

Paul, she said, you must hear what this lady has to say, about the passageway and the little girl.

As I explained again what had happened, his eyes began to light up as though he'd suddenly found a reason to take interest in the world again. Local History, it turned out, was his passion and you couldn't get more local than the passageway outside his shop's front door.

It's the Bridesmaids' Curse, he said smiling, when I'd finished. I've heard tales once or twice of strange events at weddings in the church here. I met an old man who claimed to have been at a wedding there once when it happened. And I've found a 19th century account in a privately printed pamphlet. The gist of both stories was the same. A couple of the younger bridesmaids either fainted or screamed as they followed the bride up the aisle. When the ceremony was over and they'd been calmed down, they told their mothers they'd seen a small dirty girl in white rags standing behind the altar. She'd had her arms out, beckoning to them. They were terrified of her.

The church, of course, has done its best to hush it all up, he said. It would be bad for the wedding trade. The Church is a business like any other and has its interests to protect.

Paul, his wife exclaimed!

Well, you know what I mean, he replied.

But what I don't understand, said his wife, is why this ghostly girl in rags should show herself to this lady now. She's not an impressionable young bridesmaid, she laughed.

Perhaps the girl believes that you know what she wants, said Paul, turning to me. Do you?

I think I'm beginning to have an idea, I said. I'm just not sure that I am going to be able to afford it.

They both looked at me puzzled.

I promise I'll let you both know if I manage it, I said.

Back home with Sally, we talked through what I was thinking of doing. For I had come to realize that there was nothing 'dramatic' about the ragged girl. This was no Revenge Tragedy in which evil had to be avenged by some determined and violent ghost. It was simply a case of this little girl needing something. Her presence was a request, not for solidarity or support, but for an object, for something that was rightfully hers.

In short, I knew what I wanted. It was just that neither Sally nor I had the money to pay for it.

Sadly, it's not something we can have a Church Raffle to raise the funds for, she laughed. Not for the laying of ghosts, even though it would be in this particular Church's interests to fund you.

Help, when it came, was in a letter from London. My agent, God bless her, had managed to sell the US rights to my book on the Pleasure Gardens, even though I hadn't yet written it. She had enclosed a cheque for £250, an enormous sum of money in those days, which was my advance-payment for the rights. They'd be royalties in due course, as and when I'd got the book finished. I did a quick dance around the room and then showed the letter to Sally. I cashed the cheque the next day and rang a shop I knew in London to make sure they'd be open on my next free Wednesday.

For I knew what I wanted. One of the books I'd used for my research in the library was a rare copy of 'The Sunday Ramble'. It was a late 18th century poem satirizing the world of the Pleasure Gardens and the Spas. It had a frontispiece engraving of Bagnigge Wells. Along with the ornamental fishpond with its famous goldfish, and the drama in the foreground of a small serving-boy being tripped over by stray dogs and losing his tray full of cakes, there was a young couple in love taking their air in the Gardens. The tall slim woman looked to be about 18 or 19 years-old and she was wearing the very best of contemporary fashion. A flat straw hat, decorated with ribbons and tilted forwards at an outrageous angle on her ornately piled up hair. Her long dress was made of silk with sleeves to the elbow and lace trimmed. You could just see one neat and up-market shoe beneath the silk of her long dress. That was what I wanted.

When I got to London, I went straight to the shop in Kensington Church Street. It was one of several very plush and expensive Antique Shops there at that time. But it was different from the others in that it specialised in selling antique dolls and toys, the kind that you would rarely find of that age and in that condition outside the biggest Auction Houses.

The shop was an Aladdin's Cave of lost childhoods. In addition to the Georgian and later dolls and the Edwardian teddy bears, there were cabinets full of all those Victorian optical games and illusions. There were elaborate fold-out printed Peepshows cut carefully from card, illustrating landscapes, vistas and Royal Processions. There were Zoetropes and Praxinoscopes and toys whose names I didn't know. And then there were the German wooden carved Noah's Arks, each with its hundred animals or more. They were all toys that would have been expensive when they were new, let alone a hundred years later and when they were still in such immaculate condition.

My entry ticket to this Aladdin's Cave was the generous advance from the US publisher, and I spent nearly all of it on what I needed. It was an 18th century wooden doll with jointed arms and legs. She was twelve inches high and dressed in silk and a straw hat with ribbons, as near to the Bagnigge Wells lady as I could get. The only difference was that this doll had the traditional brightly painted red cheeks which would pass as great beauty in the eyes of a 5-year-old girl. The doll was perfect. It looked as though it had been kept in a drawer wrapped in tissue paper for two hundred years or more. It had certainly never been played with. It looked as new as if it had just come from the doll-maker's shelf. A present any 18th century little girl would be proud of.

Later that night, Sally and I sat with our whiskies in front of us, admiring the Bagnigge Wells lady who sat watching us so contentedly from high up on the mantelpiece.

Do you want me to come with you, said Sally?

No, I think my best chance is if I do it on my own. But thank you for the offer. I confess I'm still always very nervous when I'm with her. I know I shouldn't be now that I've begun to trust her. But you can never be sure, can you? I suppose it's because you're standing on the very edge of the precipice, at a place where two worlds meet. You sense that one false step would be all it would take to finish you. And there you stand, knowing that you have to put one foot forward. I've never done anything like this before, where you can only get round the terror with a sheer effort of will. But then there's more to life than what's in our comfort zone. Part of being an adult is to learn to get used to it. Even this.

The following evening, I stood on my own in the silence of that cold dark passageway. It had rained earlier in the afternoon and the paving stones were black and shiny in the light of the streetlamps. I could have been on the wet rocks beside the ocean as the tide drew out. But there was no suck and drag of the sea. Just the quiet fast beating of my heart as I waited for what would come.

I had brought Sally's old wickerwork shopping basket which I hoped would be familiar and unthreatening to a child from the 18th century. I put it on the ground by my feet to be ready. All I had to do was to wait and hope that nothing and no-one would now turn up to interrupt us.

Without sound or warning she was suddenly there, standing as she'd always done twenty feet away from me, a small mud-stained girl in a filthy white shift, her arms outstretched towards me, beseeching. We stood there in silence for a minute or more before I found the courage to bend slowly down and take the doll from the basket.

I stood up and held the doll out in front of me, as far as my arms could reach. I'm ashamed to say I didn't have the courage to step forward.

The first thing I saw was the sudden smile that broke out on the girl's fixed sad face. It was as though life had returned to the dead. The next thing I knew, there was a slight tug as the doll left my hands. The little girl was now standing six feet away from me clutching the doll tight. She was hugging it, cradling it, singing to it in words I couldn't hear. And as she sang and held the doll ever more tightly, I could see that the human fingers which held it were now turning to bone.

I didn't have the heart to look at her face. I just didn't have the courage to do it. I was spared by a sudden movement as the girl spun round, still clutching her doll, and darted away towards the churchyard, so swiftly that the bones of her feet did not touch the ground.

I never saw her again. I don't suppose anyone did.

The truth, of course, is that we do not all have the "unshakeable conviction" of the Reverend Grailes. Many of us will need something more to help us, if we are to sleep through that long dark night.

# 12 CLOSE TO THE WALL

This would have been Harrington's turn to tell a ghost story at our annual reunions. So we paused when the coffees and port had been served to observe a minute's silence in his memory and in gratitude for the generous bequest in his will which was to fund our annual reunion dinners in a an upstairs dining-room at Rules in Maiden Lane "in perpetuity – or until the money had run out". We turned to Stephen, the only Vicar amongst us, for a formal blessing or a speech but he just smiled and raised his glass, "To Harrington, God bless him!"

"To Harrington!" we chorused.

Well, it falls to me then, said Stephen, to step in and tell the next story. Can I just say that it's always a treat for me to come to these reunions? Not just to meet you all, but for a chance to spend a day or two in the Big City, a far cry from my windswept Derbyshire.

I've been struck the last few times I've come down here how British Rail has been selling off every last scrap of land as you come into the big cities for development. Where twenty years ago there were weed-covered sidings with splendidly archaic rolling-stock left there to rust in peace, today there are high-rise luxury flats gleaming in their silver, copper or plate-glass fascia. I used to like spotting that old rolling-stock; wagons, engines, carriages – even one of those old chocolate-coloured coaches from the 'Brighton Belle' if you were lucky. Ah well, it's progress I suppose.

The story I am going to tell you is also about infilling, albeit outside the big cities. And, like Rachel, I should apologize at the start that the story is not mine. It's one I heard a couple of years ago from a friend of mine, a fellow Anglican Vicar, but a lot more interesting than most of us.

It was a couple of years ago I first met him when he was in his late 30s. As I say, he was unusual for a Vicar. He'd been an Army Officer for fifteen years. He was in an Infantry regiment and had served all over the world. He'd done two tours for the UN as a peacekeeper. When he finally had to admit that his vocation for the Church was stronger than his love of the Army, he'd just done three years as Assistant Military Attache at our Embassy in Kiev. They'd taught him Russian for the job. I presume they knew what they were doing.

When I first met him, he'd already spent a couple of years as a Vicar in a small Fenland town in East Anglia, a far cry from some of the exotic places he'd served when in the Army. We were thrown together by a request from the bishops that we work up a paper on the Immigration crisis and the Church's response to it. Similar pairs of Vicars had been chosen to prepare papers on other pressing social issues. Once done, we were all to meet at Lambeth Palace in late October for a three-day seminar to discuss and finalise our work. The papers would then be put to the bishops who would produce a final Church strategy on each issue.

You probably think this smacks of hubris, the dear old Anglican Church setting itself up to resolve the world's problems. But then I've always thought that the important thing about an honest broker is that they're honest. It's not a question of size or power. Let's face it, in the last thirty years it's been the Norwegians who've come closest to getting a Middle East peace deal. And the Catholic Church, of course, has had a lot of success at Peace and Reconciliation. What's needed is skill, patience and determination. My friend would add to that a quiet ruthlessness of purpose. You need as much of that to stop a war as to win one, he says.

Anyway, I and my new-found friend, still a pen-pal at that stage, went scuttling around the academics, experts and Charities hoovering up the background on Immigration in all its forms. We didn't have a big travel budget for our preliminary research, but I toured the Universities in Sheffield and Leeds while he did the same in Cambridge and Norwich. We had a fair number of long late-night phone conversations and, by swapping texts by email, we hammered out our "Strategy Document". I'm proud to say we got it down to one page of A4. From his Army and peace-keeping experience, my friend was adamant that any strategy longer than that was just unworkable waffle. I tended to agree. We weren't a committee. We could take decisions.

By late October, when we met for the first time at the Lambeth Palace Seminar, we had a finished text and pushed it forward strongly in the discussion groups. It passed pretty well unchanged. The strategy was quite simple. Immigration could only be stopped at source. Once people were on the way, it was too late. Stopping it at source meant Conflict Resolution to clear up the war zones they were leaving, Economy Building to reduce the flow of economic migrants and tough Law Enforcement action against the people smugglers and criminal facilitators in the countries of origin. Conflict Resolution was where we saw a role for the Anglican Church. We suggested starting small with political reconciliation in Zimbabwe before moving on to India/Pakistan where Conflict Resolution might prevent a Nuclear War. It was punchy, heady stuff, but it was achievable – in our eyes at least.

After the final drinks session of the Seminar (orange juice and nut-free crisp products), the two of us were feeling quite pleased with ourselves as we left Lambeth Palace and made for a small back-street Pub that my friend had once been to before. Both of us had decided to stay over the extra night in London to treat ourselves to an exhibition or, in my case, the second-hand bookshops in the Charing Cross Road before going home on the Saturday afternoon.

We both felt we'd done a good job as we sat there in a quiet corner of the quiet Pub, with our dog-collars on and our pints and ham and cheese sandwiches in front of us. It would be another month before our short, punchy single-page Strategy would emerge from the bishops, watered down and spread out into three pages of platitudes and good intention. All without structure, direction or commitment. Not an ounce of our plan left in it. But on that wet Friday night in late October in the quiet Pub we could still bask in the satisfaction of our own achievement. We may not have solved the world's problems, but we had shown our masters the way forward.

It's five years since I was last here, but this place hasn't changed at all, my friend said. The same 1950s paper Christmas decorations were hanging over the mirror then, and that was in mid-Summer. It's all clean and dusted, though. You can't fault the Management for that.

I saw him glance across towards the Bar where a formidable-looking lady in her late 60s (twinset, elaborate perm and glasses with pale-blue diamante frames) was despatching a pile of ham sandwiches with an electric bread knife. There was something unnerving about the whir of that knife and the assurance with which she handled it, but you got used to the sound the longer you sat there, until it became just background noise.

Let me tell you a strange story, he said, looking back from the lady with the bread knife. I suppose you could say it, too, is about migration, of a kind. It's something that happened to me two years ago, soon after I'd arrived in the parish. Baptism of fire would be too strong a phrase, but it was odd. A good introduction to being a Vicar, I suppose. He paused to take a sip of beer and then began.

I don't know how well you know East Anglia. It was all new to me when the Church sent me there. Some of the churches there, mine included, are built on small mounds just above the

145

level of the surrounding fields. In the days before the fens were drained in the 18th century, the churches would have stood out like islands in the sea when the landscape was flooded at the worst times of the year. My own church and its old graveyard are on a small hill about twenty feet above the level of the field on one side and the houses on the other. Walking up the path on a Sunday morning, I always feel that I'm a soldier again, but a soldier in the Middle Ages entering a motte-and-bailey Castle.

But this castle's only defence is a four-foot wall which runs round the edge of the graveyard. My predecessor had put a wooden bench raised on bricks looking out over the wall towards the field on one side. From the bench, you could look out over the steep bank, thickly covered with brambles which didn't look as though they'd been disturbed for hundreds of years, and then down across the green field. Sadly, this country view wouldn't be much use to me, and I wondered if that was why my 60-year-old predecessor hadn't seemed too upset about choosing to retire a few years earlier than he should have done.

For the field belonged to the Church Commissioners. The villagers had been allowed to use it as pastureland for as long as anyone could remember. But the modern-day villagers no longer had a cow or a couple of goats which they needed to pasture. So the Church Commissioners had decided to sell off the field for development. There would be a dozen two-storey houses for commercial sale and a further two smaller houses for social housing. It was this last which had got the proposal through the Planning process. Anyway, there would be no field to gaze out over on a sunny summer afternoon. Like everyone else, the Church Commissioners needed an income.

The builders had arrived just as I took over as Vicar in the parish. There was already a portacabin in one corner of the field for a Site Office as well as three caravans for the men that were going to do the initial hard work, clearing the site and laying the foundations for construction. In my first few weeks there I got used to the sound of the diggers and the machinery and later to the lorries that were always coming and going. With my military background, I was used to getting on with things and to taking things as they come. It wasn't as though the building work was going to last forever.

Some of my parishioners, though, took umbrage at the change to their quiet lives and routine. The strange thing was that it wasn't the noise of the lorries and construction that rankled with them. It was more the "activities" of the building workers in the evenings and on Sundays, their one day off. I started to hear grumbling in the village and at the Church Hall. There was a lot of muttering about foreigners. Most of the workers on the site were Poles, apparently. The construction company had a track record of hiring cheaper but qualified labour from some of the newer EU countries. What seemed to bother my parishioners was what they termed "the litter and the loitering".

At this point, I should probably mention the weather, he said, stopping to drink some more of his beer. I remember when I was at Staff College I read a first-hand account by a British Officer who'd served with the Chindits in Burma in World War Two. The book was 200 pages of gruelling jungle adversity, hard fighting and continual casualties during the column's two-month campaign. On the very last page, almost as an afterthought, the author mentioned in passing that, of course, it had rained solidly, day and night, every day of their campaign. I remember putting the book down and reflecting on the sort of kit they'd had in those days. No light-weight waterproof Goretex. What the author was saying, almost as an aside, was that it had been two months of Hell.

I remembered that when thinking of those Polish workers. For it had started raining at the beginning of October that year and it didn't stop till mid-November. Global warming, climate change, whatever, the fact was that the rain never seemed to stop. It rained while they were clearing the undergrowth from the field. It rained on a sea of mud as they and the diggers got to work on the field to prepare for the foundations. It rained on their each and every Sunday day-off. In the evenings, you'd see them sitting in the rain in groups outside the caravans, each one of them smoking with a can of beer in their hand. Not much was said.

Anyway, two of my parishioners arrived one Saturday as a delegation to complain to me about the "litter and the loitering" and to ask if I could get something down about it. Talking through the problem, the empty beer cans and fag packets all over the place, it seemed the real issue was the Poles use of the Cricket Pavilion. They would sit on the Pavilion veranda all Sunday outside the locked-up Pavilion, leaving more litter and rubbish.

What do you use the Pavilion for in the Winter, I asked?

There was a bit of foot shuffling and it transpired that the Pavilion remained locked from October through till early March.

Well why don't we just open it up, I said? Make a virtue of necessity.

Which is what we did. With the help of the Church volunteers, we rounded up some more deckchairs for the Pavillion and installed a tea urn. In fact, we installed the Anglican Church's answer to all problems – a trestle table, mugs and plates, sandwiches and biscuits and as much hot tea as you could manage. And it worked. It became a Sunday social centre for the Poles. Some of them even started coming to my services. Which is when I got to know them better and realized they weren't Poles at all.

I remember standing in the Pavilion on a Sunday afternoon. Groups of 'Poles' were sitting and talking, playing cards. A few sat on their own on the floor with their backs to the wall, fiddling with their phones, sending endless texts to their families back at home. It was the only link they had.

Plonking myself down in one of the deckchairs, I greeted them in my limited Ukrainian and then carried on in Russian.

You lot are Ukrainians, aren't you?

There were some sheepish grins and smiles before their foreman introduced himself as Yuri.

You won't tell them, will you, he said? You won't tell the Police, the Authorities? You see the company that employs us is Polish, but all the labour it supplies throughout other EU countries is from Ukraine. We come here as Polish EU citizens. We need the work, you see. And we work well.

No, I shan't tell them, I said.

At which point there was a lot of bear-hugging and shaking of hands. Someone had already told them I'd been a soldier and they seemed to like that. The word of an Officer, I guess.

From then on, the Ukrainians and I were best friends. They'd turn to me if they needed someone to sort out a problem with their managers on the Site. Yuri and I got on particularly well. He was a native Russian speaker from the Donbass. He was also old enough to have served in the Soviet Army in Afghanistan and we had plenty of stories we could swap about our experiences. The only gulf between us was my refusal to join him in getting drunk on a Saturday night. But then Russian drunk is not like our drunk and he seemed to accept my excuses about having to be sober for Church on Sunday morning. The drinking aside, we were best mates. He even shared some of his salo (Ukrainian pig fat) with me, which he kept carefully hidden away in a Tupperware box. I could have done without that, but friendship is friendship.

The problems began half-way through October. The Ukrainians had finished clearing the field and some of them had set to work cutting back and digging out the ancient brambles from the slope which led up to the graveyard wall. The developers wanted the slope "landscaped". In other words, they just wanted a bank of smooth grass. I must admit I was worried that the whole slope would come sliding down when they dug out the brambles. It was probably the brambles that were holding the slope together. My real worry was that we'd lose the graveyard wall at a time when I didn't have a very big budget for Church repairs. But the slope held and the Ukrainians turned their attention to the foundations for the houses. All the time, the rain kept on, now sloshing down the bare slope and onto the field.

I first heard of the problem when Yuri came round to the Vicarage one wet Thursday night and I poured him a vodka. Something was troubling him, but it took him a long time to get to the point. It was almost as though he was embarrassed by what he was going to say, as though he was going to let his country down by talking. It was the third vodka before he started to open up.

You've been in the Army, he said. You know what it's like when you are going to take men into battle for their first time. A few of them go to pieces. A few of them come up with elaborate reasons to remove themselves from harm's way. They pull strings, if they have them, use contacts to get themselves a transfer. And their subsequent careers often do quite well because of it, he added, laughing. Most of us, though, just soldier on. After all, that's our job.

Well, I'm starting to see that sort of panic amongst a few of my Ukrainians here – and I don't know why. I feel stupid telling you this. But it feels like when you are getting ready to go into enemy-held territory. But why? There's no danger here. This is not a War. We're on a building-site in England.

Yuri stared down at the vodka glass in his hand for a moment, then raised it to his mouth and tipped it down. Bozhe moi (My God)! It's all very strange.

I made the right sort of sympathetic noises but there was nothing I could really say. If he didn't know what the problem was, then how could I?

Whatever it was, it seemed to be infectious. For over the next few days, some of my parishioners started to show signs of being nervous or jumpy. If it hadn't been for Yuri, I'd have said it was just the continual rain that was wearing down. I thought back to that Chindit Officer and I wondered if they just lacked his patience and perseverance.

Anyway, I did my best to cheer them up, calm them down and keep them on the road. It's always the same in those sort of situations. If you were to stand outside yourself, you'd see that you'd become a cheap parody of one of those Officers in some old British World War Two movie, walking through the platoon with a cheery word for everyone, not saying much but always upbeat and determined, setting the tone for them to follow. Leading by example. But it's best not to over-analyse leadership. You just get on with it. Some of the parishioners seemed reassured by my act.

It was Yuri who put his finger on the problem when he came to see me again one evening the following week.

There's a young boy working for me, he said, 19 years old and never been outside Ukraine before. He's tough, though, and straight talking. He doesn't seem to be afraid of much. The others like him. He's become a sort of mascot for them. Anyway, he came to me last night and told me what the problem was.

Apparently, a few of the men have been claiming that they've been seeing strange things, people, at night in the darkness on the edge of the field. They were terrified but they hadn't hung around long enough to give a good account of what they'd seen. This young kid is made of stronger stuff. He'd sat out on his own in the rain and the darkness all last night, waiting to see what would happen. And he hadn't run when it had. He's the sort of boy I'd have liked for a son, said Yuri.

He said there were people there, strange people, wearing what looked like rags. But he only saw five, four men and a woman. They didn't seem to talk to each other. They were quite close together, but they all seemed to be on their own, in their own world.

I asked him whether he'd been afraid, said Yuri, but he said they just looked very sad. He'd felt sorry for them. They didn't do anything and, after a while, they just drifted away, up the slope.

I tried to have it out with the men earlier this evening, said Yuri. I got the boy to describe what he'd seen. Some of the men, though, started talking excitedly about blood, about bloodstains they'd seen on our visitors' clothes. There might have been, said the boy. Then again it might just as well have been dirt. They looked to him as though they'd been sleeping in the mud.

Yuri looked at me for some sort of steer. After all, I was a Vicar not just a soldier. I was supposed to understand what couldn't be understood.

I said that I'd come down to their caravans the next evening and talk to his Ukrainians. We sealed it with another vodka before he left.

In the morning, I went round to see one of my more level-headed parishioners. She was the former head of the Parish Council. She'd been the local District Nurse when she was younger and had moved to Parish politics when she'd retired, if you could call Parish affairs "politics". In her case, she was just one of those people who naturally help and organize and solve problems. Yes, she was a leader, a natural one. Needless to say, she'd heard about our problem.

Several of our neighbours claim they've seen things, she said. You know what folks are like. One of them gets the jitters and suddenly we're all running around like headless chickens, convinced the worst is on its way, whatever the worst might be.

I take it you're not one of them, I said.

Not one who's seen, or not one who's headless, she laughed? No, I haven't seen anything, but then I don't get out as much as I used to.

And where have they seen these things, I asked? In the graveyard?

That's what you'd expect, isn't it? But no, it's the other side of the wall, down on the slope towards the field, or the building-site rather. Where they've just cleared all those bushes away.

What do you think it is, I asked?

Ah, now that's your field, Vicar, she said laughing again. I'm afraid you'll have to get us out of this one. I'm happy to help, of course, but I don't think this is something for a District Nurse. Although I'll be happy to come out of retirement and treat the wounded, she added chuckling. But I hope it won't come to that. Why don't you go down there and say a few prayers, she said grinning?

Which is exactly what the Ukrainians said when I met them later that evening. Although none of them, not even the brave 19-year-old, seemed to treat it with the same levity as our retired head of the Parish Council. I guess she was made of sterner stuff.

I agreed that I would do it, whatever 'it' was, the following evening. That seemed to calm them down. The only thing I did pray for was that the local Press didn't get wind of all the rumours and jitters. I didn't imagine that my Bishop would take too kindly to a novice Vicar saying prayers to placate a slope of rain-washed mud. It would look a bit too medieval for the modern Anglican Church.

Luckily, the Lord took pity on me the following afternoon. The rain that day had been particularly heavy and, at around 3pm, work on the building site came to a temporary stop when one of the Ukrainians saw a human skull emerge from the mud and slip down the slope.

This was a problem for which there was a practical solution. In this case, a couple of quick phone calls to the Police and to the local County Archaeology team. The Police arrived the same afternoon and the Ukrainians made themselves scarce hiding away in their caravans. Yuri did the honours for them, claiming he was the one who had first noticed the skull on the slope. The Police took one look at it, decided it was "very old" and took it away in a black plastic bin-liner, suggesting that this would probably be a job for the archaeologists.

Which it proved to be. They arrived the next morning and, having exhumed the rest of what turned out to be a male skeleton, they asked the Police for its skull back. It took a week for the science to date the skeleton to the Middle Ages, 1200-

1450 to be more precise. With the Police stood down and with the driving rain exposing more human bones on the muddy slope, a team of six archaeologists spent another week searching the slope and exhuming more complete skeletons. They were all adults, one woman and four men. They seemed to have been buried in shallow graves, all during the Middle Ages. The overall date range for the burials for all five skeletons was between 1100 and 1450. There was nothing to link them except for the fact that each had been buried with a simple metal cross, of various designs and styles.

By this time, the Press had arrived and quickly started to treat us to sensational headlines on "village mass murder" and "the slaughterhouse slope". But even the copy editors lost interest and moved on to other scandals and horrors when the County archaeologists issued a more factual statement with timelines and scientific evidence.

Meanwhile the Ukrainians continued laying the foundations for what would be 'Church Close', 'Churchyard Close' having been judged too off-putting for potential purchasers. Some of the Ukrainians still claimed that they saw the ghosts of the dead walking on the slope in the evenings, but the 19-year-old, who sat out in the rain again for a whole night, said he saw nothing.

The slope still being Church land, unlike the field below, one of the archaeologists came to me to give me their conclusions before they issued a further press statement.

What do you know about suicide in the Middle Ages, she asked me?

That it was illegal and proscribed as a mortal sin by the Church, I replied.

That's right. And how were suicides buried?

Outside consecrated ground, I said, beginning to think I was back at school being tested.

Not just that, she said. Suicides had to be humiliated in death.

154

Their property was confiscated and they were usually buried at night in secret, often face-down beside a crossroads and with a wooden stake driven through their hearts. It was as if the Law and the Church were joining together to obliterate both them and their memory.

I shan't defend my predecessors, I said. Luckily times have changed. But why would these bones be on this slope, if their bodies were buried at the crossroads?

My guess, she said, would be that there must have been times when the relatives managed to exhume the bodies. After all, gossip gets round in a small village and freshly dug earth is difficult to hide. There must have been times when the relatives went out at night, dug up the body and took it up to that slope, to rebury it as close to the Churchyard wall as they could, as close to consecrated ground as they could get. They'd have cut the turf or the topsoil and replaced it when they'd finished. They'd have done the best they could. After all, it was a labour of love for them, something they were determined to get right.

Before she left, I asked her what the bureaucracy would be for my seeking the return of the skeletons for burial.

What are you going to do, asked Yuri, when we sitting over a bottle of vodka one evening a few days later?

I am going to bury them properly, over the wall in the churchyard, so their souls can return to God, I said.

Two months later, on a cold but dry December morning, I performed my first burial service. The roofs of the new houses could be seen over the churchyard wall, just awaiting the tiles. Yuri and the Ukrainians had moved on to another building site somewhere, hopefully not beside a graveyard. Perhaps they were working on British Rail land besides the tracks in some big city, preparing the ground for gleaming luxury apartment blocks, a world away from the Middle Ages and from the mud of my Fenland village.

My parishioners turned out in force, along with the County

155

Archaeologists. Armed with our more enlightened approach to the tragedy of suicide and sanctioned by the Burial of Suicide Act of 1823 and subsequent legislation, I committed the souls of this one woman and four men to the protection of God, laying their ghosts in consecrated ground. As we turned to make our way to the Cricket Pavilion for the refreshments organised by the Church volunteers, I just hoped that somewhere and somehow the souls of these five people and those of their relatives, who'd risked much to move them, could see that they were over the wall at last. It was strange to think that they had the Church Commissioners development department and a bunch of hard-working but illegal 'Poles' to thank for that.

# 13 THE HAND OF JUSTICE

I think I've already told you that I don't believe in ghosts, said Abigail. But then you would hardly expect me to. As a lawyer, I have spent my whole life either presenting evidence as a barrister or sifting it and interpreting it as a judge. I have been guided by precedent and steered by intellect. Every decision I have taken has been the product of reason. What we do as barristers is to present each fact in a way which strengthens our argument and rules out all possibility of an alternative. Someone once said that our job is to corral the truth. We stand before the jury with all their doubts removed or accounted for. If we are good at our job, we leave them with no choice but to accept the result we have delivered for them. It's this final certainty which has always appealed to me, a certainty which is arrived at through hard work and logic. As a judge, it is a joy to watch a good barrister construct their case, destroying all counter-argument as they do so. Even if that leaves little work for the judge to do.

And so I don't have a ghost story to tell you. What I shall do is tell you about something that happened right at the start of my legal career, when I was still in pupillage. It's a sad story and hardly the stuff of after-dinner entertainment, but it was something that affected me deeply at the time and which I have never forgotten. A warning of the fragility of reason, I suppose. It concerns the destruction of a mind, the mind of someone I respected. I have decided to tell you the story now because of something I learnt recently, in the last couple of months. I wouldn't go so far as to say that it raises a question-mark over what happened, but it is curious and, for that reason alone, you might find it interesting.

There were two reasons I decided to apply to our college. The first was that it offered me the chance to split my degree between History, which I loved, and Law which would be my future. The second was the scholarship it offered to its Law graduates to help them pay for their first years as a barrister after graduation. In the old days, you didn't become a barrister unless you had private money of your own. Even when we graduated, the college scholarship was what made it possible for me to go into pupillage as a barrister. Without it, I'd have been forced to qualify as a solicitor instead. I am very grateful to the college for that scholarship help.

I was lucky after graduation to secure a year's pupillage at an old and distinguished Legal Chambers in London. Their work was predominantly Criminal Law, "pure barristering" as one of my new-found colleagues at the Chambers described it. We were there for the love of the profession and for the satisfaction we derived from deploying its skills. None of us would accrue the wealth we'd have acquired in Commercial Law.

At first sight, it was a bit like college. There were the same 18th and 19th century staircases with the residents' names painted on wooden boards by the door. There was the same sense of peace in the courtyards and the quadrangles. It was only indoors that you sensed the change. The intellectual analysis and thoughtful consideration were still there. It was just that, in the Chambers, there was a drive and a pace which college had lacked. Perhaps it was because the deadlines came by the day rather than the term. It was like a perpetual scramble up a slippery ice-covered hillside. Reason and intellect were what drove you forwards. You knew that if you made the wrong decision or acted without due knowledge of precedent, then you could find yourself sliding inexorably back. With no disrespect to college, I felt that I had to keep my wits about me more in the Chambers. There was no margin for error, none at all.

The two barristers I worked most closely with were those who were to supervise my pupillage. The more junior, Helen, was in her late twenties, phenomenally hard-working and phenomenally serious. I don't think I once saw her smile in the year I was working alongside her. I can't fault her for the help she gave me, for the advice and the direction, nor for the thoroughness with which she set about this, her first, experience as a teacher and guide.

But it would have been a somewhat dry and dour year if it hadn't been for the more senior barrister who oversaw my pupillage from on-high, so to speak. Terence Macleise QC was well-known amongst his peers for being a character. He was idiosyncratic and, albeit in the most polite of ways, always strongly opinionated. He was never going to conform sufficiently to rise to the top of his profession and was thus both admired and slightly pitied by his more ambitious colleagues at the Bar. What set him apart for me, apart from his sense of humour, was that he was the only barrister in the Chambers who seemed to step back and consider how the judgements passed down in Court actually reflected or impinged on wider social issues. I enjoyed my weekly sessions with him, at which he'd always insist I join him in a glass of madeira. I think the ceremony of this appealed to him as much as the alcohol. It was always the same, the way he would walk to the cabinet to take out two of his six 18th century sherry glasses, each different and each with that slight roughness under the base where the pontil had been snapped off by the glassblower. This was always followed by the triumphal smile with which he would produce the cut-glass decanter. This small, balding, middle-aged bachelor clearly enjoyed his rituals and his routines.

Presiding over the whole pyramid of the Chambers, like a God veiled from his worshippers, was their senior judge, The Honourable Mr John Smith, known to us as Sir John. That at least is the name I shall give him. You could work out his name fairly quickly now on the Internet, but I shan't repeat it here because of the story I am about to tell you. I admired him, you see, and respected him.

I say 'veiled from his worshippers' because, when I joined the Chambers, he was a somewhat aloof, remote and indeed tragic figure. He lived for the Law and had excelled at it. As a barrister, he had been a master of his brief. As a judge, he had navigated his way with logic and precision through the most tortuous or troubled of cases. When he summed up a case for the jury, his intellect and his choice of phrase would quickly become gospel in the legal profession. He certainly was someone who had never put a foot wrong in his whole legal career. The only chink in his somewhat austere manner had been the fact that he had doted on his only daughter.

And there lay the tragedy. For, just over two years before I arrived at the Chambers, his daughter had died in a freak accident in her second year at university. She'd been sitting on a windowsill at a party on a warm early summer evening in college. She and everyone else there had drunk too much. She leant back too far and fell two storeys onto the paving stones of the quadrangle below. No-one was to blame and no-one could say exactly how it had happened. More importantly, no-one could tell The Honourable Mr John Smith why it had happened. Her's was a meaningless and tragic death.

Terence Macleise was the one who told me of the aftermath. When I tried to broach the subject with Helen, I just got nervous evasion. According to Macleise, the judge and his wife were quite understandably destroyed by the tragedy. Sir John, with his austere brilliant mind, had withdrawn into himself. It was a year before he returned to the Chambers and to his work in Court. Macleise was telling me this so that I should be warned in advance when I met the judge. I should make allowances if Sir John was unduly sharp or brusque with me, as he had been with others since his return to work.

As it was, I think I only met Sir John three or four times one-to-one during my first year at Chambers. He would call me to his room every few months to ask about my progress and how I was enjoying it. To tell you the truth, I hadn't expected to hear this austere man use the word 'enjoy' in connection with the Bar, certainly not given all that I'd of him from others. Even Macleise seemed surprised when I told him. Macleise could only conclude that Sir John had taken a shine to me because I perhaps reminded him of his daughter.

The early weeks turned into months as I shadowed Helen in her casework, slowly building up my knowledge of the intricate procedures a barrister must learn to achieve the results they require, all those seemingly arcane channels which their intellects and knowledge must follow. With that, and the endless reading of and around the cases, it was a punishing regime. In some weeks, the only bright spot would be my hour with Macleise and his madeira. He had a way of putting everything into context, even hard work and misery, and I never left his room without a smile and a lighter step.

As I say, I always looked forward to my catch-ups with Terence Macleise and I was surprised when, at one of our weekly review sessions, with his glass of madeira in his hand, Macleise became suddenly and quietly more serious.

I have been thinking how to raise this, he said. Indeed, I have been thinking whether I should raise it at all. It's quite a lot to ask of someone still in pupillage and I should quite understand if you were to feel unable to help me and the Chambers with what I am about to suggest.

I had no idea what was about to come and I didn't know what to say, so I just sat there in silence turning the sherry glass in my hand, feeling the rough mark where the pontil had been snapped off.

Seeing me look nervous, Macleise was quick to reassure me.

We, the Chambers, need your help, he said. It concerns Sir John. I shall tell you what the matter is and then you will decide whether you can help us. Either way, you must not repeat what I about to tell you. Can you agree to that?

I nodded and he went on.

Sir John was the best and most gifted barrister of his generation. As a judge, his work has been of the very highest quality. In years to come, the textbooks will be filled with the intellectually precise and majestic prose of his judgements. The problem, though, is this. Since Sir John has returned to Court, after his daughter's tragic death, it seems that his sense of judgement might have begun to fail him.

Macleise paused to look out of the window to the dark bare branches of the Winter trees in the courtyard. Their sombreness seemed to affect what he then said.

His recent judgements, the way he has summed up and steered the juries, have been 'wayward'. That is the word I would use. He has departed from the logic of the evidence. Put simply, his judgements have made no sense. It's not good for Sir John, it's not good for the Chambers and it is certainly not good for the Law. All in all, we find ourselves in a bit of a mess.

What I am going to ask is whether you might help us by being a fresh pair of eyes. I and the Senior Clerk could arrange that you would spend an appropriate part of your time in Court shadowing those cases over which Sir John is presiding. He likes you. He would accept your presence at the back of Court as quite natural. We, at the Chambers, need you to observe him at work in the Court. Perhaps you can identify first-hand some clue in his behaviour, in the way he handles the cases, which might help us to understand what is going on. He has one of the greatest minds in our profession and something seems to have gone wrong.

Having unburdened himself, Macleise moved quickly to pour us each another madeira.

You don't have to decide now he said. Go and think about it over the weekend.

Of course I shall help, I said. You know that I am very grateful for my pupillage here and that I am keen to help the Chambers in any way I can.

Thank you, said Macleise, looking immensely relieved.

What we badly need here, he said, pausing to sip his madeira, is your intellect and your powers of observation. Watch him in Court. Follow the proceedings but always keep your eyes on Sir John. There must be something in his manner or behaviour which might give us a clue and shed light on his recent rather peculiar decision-making.

And so I spent two weeks of my precious pupillage neither shadowing Helen nor embarking on my own rudimentary casework but, instead, seated at the back of the High Court patiently observing Sir John and his 'peculiar decision-making'.

The case I was to follow was a murder trial. A young mother of two had been attacked and killed one afternoon in her own home. Her baby was asleep in her cot in the living room. The mother was in the kitchen showing her 3-year-old son how to make shortbread when she was assaulted and killed. The Police, therefore, had a witness.

The little boy would say nothing. All he would do was to curl up in a foetal position whenever the therapists or experts tried to speak to him about what had happened. The Police breakthrough came when they confronted the little boy with the 18-year-old son of his next-door neighbours. Nowadays there would be a scientific term to describe the neighbours' son and support groups to help him and his parents. Back in those days, the 18-year-old was just 'strange' and his parents had to do the best they could with their permanently angry and withdrawn son.

The little boy had started to shake uncontrollably when the 18-year-old was brought into the room. He would say nothing but his terror was proof enough in itself.

The Police questioned the 18-year-old for ten hours. He eventually confessed to the attack and to the murder and described how he had taken the knife from the dead mother's kitchen-drawer, a knife which he'd abandoned blood-stained on the kitchen floor. He refused to say why he had attacked his neighbour, whom he knew well and had always seemed to get on well with. The psychologists who reviewed his statement and behaviour referred to his history of pent-up anger and suggested that something in his mind had just snapped. It was common apparently in such cases for a killer to be left with an imperfect or hopelessly blurred memory of what had happened, of what they had done.

These were the bare bones of the case which were fleshed out at length during the two-week trial. A trial that was made more complicated when the 18-year-old retracted his confession three days before the trial began. The prosecution barrister, snapped out of his complacency, had used those three days to go over yet again each last scrap of Police evidence and he appeared confident and unruffled when he appeared in Court on the first day.

I don't know how many of you have attended a High Court trial, said Abigail.

I have, interrupted Lance, grinning. I've been at several.

Abigail smiled at him and continued, undeterred.

I shan't bore you with the procedure and the ceremony, she said. After all, this story is not about the Law. It's about Sir John and his 'wayward' decisions. And it was Sir John whom I was there to observe.

During the first days when the prosecution was presenting its evidence, Sir John seemed detached from the Court and its proceedings. There were times when he would spend whole minutes staring at the ceiling as if he was trying to compute its exact size in square feet. At other times, he would seem entranced by the way a pigeon walked along the ledge outside the window. He wasn't daydreaming. His brain was clearly working and he appeared inordinately interested in what he was seeing. It was as if he was an ornithologist in a jungle observing some undiscovered species of parrot. There were times when he seemed almost entranced. However, just when the prosecuting barrister was on the point of losing patience with his judge's indifference, Sir John would butt in with some penetrating observation on the barrister's conduct to pull him up on some precise point of legal procedure which proved that he had followed every moment of the barrister's work.

Sir John's mind was patently capable of existing in several spheres simultaneously. He was undoubtedly following the trial, as was his job, but it was as if he didn't really need to. It was as if he knew the result.

At the time, I put this down to the strength of the Police evidence. Even with his confession withdrawn, the case against the 18-year-old neighbour seemed insuperable. For a young barrister doing her pupillage, it was a depressing experience. It was as if the whole legal process was merely an exercise in going through the motions.

I remember putting this to Terence Macleise one evening after the Court had adjourned for the night. He nodded but cautioned me against taking anything in the High Court for granted. The unexpected could and did happen, even in a setting where the protagonists, the highly qualified barristers, were unlikely to make a mistake. Fate could still intervene. He agreed with me, though, that this was an easy case for Sir John to preside over. The evidence largely talked for itself.

Over the following few days, the prosecuting barrister teased out from his witnesses a steel frame of guilt with which to surround the 18-year-old neighbour. The confession (albeit withdrawn) with what he had said about the knife, the terrified reaction of the murdered woman's small son, the passing delivery-man and the other neighbours who had seen the 18-year-old leaving the murdered woman's house shortly before her small son ran screaming into the street and attracted the attention of a passer-by. The various expert testimonies of the psychiatrists only added a further comforting layer of science to the prosecution case.

None of this evidence, however, elicited any form of facial response from Sir John. It was just that, from time to time, I would catch him glancing at the prosecuting barrister with an expression of mild pity, as if he were watching someone who didn't know how to play chess attempting to respond to his opponent's complex opening gambit. I almost expected to see Sir John shake his head as though the barrister had completely lost his way. I don't suppose anyone else left the Court in the evening with that same impression, but then I don't suppose anyone else there had spent the whole day watching Sir John.

I remember when I described this to Macleise he became quite excited, almost knocked over his glass of madeira. As nice as he was, Macleise switched into professional barrister mode and started to cross-question me on every last nuance of expression on Sir John's face. He clearly thought we were getting somewhere but, for the life of me, I couldn't see where. He congratulated me and urged me to keep up my good work.

When the defence barrister took over the following morning, there was little sign of a complex opening gambit. He had to use the material at his disposal and it was as though he had just two pawns to pit against rooks and bishops. He did his best with a string of witnesses to testify to the 18-year-old's essentially harmless nature. Yes, he was withdrawn and, on occasion, rude or surly, but they had never seen him violent. Perhaps sensibly, the defence barrister stuck to calling 'ordinary people' as his witnesses in the hope they might convince the jury with their common-sense. But the jurors sat largely impassively throughout this evidence. It was as if they had made up their minds on the strength of the prosecution evidence. And who could blame them?

The defence barrister didn't stray into calling expert psychiatric witnesses. I think he just hoped that he could portray his client as harmless but 'strange'. Further recitation of scientific terminology by the psychiatrists would only be further nails in his coffin, even if these expert witnesses were speaking in his support.

I was puzzled by Sir John's reaction to the defence case. For almost the whole time he sat there studiously impassive. There were just a few moments when his face betrayed any personal involvement or judgement. And where I would have expected to see suppressed irritation or perhaps just boredom (the prosecution evidence being so clear-cut), I glimpsed quiet concurrence. Once again, it was as though he knew more about this case than anyone else in the Courtroom.

I had expected Sir John, of course, to carry himself with assurance and self-confidence on the Bench, but I had never seen anyone look so in charge of events. It was like on the TV News when you see footage of the UN Security Council, the Ambassadors there supported by a small phalanx of their Counsellors and advisers, sitting behind, ready to pass a note of hand-written advice with some pertinent fact, should it be needed. But there was no-one standing behind Sir John. Nothing but empty space between his back and the wall.

It was this last point that Macleise focussed on when I briefed him later in his room at the Chambers.

It's not that I wouldn't expect Sir John to be self-assured, said Macleise. It's just that your impression was that he was almost unnaturally so. It's your impression of Sir John that's the most important thing here. It's why we've asked for your help in attending this trial. I suppose all we can do is wait and hope that we'll learn more as the trial goes on. It's his summing up which will be the most important thing. Watch him like a hawk then.

Do you think he's communicating with someone in the Courtroom, I asked? Is that what this is all about, undue influence?

Macleise smiled and shook his head.

No, I don't think Sir John is a witness to be intimidated or a jury to be nobbled, he laughed. Whatever is going on is inside his head. I'm sure of that. Just keep your eyes on his face. Sooner or later, he'll reveal more.

As I shut Macleise's door gently behind me, I was beginning to feel distinctly uncomfortable with the task he'd set me. I have always done my best to keep to a straight line in life. This was all a bit circuitous, even devious, for my liking. If Macleise and the others thought Sir John was insane, driven mad by grief, why didn't they just say so? I've always preferred honesty and plain-speaking. Surely a psychiatrist would be better than I was at interpreting Sir John's behaviour.

Luckily, it was Friday evening and, when I left Macleise, I hurried off to Victoria Station to catch the train to Lewes. I was going to spend two nights there with a friend from college. Walking on the South Downs with her and her dog helped blow some fresh, clean air into my lungs and get rid of the now somewhat unpleasant taste in my mouth left by what I was beginning to see as my 'snooping' on poor Sir John.

By Monday morning, all these personal emotions had gone and I was 100% professional. My colleagues in the Chambers wanted me to observe Sir John's behaviour during the trial. It was important not just for the Chambers but for the Law itself. That's what Macleise had said, and I did believe I could trust him. He was a decent man as well as a good lawyer.

Monday was devoted to Sir John's summing up. It was a tour de force and completely unexpected. For a man who had at times seemed distracted or comatose during the trial, Sir John employed his superb brain to martial every fact in support of the direction he was asking the jury to travel. There was no passion in his voice. This was no dramatic performance. Every word he spoke was with quiet assurance and complete commitment. There wasn't a shred of doubt in his brilliant mind. All was brightness and clarity like the sunlight reflected from one of Terence Macleise's cut-glass 18th century sherry glasses. His summing up was illuminating. I and the jury and everyone in Court, perhaps even the prosecution barrister, came to see that we had spent the last week in darkness and error. Sir John's crystal-clear, rapier-sharp arguments set out to convince us that the 18-year-old was innocent.

He systematically broke down every fact he could in the

prosecution case and cast doubt on those facts he couldn't destroy. What had the witnesses actually seen? Was the murdered woman's small son terrified of the accused on that one occasion, or had he always been scared, as any young child might, by the accused's 'strangeness'? The jury would need to be sure of these points, beyond all reasonable doubt, should they pass a verdict of guilty.

I know my job was to watch Sir John, but I saw the prosecution barrister's face grimace as he saw all of Sir John's skill and intellect being employed to such a misguided purpose. In the barrister's eyes, the judge was perverting the course of justice.

As for Sir John, I saw a slight glimmer of a smile on his face as he finished. And perhaps, I can't be sure, he turned ever so slightly, started almost, as though someone he trusted had stood behind him and laid their hand on his shoulder. For, as soon as he felt the touch, his face became calm and serene as though he knew he had done his job well and was satisfied with it. He sat there impassively on the Bench suffused with joy while the rest of the Courtroom sat in stunned silence. Only the 18-year-old made a slight sound and I could see that he had begun to cry.

The jury shuffled out and it took them two and a half days to reach their verdict. When it came, they were split. But by a majority they found the accused innocent.

Sir John thanked them for their work and their application. He then pronounced a verdict of murder by persons unknown.

The Press reporters ran down the Court corridor to the phones. By the next morning the Tabloids carried headlines denouncing a miscarriage of justice and demanding that Sir John be sacked. The dead woman's family issued a statement demanding justice. The Tabloids then picked this up the next day and launched a public campaign, issuing tear-out forms on their inner pages for their readers to fill in and send to the Home Secretary, demanding that 'the hand of justice' should deliver fit punishment to the guilty.

So what happened, asked Macleise when we met in his room on

the evening of the end of the trial? What did you see?

I described as best as I could Sir John's masterful but seemingly perverted summing up in which he seemed to employ all his skill and his lifetime of experience to push back against the evidence. I confessed that I had never seen anything like it, a supremely rational man standing in opposition to Reason. But I had to admit that I was still mesmerised by the power and precision of his arguments.

But what did you see, repeated Macleise?

What I saw was that slight turn of his head as he brought his summing up to its conclusion. I saw that slight wince as though he'd felt a hand on his shoulder and then that look of contentment and joy when he saw that it belonged to someone he trusted.

And loved, said Macleise?

I suppose so, I said. But what does it mean?

Macleise smiled. I think neither you nor I are in a position to say what it means, he replied. All I can tell you is what I think the result will be.

The end of Sir John's career, I asked?

I suspect that there will be private meetings later tonight, he said, involving the Master of the Rolls and others. My guess is that Sir John will be asked to retire.

And the case, I asked?

There will be a retrial, I imagine. The prosecution will plead gross miscarriage of justice, and they will be within their rights to do so. After all, a judge is not a barrister and a summing up is not the place to argue a case. Sir John exceeded his remit, to put it mildly.

Macleise proved to be correct. Sir John was asked and agreed to retire quietly, to withdraw into obscurity. There was a retrial with a new jury and, second time round, the undisputed strength of the evidence resulted in conviction for murder. The 18-year-old was sectioned and went not to prison but to a secure Psychiatric Facility.

It was undoubtedly the most dramatic event of my pupillage, said Abigail. But, like all dramas, it receded into the distance with time. The Chambers recovered and the Law recovered. The Tabloids, speaking for the Public, were satisfied that justice had eventually been done.

And I admit that I had completely forgotten the case until a couple of months ago when the Police charged the young woman's actual murderer. He was a retired travelling-salesman who used to work door-to-door in the days when there was more of that sort of thing. He was involved in a 'domestic', as the Police say. He was arrested and charged for beating his wife with a steak hammer. Mercifully she survived. As part of the subsequent investigation, he was DNA tested. That matched with material evidence from a murder case of a woman twenty years before. They then interviewed those companies that had employed him which were still in business and combed the records of those companies that had kept them. One of his area rounds coincided in date and time with the murder of the young woman in Sir John's last case. They still had the kitchen knife that killed her and the DNA matched. Sadly, there was no happy ending for the 18-year-old. He had died in a Psychiatric Institution ten years ago.

So what do you think happened at Sir John's last trial, we all asked?

I am a lawyer, said Abigail. It is not my job to 'think' as you call it. My job is to present the evidence with logic and reason, "to corral the truth". I have no idea why Sir John acted as he did in his final summing up. There is no way I can see that he could have known more than anyone else in that Courtroom.

Unless, said Lance, Sir John had spoken to someone who did know more. Perhaps to someone who had spoken to the victim?

You mean a witness to the crime, said Abigail?

No, I was thinking more of someone who might have spoken to the victim after the event, said Lance.

Ridiculous, said Abigail, as if that was sufficient to close down all discussion.

After we'd sat in silence for a while, one of us, I can't remember who, asked Abigail what had happened to Sir John after his 'retirement'.

He died a few years after the trial, she said. He invited me to his house in the country for Sunday lunch once. It was an embarrassing affair. I was the only guest with Sir John and his wife. She did her best to keep the conversation going but she was clearly wrecked. She'd lost her only daughter to a tragic accident and now her husband to insanity. For insanity it was, however mild his behaviour.

I remember after lunch he took me for a walk round his large garden. When I asked if there was anything I could do for him or his wife, anything I might bring them from London, he just shook his head and smiled.

That's very kind, he said. But you see you mustn't worry about me. I've been right as rain ever since my daughter came back.

# 14 STAVRAKIS

In my case, said Richard, it always seems to be illness that brings me up against ghosts. The worst time was when I was medi-vacced from a job in Mozambique. I had been there for over three years working in the field with a small team of local staff. And we had been very busy. The country was still in a mess after the Civil War. The farmers that were left were only just beginning to return to their land. We had to start with food distribution and a medical programme before we could move on to irrigation and seed projects and literacy campaigns to try and help restart what schools there were. The only thing that helped us, and it was a big help, was that the Civil War remained dormant and we were spared drought, floods and locusts for the whole three years. It was as though the Gods looked kindly on us and allowed us some breathing space to rebuild in the wreckage of this man-made disaster.

My own experience of such jobs has been that you can run for several years on nothing but adrenalin. The adrenalin buys you time, but it won't keep you going forever. I remember that when the low point came, it was without warning. There was no dramatic trigger, no sensational event. It wasn't caused by any unforgivable error on my part. It wasn't as though I had done anything to deserve it. The collapse just happened all of a sudden. My body had enough and it shut down.

Comatose in the back of a Land Rover, I was bumped down to the capital where, unbeknown to me, I was diagnosed with Weil's disease and put into an isolation ward. You catch Weil's disease from rat-infested water, apparently, so there was some logic to it. The doctors told my Programme Manager that I had a 40 % chance of survival. Luckily for me, the whites of my eyes turned yellow after three days and the doctors were able to downgrade the diagnosis from Weil's disease to jaundice and glandular fever. There was a logic to that too, overwork and exhaustion being a contributing factor.

All I can remember about those three days of fever in that isolation ward were the things that weren't there, the illusions and the hallucinations. You all know what fever is like, I suppose. It's the time when the devils emerge. It starts with those simple misconceptions – that the curtains in your room are in flames, that you are about to be burnt like a childhood Guy Fawkes on some back-garden bonfire. But then the hallucinations move to another level and it gets far worse when you realize that this mortal danger is directed against you personally, that there are practitioners of hate who have singled you out for this torture.

The 'people' or things you see will be determined by your background and experience, by images you've seen when sane. We all have our custom-made demons ready to emerge when fever or insanity offers them the chance. Some of us will see smiling men in medical gowns, walking forwards with hypodermics in their hands. Others will see soldiers and weapons. I, being an old-fashioned romantic, saw the real thing - devils in all their glory. Horns and talons and evil faces. Evil, small devils in all the colours of the rainbow. Whole swirling clouds of them in all the colours except those we associate with human beings.

The red ones seemed to be in charge, laughed Richard. I do remember that. But what's the point of describing such madness? The only thing you need to know is that it was Hell

174

on Earth and that, for me, it was completely real. In fact, it was the only reality there was. It was my misfortune to have been condemned to it.

If it gets very bad, then the doctors have to put you into restraints, for your own good, until the fever passes. That happened in my case. I guess the ghosts and the devils that I saw were the really powerful ones. Perhaps I have a better imagination that I give myself credit for. Either that or I'm more stupid than most people. Anyway, it was real for me and I felt doubly wrecked when it was finally over.

I did my best to argue that I should be allowed to remain in-country to recuperate, but the truth was that I couldn't stand up unaided. I had to accept that, to others, I must still have looked close to death. And so the decision was out of my hands and I found myself, a complete fraud in my eyes, medi-vacced to Athens sitting upright in a seat on a commercial flight. I wasn't on a stretcher and I certainly wasn't my idea of a deserving case. But I have to admit that I was grateful to be allowed to sit there on my own while the aircraft emptied at Athens airport before the ground staff brought the wheelchair to take me off. I wasn't a hospital case, but I did need looking after for a few weeks until I could walk properly again.

Athens had been a compromise between my Aid Organization which wanted to send me back to England and my own preference to remain closer to my work in Mozambique. My Programme Manager, Yianni, was Greek and he'd suggested I could stay with his parents in Athens. They had a big flat, mostly empty now that their children had moved out, and they'd welcome the company. His mother had been an English teacher while his father had been a Professor of Philology. They'd welcome the chance to use their English again.

I found Yianni's smiling parents waiting for me at the foot of the plane steps, watching as the crew members helped me down. They even had a large taxi parked right up against the plane. Security wasn't as tight at Athens Airport as it is now and being a retired Professor of Philology clearly brought you more influence than it would in London. So there they were, ready to bundle me off to their home on Lykavettos Hill in Kolonaki in the centre of Athens as soon as the taxi driver had put the folded wheel chair in the boot. I asked about Immigration checks and they laughed, saying they had a card I could fill in which they'd pass later to their friend the Chief of Police. Philologists there obviously moved in strange circles.

It was the middle of March and a beautiful Spring had already arrived. Their flat was on the top two floors of an apartment block on the ring-road round Lykavettos Hill. I spent every day for weeks sitting out on their balcony, gazing out at Athens stretched out below me, the Parthenon shining in the middle distance and, on clear days, the bright-blue sea beyond. It was as close to Heaven as you could get. Albeit a noisy Heaven with the constant honking of the car-horns and the pigeons swirling up around the church dome below me every time a lorry back-fired.

But there were other more pleasant sounds which became part of my daily ritual as I sat there. The neighbours throwing coins down to the Balkan street musicians playing their clarinets and accordions as they passed. The long litany of houseplants, flower-pots and sacks of compost recited by a gravel-voiced man on a tannoy from his Toyota pick-up truck which cruised the streets each day drumming up custom for the wares in the back. A voice which came from a lifetime of chain-smoking.

Apart from mealtimes, Yianni's parents would leave me alone on the balcony with a selection of English books from their library. It was the late afternoons and early evenings, the hours before dinner at 9pm, that we'd all sit together out on the balcony, the two of them wearing overcoats and hats "against the chill".

The first few evenings they set about working their way through the great works of English literature. What did I think? What did that precise phrase mean? But the truth was that my A Level in English Literature could only take me so far. They had both read far more widely in English than I had. I must have been a disappointment to them, but they did their best not to show it. Yianni's mother would drift off to the kitchen to get on with the

176

dinner while his father would pour me another ouzo, clink out the ice cubes from a small metal bowl and turn the conversation to the many other things that interested him. Folk beliefs and folk customs were a hobby of his, that and tracing their survival in the backwaters of folk culture.

Pointing to the Parthenon, he said the old Gods are still with us, you know. Out in the country, some farmers will still leave offerings of honey for the gods and spirits. People will tie holy rags to the trees. You had the same in England, of course. Farmers would make the pilgrimage to Canterbury and return with holy water to pour on their fields. The old ways die hard. Which is good, I think. It's a form of continuity, the shadows of the past. Why throw out the past just because we're modern and up to date? We ourselves will look old-fashioned in a hundred years' time.

But dinner was ready before he could develop his theme. It was the next evening when he started to talk with passion about these folk beliefs and traditions, about the old gods and ghosts and the vampires that walked the Greek countryside.

These beliefs may be naïve and simplistic, he said, but that's because they're elemental. They are perhaps the last enduring link with the old religions. They are the small man's religion. They are what he will place his faith in. That's why they've survived in popular culture. They may not be for the "pen-pushers" as we say in Greek, for the educated elite. But they are what the uneducated man will turn to when his back is against the wall and he needs help. For that's what folk art and folk culture is, I suppose. It's a prop and solace for the common man.

At which point he burst out laughing. What a pretentious load of rubbish, he exclaimed. I'm at risk of straying into 'karagiozilikia' as we say in Greek, idiotic, childish stuff.

Have you heard of Karagiozis, he asked? Oh, then I must tell you, and he paused to pour us each another ouzo.

Karagiozis is the hero of our shadow puppet theatre. His roots go back to Ottoman Greece. You can still see performances here in Athens in the Summer, though it has been pretty well finished off by television now. Karagiozis is the absolute epitome of the poor man, the little fellow, the downtrodden. He's oppressed by the Ottoman ruling-classes and beaten up by their police and soldiers. He's always starving and always wanting nothing more than a square meal. He lives in a run-down hut with his starving children across the stage from the Vezir's grand palace. But Karagiozis is much more than this. He's wily and cunning and funny and capable of a hundred disguises. With no education he still manages to pass himself off as a lawyer or a doctor or a journalist, even a Chinese Mandarin speaking fake Chinese to fool the Vezir into giving him money.

Yianni's father then took me through the plots of a dozen or more shadow puppet plays before dinner was ready. Plays with Karagiozis and plays with heroes of the Greek War of Independence, of Byzantium and even Alexander the Great – the Greek shadow theatre in all its glory.

The following evening, I was expecting more about Karagiozis and I was surprised when Yianni's father became suddenly more thoughtful. He stared out in silence at the Parthenon for several minutes before he began speaking.

One of my school-friend's fathers was a Karagiozis performer, he said, before the War, when we were at high-school. That's how I got to know more about Karagiozis and the shadow puppet tradition. The family were very poor, from one of the roughest parts of Piraeus. My friend was always embarrassed because he didn't have the money to stand us coffees. Which was why I think he was so proud one Spring day when he could invite us all to one of his father's Karaziozis performances in the Plaka. His father would tour the islands in the Summer and do the best he could to make ends meet with performances in Athens over the Winter.

My friend said his father was giving us all free tickets, but I'm sure he repaid his father later. The family were on the breadline. They lived a world away from the rest of us with our Kolonaki flats and our business and professional parents.

After the show, my friend took us behind the white sheet screen to introduce us to his father. He was a middle-aged man in a worn-out dark suit, shirt buttoned up to the collar but no tie. I remember he had an impressive and much cared-for moustache. I was surprised by the mildness of his voice, so removed from the gravelly, raucous voices he'd used for some of the puppets during the performance. It was a hallmark of the old Piraeus Karagiozis performers, he told us, proud of the tradition he was part of. It was a tradition that would have been impenetrable for anyone but a native Greek-speaker. But then Karagiozis was designed by Greeks for Greeks.

He kept his treasured puppets in a small brown suitcase. Flat leather puppets brightly painted and re-painted over decades. There was Karagiozis in his rags and in his hundred disguises. Karagiozis as a priest, as a doctor, as a detective or secret agent with a revolver in his hand. There were puppets for all Karagiozis's friends and for the Greek heroes with their swords, for the Vezir and his Turkish soldiers with their rifles. Puppets for animals, puppets for devils, for flying machines and tanks. It was endless. My friend's father took out each one to show us before returning them lovingly to the old, battered suitcase that was their home.

If you're here one Summer, Yianni's father said, turning to me, we must take you to a Karagiozis performance. I could talk you through the plot in advance. It's quite a spectacle and worth seeing, even if it is by Greeks for Greeks.

Did your friend follow in his father's footsteps with Karagiozis, I asked?

Yianni's father stared out at the Parthenon for a while before replying.

No, I am sad to say he was killed in the War, he said. It's a long story. I'll tell you one day, if you like. That's if you don't mind sad stories, strange stories. But I think that's my wife calling us in to dinner.

179

It wasn't until the following week that Yianni's father returned to the story of his dead school-friend, making sure our glasses were well-filled with ouzo before he started.

To the past, he said, raising his glass, and to the heroes we have lost.

When the War began, I was at university studying English and French. My friend was a clerk in a lawyer's office. His parents were so proud of him. In their eyes, he was 'settled' and 'established'. He was on his way to a financial security they had only dreamed of. The War, of course, put an end to all that.

When Italy invaded, my friend and I clamoured to be allowed to join the Army that was pushing Mussolini's troops back into Albania, winning part of the Greater Greece we had always dreamed of. They were heady days and we were thrilled when we finally got the go-ahead to begin our military training. It was perhaps lucky for us, though, that we hadn't finished that basic training before the Germans invaded Greece to take the pressure off their failing Italian allies. The Germans blitzed their way South, driving the Greek and allied armies before them. Before long it was a rout with allied soldiers trying to get a ride on any boat that could take them to Crete or to Egypt. In Athens we just watched in horror as our country became part of the Nazi Empire, divided up between the Axis Powers, with the Germans taking control of Athens itself, presumably not trusting the Italians to look after the capital.

It was my friend who came to me with the offer of Resistance work. Some of his father's Piraeus contacts were amongst those trying to organize small boats to smuggle allied soldiers out of Greece so they could escape the POW camps and fight again. Over the following weeks, these separate groups gradually came together under the leadership of a directing cell in Athens headed by a Greek Navy Officer. The Organization, as we called it, was so successful collecting allied soldiers, holding them in safe-houses and shipping them out that it came to the attention of the British in Alexandria and Cairo. I still don't know if that was a good thing, but the British could provide the funds and facilities we didn't have.

The British end of our expanded operation was run by an enthusiastic Officer from Alexandria. He set up a base on one of the Greek islands in the Italian-held zone. The plan was for us in Athens to ship out the allied soldiers to this island in small batches. Once enough had gathered there, then a British submarine would pick them up and take them to Alexandria. It was a big risk using one of the Allies' precious submarines for something like that, but when you think that there were shot-down pilots amongst the allied troops we were helping, then it made sense. Pilots were a commodity in short supply.

As for those of us in Athens, we were just heroic amateurs at that stage. It was before I'd escaped to Egypt and been trained in conspiracy. It was before we'd learnt that there are times when you have no choice but to cut your losses and run. The leaders of our Organization did the best they could for us, to teach us, to train us on the job, to make us understand the essential value of security. We all had code-names, of our own choosing so we wouldn't forget them. I and my friend used the names of Karagiozis puppets. I, as a university student studying languages, was Dionysios, the comically Westernised character in his suit and Western clothes. My friend I christened 'Stavrakis', the sharp-talking 'mangas' tough-man character, the hard-man from Piraeus. That was my joke, I guess. For my friend was the mildest of young men, as mild-mannered as his father. He was quietly determined but he was not someone to raise his voice or boast. He did come from Piraeus, though, so Stavrakis it was.

Our role, mine and Stavrakis's, was to collect allied soldiers in groups of two or three and walk them from safe-house to safe-house towards those quiet areas of the coast where they would be picked up at night by small boats. We'd tap out a code on the front-door and then be followed at a safe-distance by our charges, many of them not much older than we were.

We carried on like this for a couple of months, becoming more quietly confident with each passing week. We began to feel that we were not only contributing but winning. It was absurd to feel like that, but the very fact that we were doing something made us sure that we'd be one day victorious. All the hopelessness had suddenly gone from our lives. We could look at the German soldiers in the streets and smile. Our secret world would eventually destroy them.

The truth, of course, was that we were living on borrowed time. It was just that we didn't know it. The few Piraeus criminals in our Organization had a street-wise sharpness which had helped them survive against the Police and the Greek authorities. But even they were no match for the ruthless skill and the discipline of the German Secret Services. The latter, I suppose, regarded us as only half-human and would treat us worse than animals to get the information they needed when they caught us. But that was still to come and we had no idea of the fate that lay in store for us.

When the crash came, it wiped out almost everything. The allied soldiers out on the island were all rounded up by the Italians. The Germans went house-to-house and arrested nearly all of us in Athens, including the Greek Navy Officer and our leadership cell. Stavrakis was arrested when he went to a safe-house to warn them, only to find the Germans were already there. I escaped out of a back-window of a safe-house when we heard the German soldiers break down the front-door. They even managed to capture the British Officer who was running the whole operation. He was on the island at the time the Italians arrived and they handed him over to the Germans in Athens for interrogation.

I imagine the real loss for the British was when the Italian Navy managed to intercept and destroy the British submarine on its way to the island to pick up the allied soldiers there. At that stage of the War, a submarine was difficult to replace.

I hid out in a cousin's attic in Athens for months before I managed to make contact with a Piraeus small boat owner who agreed to smuggle me across to Alexandria. My cousin would feed me all the latest news he could pick up about Stavrakis and the others who'd been arrested. Stavrakis's mother and father would take it in turns to stand outside the prison gates, waiting and praying. His mother would stand there all day trying to

182

give in food parcels for him which were always rejected by the guards. His father would stand there in silence all night. Their vigil came to an end when the Germans pinned up a notice outside the gates listing all those who'd been executed. Stavrakis's name was on the list as was that of the Greek Navy Officer and the British Officer who'd been captured on the island.

In the weeks I remained in hiding, I received two other pieces of news. The first was about Stavrakis's father. He'd left home one day on his bicycle with his suitcase of Karagiozis figures and the bundle of sheets and poles he used to stage a performance. His wife never saw him again. Two weeks later his bicycle was spotted by a passing fishing-boat on the beach at Rhamnous, beneath the old Classical ruins. When the fishing-boat saw the bicycle still there on their return, they landed to investigate. They found it lying on top of his neatly folded jacket and his shoes, his bundle of sheets and poles beside it. They had them returned to his wife. There was no sign of the small suitcase of Karagiozis puppets. His wife guessed that he'd walked out into the sea with them, to drown with him.

The suitcase, however, did turn up a few weeks later when a shepherd found it stuffed between a couple of slabs in the ruins of one of the Classical Temples up on the hill at Rhamnous. The puppets were gone, presumably stolen by some child who'd taken the puppets and then hidden the suitcase to cover their theft.

The second piece of news was just as dramatic although it concerned someone I didn't know. A senior German Officer was assassinated on the road back from Marathon towards Athens. He and his driver and escort were returning from visiting the site of the ancient battlefield. No other details were given but it led to another round of executions of prisoners. With our Organization destroyed and no other Resistance groups we knew of in Attica, we could only assume that the assassination had been carried out by British commandoes. It was a mystery and one which deepened when I got to

Alexandria and my new-found British friends there denied it had been their operation.

But it was something which was pushed to the back of my mind in the busy years that lay ahead. I finally got my training in conspiracy. I spent the rest of the War travelling in and out of Occupied Greece as a courier and later as a co-ordinator for the Resistance. I saw more of Greece than I ever saw before or since. When the War was over, I chose not to follow my Greek Resistance colleagues into the Army, the Police or Politics, preferring to go back to university. I then did a doctorate at Oxford. After that I was offered a teaching post at Harvard but turned it down to come home to Athens. I spent the rest of my academic career in Athens. I missed my homeland, my friends and the climate. And sitting on a balcony in the evenings drinking ouzo, he laughed.

It was not till twenty years after the War that I learnt something which made sense, to me at least, of what had happened to Stavrakis's father and of the assassination of the German Officer on the Marathon road.

One of my colleagues at the university was researching the operations of the German Secret Service in Greece during the Occupation. He knew of the minor role I'd played in that first Athens Resistance Organization and he came to me with a translation he'd made of a German report he'd unearthed in an archive somewhere in Europe. It was the German secret report on their investigation into the assassination of Major Muller on the Marathon road.

Muller, it seemed, was the architect of all German "counter-bandit" strategy in Attica at the time. He was a dynamic and enthusiastic Nazi Officer more interested in quietly liquidating all threats to the Reich than in taking credit for the operations he inspired. He was the one who had master-minded the rounding-up of the allied soldiers on the island, the destruction of our Organization in Athens and the subsequent interrogations (for which read torture) which gave him the information he needed to help the Italian Navy intercept the British submarine. He even decided which and how many of the prisoners should be executed.

It was obvious from the report that what troubled the Germans most was how the British, who were in full-retreat, had managed to pin-point Muller's secret role and then send commandoes to assassinate him. For there was no-one but the British who could have done it. However, the annex to the report, which included eye-witness accounts of the assassination by Muller's driver and escort, begged more questions than it answered.

There was the driver's account and that of the two soldiers on a motorbike and sidecar who'd travelled just in front of Muller's car. Muller, a Classicist when at university, had enjoyed his trip to Marathon more than his driver and escort. On the way back, though, the latter were cheered up thinking of the beers they would have back in the barracks.

All was well until two things suddenly happened. The first was that the escort bike suddenly disappeared into a grey cloud on the road ahead. The second was that a tall young woman in a white ball-gown and wearing some sort of gold-coloured tiara walked out of the cloud towards Muller's car. The driver slammed on the brakes and the woman just stood there smiling at them. The driver thought she was probably insane. She looked like some refugee from a travelling theatre. Muller and the driver got out of the car, Muller with his Luger pistol in his hand just in case. At which point, the woman held up the small suitcase she was holding and smiled again as she tipped it open in front of them.

At this point the driver's account became less clear. He described seeing a swirling cloud of small, coloured figures, like devils, surging forwards to envelop Major Muller who started screaming. The driver ran back to the car for his rifle, but the cloud was upon him driving him back down the road to Marathon. He ran until he dropped unconscious.

He only came round when the two escort soldiers arrived running up to him along the road with their submachine guns in their hands. The two were battered and dazed and bruised.

They described how they'd turned their bike round and tried to drive back through the cloud towards the Major's car, only to smash straight into a wall of iron. A few minutes later both the wall and the cloud had gone and they were able to run back past Muller's dead body till they found the driver lying in the road.

The upshot was that the two escort soldiers were reassigned to light duties while the driver had to be sent back to Germany to a psychiatric institution. The report ended with some speculation about a new British secret weapon. But some senior Officer had later scored through the sentence and written the word "Unproven". Which was where the report ended.

Yianni's father poured us each another ouzo before he went on.

The report made sense to me, he said, although I'm not sure that 'sense' is exactly the right word. You see there are two Classical Temples at Rhamnous. I don't know, but I suspect that Stavrakis's father's suitcase was found at the Temple of Nemesis and that it was he himself who had put it there with his Karagiozis figures still inside, wedging it carefully between the two slabs as he prayed to the Goddess. His final act of faith before he wheeled his bicycle down to the beach, laid his things on the shore and walked out into the sea to drown.

# 15 ON THE BRIDGE

What you've always been too polite to mention, said Lance, is that I'm a thief and that I steal other people's possessions, some of them hard-won.

It was Lance's turn to tell a ghost story at our annual reunion and, as always, he had a way of arresting our attention. It was as though that upstairs dining-room at Rules restaurant was suddenly transformed into one of those small, almost intimate, Elizabethan stages and Lance was the lead actor striding out in front of us, intent on making his presence known.

Lance paused to look round the table at us, before giving us yet one more of his knowing smiles.

Perhaps it's time, then, that I offered you all a few thoughts on the nature of theft, as I see it. From my angle, so to say. Nothing too serious, though, and all in the best spirit of entertainment. I wouldn't want to ruin the good meal we've just eaten.

Lance took a final sip from his glass of port, looked down at the empty glass lovingly and then began.

It was a freezing cold grey February morning when I was much younger that I first met old Tony. A freezing grey morning in a freezing Victorian prison. I don't know what I'd done to deserve that. Well, I do, actually. I'd burgled a string of big houses in the Home Counties. Silverware (I've always liked Georgian) and jewellery mainly, things easy to carry and easy to sell. I had a good run of ten or eleven months working on my own before I was caught with a nice but too distinctive oval Irish Georgian snuffbox in my pocket. I remember it had a Dublin harp hallmark and I'd just taken a fancy to it. I'm not a collector, never have been. I kept it because it was useful. I wanted it to keep mints in, to carry in my pocket. Because of that snuffbox I was convicted and sent down, for six years that time.

I had the misfortune to arrive at that old red-brick prison just as the warders were trying to deal with an outbreak of some virus. They were hoping to put the lid on it and stop it spreading by keeping the prisoners locked up for 23 hours a day. So, no hours in the workshop or digging in the vegetable gardens. A half hour's walk round the yard if we were lucky. For the rest of the time, it was just you and your cellmate for company. In the end, I had no complaints. I could have done a lot worse than old Tony.

Tony was a railwayman by profession and a thief by nature. He'd also been born in London, so we had that in common as well. He'd worked for many of the old railway companies over the years and he'd stolen from all of them. It was almost an illness for him. He stole and stole and sooner or later he'd get caught. Usually, it was sooner because of the scale of his thieving. He wasn't someone to do it discreetly or in moderation. If he saw something, he'd take it. And if there were dozens of them, he'd just as likely take the lot.

He couldn't help himself, I suppose. He was not a professional thief by a long chalk. I'd never have worked with him. I could see he'd be trouble right off. A walking conviction magnet, he was. As I say, for him it was an illness. Kleptomania we might have called it then. I expect there are even fancier names for it now. He wouldn't end up in prison today, that's for sure. They'd be trying to cure him somehow, wean him off it. 'It' being an addiction, like gambling or drink. In those days, they'd just bang you up. An example to others, as if the others were ill in the same way.

Tony just couldn't help himself. He never planned or set out to do wrong. He wasn't guilty in the same way I was. You know, he even stole my toothbrush when we were together in that cell. I don't know how he got away with it without my noticing. I found it hidden under his mattress. He honestly had no idea it was there.

When I met Tony, he was serving the third year of a seven-year sentence for robbing one of his railway company employers, Southern Region I think it was. The length of the sentence reflected the scale of his theft. Like me, he'd had a good run. Though, in his case, his unbridled robbery had gone unnoticed for nearly two years. It was remarkable really when you consider all the things he'd taken. For when they entered his railwayman's cottage, they found a veritable museum of what we'd now call 'railwayana'. You could probably get quite a lot for it nowadays at the right sort of auction.

Tony was in reflective mood, more puzzled than proud, the evening he tried to recall for me the list of what he'd actually stolen. He'd obviously walked the length of whole trains with a screw-driver taking off all those small bakelite signs the railway companies set such store by: 'Do Not Lean Out Of The Window', 'Caution Low Racks', 'Luggage Must Not Be Placed On The Floor Or Seats'. He had whole shoe-boxes full of them in his cottage. The odd thing about it was that Tony couldn't read or write. He'd just taken the signs because they were there.

His small cottage was stacked high with this stuff. There were whole collections of crockery from the station buffets. He had crates of detonators, the blasting caps they'd lay on the track to warn drivers of fog or some other danger. He even had a metal nameplate stamping machine which he must have hauled away from some terminus station. The machine was one of those Edwardian survivors like 'What the Butler Saw'. You put in an old penny and could stamp out up to 22 letters on an aluminium strip, which you could fix to your trunk. I remember when I was a kid there was one of these machines at Victoria Station hidden away by Platform 19. We'd put in a penny and laboriously turn the dial to produce a metal strip with our names punched into it, one letter at a time. You even had to pay for full-stops. The machine must have weighed the same as a washing-machine. God knows how he'd managed to pinch it.

He couldn't remember a tenth of what he'd taken when they came to arrest him, but he was glad they'd come. He said it was getting difficult to move around the house for everything he'd stolen. Prison for him was a relief in a way. He had more room in his cell, even with me there.

I confess that I enjoyed my three weeks of 23 hours a day locked in that cell with Tony. I learnt a lot from him about life on the railways. And he learnt a bit from me. You see, during the day I did my best to teach him to read and write. By the time he was moved to an Open Prison, he had mastered the alphabet, could mouth many of the words and had even learnt to write his name. I think that's what he was proud of the most. He said he'd never had a signature. And when the lights were switched off in the evenings and our lessons were over for the day, then Tony would reminisce about his work as a railwayman.

He'd talk of the smell of carbolic in the tunnels, a strange left-over from the days of steam. He described the pitch-black darkness and stepping into the nearest recess in the wall every time a train came by. He always wondered whether the passengers could spot the whiteness of his face against the wall as they passed. If they had, he must have seemed like a ghost to them. One of the many poor navvies who'd died in the making of the tunnel.

And, in contrast, there was the fresh air, more than you'd want, walking across the Balcombe viaduct, checking the tracks. He said it's a different thing altogether when you're up that high on foot with the wind blowing so strong. Not like crossing the viaduct in a warm carriage, admiring the scenery. You realize when you're that high up that life is very fragile. The mind plays tricks up there as well. There are times when it will be urging you to jump. It's difficult to explain, he said, but sometimes you find yourself having to grit your teeth and stare down at the sleepers to stop yourself from ending it. There must be devils up there in the wind.

But there was Paradise too in this world of his. For he described the Welsh poppies at an abandoned country station, one of the many that were axed in the Beeching cuts. The bright yellow flags of the flowers were growing everywhere in the sidings and up on the platforms, their tall straight stems finding their way up through the wooden slats of the broken benches. Flowers self-seeded from the station-master's garden, his small house boarded up, green-painted planks nailed tight across the windows. He described how they'd spent their lunchbreak there, sitting amongst the yellow poppies, alone with the total silence between trains.

And between it all, there were the more prosaic but welcome brew-ups in the run-down and half-collapsed plate-layers shacks. The chance to sit down on whatever you could find and take a breather. Happy just to listen to the rain as it dripped from the blackened wooden eaves and from the trees either side of the tracks. Glad just to be out of it for a short while, a tin mug of tea in your hands. No, it wasn't a bad life.

The railway was a world he'd become part of, and he was almost poetic in his depictions of the colours of his world. The green and cream paint of the Company livery on the waiting-rooms, the benches and the lampposts. The rich red russet colours of the old railway brickwork, tones that would change with the weather and with the time of day. So much more gentle than the harsh red bricks of our prison. He was at one with his world and could have stayed there and flourished had it not been for his one weakness, the thieving.

When Tony talked of the railway, you realized that he was a fish out of water in prison. He really didn't belong there. He wasn't like me, the professional thief. The railway was where he belonged. It was the railway he always thought about and it was the railway that made him thoughtful.

191

I remember late one evening we were lying in our bunks in the darkening half-light. The lights had been turned off long ago and the prison shut down for the night. I was feeling as useless as an old sailing-ship becalmed in mid-ocean. Tony suddenly broke the silence by asking me if I'd ever seen a ghost. I said I hadn't, which was true at the time. He fell silent for a while and I wondered whether he was going to tell me again of the Balcombe viaduct and its devils, or of that abandoned station with its sea of yellow poppies waving in the breeze like lost souls, the ghosts of the station-master's garden.

Speaking quietly, as though ashamed of what he was going to say, and choosing his words carefully, he began to tell me of something altogether more strange and unsettling that had happened to him years before, when he'd been working on the tracks in Sussex. This was not something he had been able to suppress by gritting his teeth, walking on and staring down at the sleepers. Whatever it was, it was still with him and still troubling him.

It was a year we went without Spring, he said. April was dry but freezing with a cold North wind. Anyone planting seeds that year would have been out of luck. May was a wash-out. It rained almost every day. We were four or five weeks from the longest day of the year and there was still no sign of Spring, let alone Summer. I suppose I was lucky in a way that I was working throughout. You just kept plodding on and hoping that perhaps the weather would change.

It was late May when it happened and there were five of us working on maintenance on the tracks there. We'd pick up our tools each morning and take the train to the nearest station to where we were going to work. That train ride was our only dry time of the day. They'd be breaks in the rain, sunny spells even, but the wet trees would steam in the haze and it was only in close-up, like the sunlight on the raindrops on the leaves, that you saw anything to lift your spirits.

It was around mid-morning and we were working in a green culvert, young wet saplings on the banks to each side. Ahead of us there was an old red-brick bridge across the railway, one of those 19th century ones put up when the railway was first built to allow a farmer whose fields had been split in two to move his cattle across the railway. They were grand and elaborate affairs these bridges for what was just a dirt track for the occasional herd of cows. Bridges without roads, standing miles from anywhere. At first sight, you'd be hard-pressed to see the purpose in them.

It was while we were working there in a lull in the rain, the warm haze rising from the grass and the trees, that I looked up and saw him sitting there on the bridge, right on the edge of the parapet, dangling his legs in the air as if ready to jump. A small boy it was, a rich kid, wearing those long shorts you see on the little kids coming out of the expensive schools in Kensington, when they come running out in the afternoon happy to be released for the day. But the bridge was arched and high, and it was a long drop onto the hard sharp stones on the tracks and I could tell that this kid was very scared.

I don't know what came over me but I just chucked my spade on the ground and started shouting orders to the others. My own mother wouldn't have recognised me. I'd never been in charge of anything and here I was like a captain on the bridge of a ship giving orders. What was even more surprising was that the others seemed to take it as natural and obeyed me without a word. I ordered two of them to stand under the bridge to be ready to catch the kid if he jumped. I shouted at the lad to run back to the nearest station for help while I sent the two others to grab a canister of detonators and run up the track in both directions to lay the blasting caps on the line in groups of three, so we could warn any oncoming train of the danger.

I then scrambled up the side of the culvert, dragging myself up by the saplings. When I reached the top, I swung round onto the dirt track and stood there panting, facing the boy, trying not to spook him into jumping. He just turned his head slowly to look at me. He was shaking with fear, but he smiled at me as though he was relieved I'd come, as if he'd seen a friend at last. I took it as a good sign, but it didn't get me anywhere. You see, I couldn't get a word out of him. He smiled alright, but he wouldn't say anything. He sat there rigid, as if he was being held tight. I pleaded and begged until I could beg no more. And then I just ordered him, quietly but firmly, to get off the effing wall and come down.

It was as though he'd suddenly been released, as if I'd scared the person who'd been holding him. He quickly swung his legs to the ground and ran towards me. I never saw a kid look so happy, so relieved. It was only six or seven yards and he was running as hard as he could, but he just couldn't run fast enough. I was moving towards him, almost near enough to touch him, when he disappeared. He was suddenly gone, into thin air. The haze had lifted and I was left there standing on the bridge on my own.

I remember I just sank to my knees, crushed by the fact that I'd failed. If I could have just got up there faster. If I'd had the brain to know what to say to him. If I'd just ordered him straight away to get off the parapet. Whatever I'd done, it hadn't been enough. I'd missed my chance and my normal life had closed in again around me.

I was brought back to my senses by the sound of three blasting caps going off further up the track. There was a screeching of brakes as the passenger train slid to its emergency stop along the rails. My mates were shouting at me from the track below. Not hearing anything from me, they came running up onto the bridge. What could I say? What was there that anyone could say? The little boy had been real. The danger had been real, but now he was gone. I couldn't explain it. The train driver who eventually came walking along the tracks just shook his head and swore at me for wasting everyone's time.

When the train had started up again and had passed us, we decided we might as well pack it in for the day and get back to the Depot to report. It was my fault we weren't going to be popular. So we picked up all our stuff and trudged back along the tracks to the nearest station. We met our lad coming towards us with a couple of blokes from the station on the way.

When we finally got back to the Depot, they just laughed at us.

194

Surely we'd heard the stories about that bridge?  It seemed that the blokes at the station knew all about it but hadn't had the heart to tell us, seeing what a state we were in.

It had happened several times before, you see.  Someone would see a small boy sitting up on the parapet of the bridge, dangling his legs in thin air, about to jump.  They'd call the Police, the Fire Brigade with ladders, all sorts.  The Police would try and talk the kid down.  Every time they moved closer, it would look as though he was going to jump.  He never said anything.  It was just his body language, the way he was acting.  He seemed trapped and terrified.

The strange thing was that this would go on for an hour or so, the line shut down, all trains stopped, no end of disruption for the poor travellers.  And then suddenly the boy would be gone.  He'd suddenly break free, climb down off the parapet smiling and run towards the policemen.  But he'd be gone before he reached them, disappeared into thin air.  God knows where he went or how he did it.

There'd be a lot of scratching of heads, but at the end of the day there was nothing anyone could do.  They'd pull down their ladders, pile back into their Fire Engines and vans and leave.  Railway traffic was given the green light to restart.  The story was that some child had been murdered there years before, thrown off the bridge in front of a train.  It was an answer of a sort for those that believed in ghosts and the supernatural.

Tony fell silent for a while and I lay there in the silence of our cell waiting for him to finish the story.

What sort of person would do that to a kid, he asked, throw him off a bridge?  You're a well-educated sort of bloke, Lance. Perhaps you could go to a library when you get out of here, have a look in the old newspapers, see if there's anything that would make sense of it.

I can see the boy still haunts you, I said.

Not the boy, said Tony.  What haunts me is myself.  You see, for once in my life, I really thought I was going to be useful.

And, with that, I heard him turn his face the wall, pull the blanket up round his shoulders and settle down for the night.

When I did fall asleep that night, it was to a land of strange dreams, to memories of one of those large houses I'd burgled in Sussex. It was about two in the morning. I'd cut out my circle of glass, opened the French windows and stepped inside. A sweep with my torch told me that I'd struck gold. Or, in this case, silver, small 18th century pieces kept behind glass in dark-wood cabinets. I lost no time in quietly filling my sack.

One of the cabinets, though was different. It was made of ebony and instead of glass, it had small painted panels showing chinoiserie scenes, similar in style to those gold-painted landscapes you see on 18th century tavern clocks. These panels, however, were polychrome and seemed even more exotic. In fact, they were truly otherworldly when they caught the light from my small torch. Each panel seemed to tell a story, a fable perhaps. For there were animals and bats as well as people in the pictures.

Fables that were nearly my undoing. I was so bound up in them that I almost missed hearing the soft footsteps moving cautiously down the stairs in the huge hall. I just had time to grab my bag and the sack of things I'd already stolen, including that oval Dublin snuffbox, and make it back through the French windows and out into the safety of the darkness of the garden before the door to the room was opened behind me. It wasn't very professional of me to allow myself to be distracted by chinoiserie. I'd allowed my mind to wander from the job.

I guess this all came back to me in the prison bunk because there'd been a bridge in one of the painted chinoiserie panels. It wasn't Tony's. It was a rickety old thing made of wood and it spanned a raging torrent not a railway. A man in Chinese clothes was standing on the bridge, staring down at a monkey holding a human skull. The only thing the dream shared with Tony's story was the same feeling of hopelessness. Whatever was happening there, there was nothing you could do about it.

It wasn't Hell as such, but a premonition of where my misspent life would lead me. The Chinese man, the monkey and the skull were a warning to me, I suppose. A frozen warning of wasted time. But it would have needed the man to have said something, if I was to understand.

Anyway, the dreams disappeared with the morning light and not long afterwards Tony was transferred to an Open Prison.

For Tony's sake, to keep my promise when I was released, I did go down to the library at Lewes and trawl through the Victorian newspapers for the local area. It seemed a nanny had committed suicide from the bridge in the 1880s. What made the story more tragic was that she'd taken the little boy she was looking after. They'd walked across the fields from the Big House with a picnic basket. But she never opened the basket. She'd taken it to use as a step to help her get herself and the little boy up onto the parapet. Still holding the boy tightly, she'd thrown herself off in front of the fast train to Brighton.

There was the usual journalist's drivel in the newspapers about why she'd done it. Thwarted love etc. The truth is that when she jumped, she'd become a closed book. How much do we ever know of people's reasons?

I just had this image which the papers couldn't provide. The driver slamming on the brakes when nothing could be done. The crockery in the dining-car going everywhere and the steward being thrown to the floor. Red wine stains on the white tablecloths. And, beneath it all, the killing of a child who had no wish to die.

I never saw Tony again. I remember, though, that when he was transferred to the Open Prison, I had a day to myself before my new cellmate arrived. It was long enough for me to discover that Tony had pinched my toothbrush again. After I'd finished cursing the old boy, I had a look under his mattress. There it was, the toothbrush, but this time there was something else there as well. It was a note he'd written in pencil on half a page he'd torn from his exercise book.

The note was a labour of love which he must have struggled to complete in the half-light after dawn while I was still asleep. It was a tour de force in capital letters, with full-stops as the only punctuation.

None of us said anything as Lance paused to reach for his wallet and take out the now much-faded piece of paper which he unfolded and passed to us to hand round the table.

TOO LARNS. WEER THEEVS NOT MURDRAS. YOR FREND TONY.

I carry it with me, Lance said, as my ID if you like. My passport as well, perhaps. It's no excuse for my misspent life but I shall show it at the Pearly Gates all the same. I don't suppose it will get me into Heaven, but it's worth a try.

# 16 THE ICE HOUSE

I think I may have short-changed you with my last ghost story, said Lance. I shouldn't want to send you all home without that slight quiver of dread. 'There but for the grace of God' etcetera. Perhaps I should leave you with another lesson I learnt in prison. If you don't mind, I think I had better break our rules and tell you a second story, something less elegiac, a touch colder. I mean they shouldn't leave you with a warm glow, ghost stories. Although this is hardly a ghost story in the true sense. Not something that M.R.James would have recognised. But then I'm not a Cambridge don.

None of us objecting, Lance picked up his glass of port and began.

Someone more impressionable than I, said Lance, might have at least sensed echoes of the crime in that Ice House. It was a cold January day when I visited and the dripping slime on the bricks inside was frosted and frozen. I could see my breath as I stood there casting my eyes around the walls. Yes, someone with more imagination would surely have sensed something of the terrible drama that had taken place there. The insane man talking at the edge of the pit, his diabolical laughter which obscured the soft approach of stockinged feet, the blast of the revolvers shattering everything with the sound of bullets being fired in a brick-walled, underground room. Someone more impressionable than I would have sensed something...

Lance smiled at us as he turned the glass of port in his hand, holding it to the light so that he might better appreciate its colour and its qualities. Lance the professional thief and consummate performer, confident that he'd captured our attention as we basked in the warmth of that wood-panelled private dining-room in a street off Covent Garden, where we'd gathered again for our annual reunion and the telling of ghost stories.

But perhaps I should begin at the beginning, smiled Lance. For what I'd like to talk about tonight is absolute power. I've often wondered what it is in that power which attracts people. I suppose it's my love of Russian history that draws me to it. You can't get away from tyrants and dictators and Tsars if you love Russian history. Even today they have them, though the current leadership like to call their system "a managed democracy". George Orwell would have had something to say about that. What is it about these people that makes them think they have the right to destroy so many lives? I'd like to think there was a special part of Hell reserved for them.

Ah well, we must count ourselves lucky if we never meet a tyrant. I never have. Although I did, when I was younger, once share a cell with a man who had briefly achieved absolute power during the Cold War and who had clearly revelled in its benefits and its joys. He was a complete head-case, of course. He was a very well-educated man, an Oxford Don no less, but I think 'head-case' is still the correct description.

He was in prison for murder, my new cellmate, multiple murder in fact, but the authorities judged him harmless by the time I was ushered into his cell to join him. I did ask once why he wasn't in Broadmoor, but they said the Prison Service psychiatrists had seen him and pronounced him sane. You, my friends, said Lance, will have to be the best judge of that.

But, as I say, perhaps I should begin at the beginning.

Even on a dull December morning, said Lance, putting down his glass of port, the great gatehouse with its twin octagonal towers, in brown brick and white stone, must have looked for-all-the-world like a castle built for Cesare Borgia. It spoke of authority, power and the outwitting of one's enemies, of subterfuge and trickery. But the two white-painted terracotta busts set in stone roundels, one on each tower, were not of Cesare's proud parents, Pope Alexander VI and his mistress, Giovanna dei Cattanei. They were a more humble but equally purposeful pair, the English prison reformers John Howard and Elizabeth Fry. For this gatehouse belonged not to a Borgia castle but to an English prison, and it was not something you could see as you sat handcuffed on a bench in the back of a windowless police van, waiting for the doors to open on your prison sentence.

It was my first time inside and I was feeling completely numb. After the procedures and the formalities, I was led along corridors and up staircases until the warder and I stood outside a strong, shut and emphatically bolted door. It's the initial feeling of helplessness as the warder takes out his bunches of keys. You couldn't move even if they let you. I can't describe it. As you stand there, it's as though your life is over.

You're a university man, said the warder to me as he pushed me forwards into the cell, you two will be company for each other. You can teach each other foreign languages, discuss Assyrian antiquities, do whatever it is you bright chaps do. And with that the door slammed behind me and I made the acquaintance of Archibald Wynters, sometime Professor of Medieval History at the University of Oxford, sometime Fellow of one of the smaller and more obscure colleges.

Call me Archie, said the small fat man in dark blue prison overalls as he held out his hand. All my friends call me Archie. Grab yourself a seat on the bottom bunk for the time being. The top one will be yours at night, of course. I'm not as nimble as I once was. And if you don't mind, I'll monopolize our one and only wooden chair during the daytime. It reminds me of being at school and helps me think.

We shook hands and I followed his suggestion to park myself on the bottom bunk.

Well, this is nice, he said. What shall we talk about? Life in general, death in particular? Ah, if only I could offer you a sherry, then we'd be set up nicely.

Who's your favourite Latin poet, he asked?

Hugh Primas of Orleans, I replied. An answer which stopped him in his tracks. He chuckled nervously, glanced at the floor of the cell, and fell silent. In fact, he didn't speak to me for the rest of that day

The trick of being in prison, said Lance, looking round the table at us again, is to show them who's boss. It applies just as much to the head-cases as to the hard-men.

We had no choice but to remain silent, bowing to a depth of experience we did not share.

I knew I'd got through to him, said Lance, when he opened the conversation the next morning, after we'd cleaned out the slops, made our beds and eaten what passed for breakfast, handed in to us on metal trays.

I've read Helen Waddell's *Wandering Scholars*, he began, but I can't say I have read as much of Primas as I perhaps should have done. He is someone you'd recommend, then?

Yes, I said. For the driving rhythm, mainly.

For the rhythm, repeated Wynters. Ah yes. Quite so, the rhythm.

And so began what became months of sparring, each of us drawing on our education, his much more extensive than mine, as we manoeuvred to keep one step ahead of the other, to wrong-foot the other if possible. The whole thing may have been silly, petty, but it's the sort of thing you welcome in prison, anything to keep your brain alive. And when he got the better of me, which was most of the time, I'd play the dumb and admiring student and beg him for the full lecture on whatever it was we'd been discussing.

I learnt a lot about medieval heresy during those months with Wynters. The Cathars, the Albigensians, had been his main area of research. He could talk for hours about Dualism. He would become animated to the point of rapture. At times I felt that he was actually preaching, that he was an evangelist for his cause. He was intelligent enough not to mistake my interest for conversion, but I guess he was just happy to have an appreciative audience. It was a tutorial he would otherwise never give.

I'd been there a few weeks when the Governor came up to me as I was doing my outdoor work, hoeing the vegetable patch.

I appreciate what you are doing with Wynters, he said. He has been here for over twenty-five years now and he hasn't had someone of his own university background to talk to for a long time. It does him good, makes him calmer, I think.

I stopped working, leant on my hoe and waited for the Governor to get to the point. You don't interrupt the Governor. You just nod and stay quiet and try to keep on the right side. There may come a time when you will really need his help, on parole for instance.

It's just this, he said. I'm very grateful but I'd advise you to be careful. You are doing us all a service by keeping Wynters calm, but I owe it to you to let you see the full background to his conviction. For your own good, really.

And so it was, during my indoor duties, helping out twice a week with the filing in the prison farm office, that I was allowed to spend half an hour at a time sitting at a much-scratched plain deal table in one corner of the office, reading my way through a complete run of newspaper cuttings on the Wynters trial, newspaper cuttings that came to me in chronological order in batches in a large plain brown envelope addressed to me

203

'Personal from the Governor'.

It's always a revelation when you see the truth about someone you think you know. I was well aware that Wynters was in prison for murder, more than one, but it was not a subject I'd ever raised with him, just as he'd never asked me about my own criminal career. Here, in the lengthy Press reports of the prosecution case, a whole world of evil was laid out before me, a world created, overseen and managed by Professor Wynters.

It started with an inheritance. His rich aunt had died and, having no children, she'd left 90% of her estate to her talented nephew, in the hope that he would use his intelligence and education to further the interests of mankind. The remaining 10% she left to the Battersea Dogs Home. The latter was undoubtedly money better spent. Wynters decided to take over his aunt's Country House in the Home Counties with its fifteen acres of grounds. There was more than enough in her extensive portfolio of shares and investments both to fund its upkeep and to kick-start Wynters' much more ambitious personal project. He negotiated a sabbatical from his college and university teaching commitments, withdrew to his Home Counties estate and set about putting his plans into action, achieving his life's ambition, if you like.

The outside world saw nothing of Wynters' plans for nine months and, even then, had no reason whatsoever to link his name to the string of very expert jewel robberies that were carried out with force and precision against London's finest West End jewellery stores over a five-week period. Still less was he associated with the campaign of brutal knee-cappings carried out all over Britain in the months that followed. Knee-cappings whose victims ranged from politicians to housewives, a brutality without apparent logic or purpose.

If we are to believe the prosecuting barrister, and his case was well-argued and clear, then the robberies and the knee-cappings would never have been linked let alone solved if it had not been for the persistence of one brave and seemingly powerless part-time member of the Women's Royal Voluntary Service (WRVS). Her husband, you see, had disappeared and she carried on her hunt for him until she reached the very end of the road, in her stockinged feet, in that 19<sup>th</sup> century Ice House, with her late father's old service Webley in her hand.

But I'm getting ahead of myself, said Lance, smiling and pausing to sip his port. For the barrister's case, as reported in the old newspaper reports that dropped out of that brown envelope in the prison farm office, elaborated with logic and precision how Wynters had created this whole Devil's edifice, and why.

He'd needed 'Officers' and 'soldiers' to carry out his plan. The first he'd found amongst his former History students at Oxford. He chose those who had responded most warmly to his seminars on Dualism and who, for one reason or another, were now at a loose end, those who (in the barrister's phrase) had so far "been unsuccessful in life". He would wine them and dine them in London and then invite them to his Country House for the weekend. And there he would weave them tales of the Cold War and the threats that Britain faced. He would draw on his own brief involvement with the British Secret Services in World War Two to elaborate and describe just how those things worked, that there were wheels within wheels, Chinese boxes within Chinese boxes, hidden apparatuses of State whose job was to keep us ordinary folks safe.

Wynters described how he, with the current rank of Colonel, headed one such secret world, operating securely and distinct from other organs of Government, sanctioned by the Prime Minister and the Monarch. Its aim was to push back against Communist infiltration into British Society, to send a warning to those who would understand. And to do this secretly, his organization had to be self-funding, self-supporting, very much on its own. This, he explained to them, was where the jewellery thefts came in. The shop-owners, of course, would be reimbursed by their insurers. The latter would be discreetly repaid by top-level contacts in Government. It was a story that was convincing enough for Wynters' audience. In short, he got his 'Officers', three of them, which was enough.

At which point in the story, the warder tapped on my shoulder.

My time was up and he took me back to my cell. Perhaps more deferentially than before, now that he knew I was the Governor's pet. The warder probably thought I was a snout.

Back in the cell with Wynters, I had to try hard not to betray my new-found knowledge. I felt he was looking at me even more slyly than usual, a half-smile almost there on his face. There was something of the animal about Professor Wynters at the best of times. Not a rat or a pig, not even a fox. For his cunning and his wiliness were coupled with something more, 'intelligence' for want of a better word. A mongoose, I think, was the animal I was looking for, but a mongoose that had gone bad. Intelligent but malign. And I suppose that's the problem, isn't it? For if someone's born with intelligence, you expect them to use it in a good cause, whether that's for the wider public good or for just solving some thorny problem of Mycenaean archaeology. You don't expect them to use their intelligence to do harm. It seems like a betrayal of a God-given gift. Like a violinist who smashes their violin.

As if reading my thoughts, Wynters rubbed his hands together and chuckled.

You know, he said, we've never yet talked about ourselves. It's all been academic subjects, our conversation. Fascinating, stimulating, absorbing but not personal.

I didn't think you academics had a personal life, I joked. I thought you were all absorbed in your subjects. I thought your research was your personal life. Except on those very rare occasions like the War, when you were all dragged from your cloisters to do great work in the real world.

Not all of us managed great work, laughed Wynters. There was Fotheringay, for example, a Fellow at my college. He went out to France before D-Day with his unit, but he was injured and sent home, unfit for active service, before he ever got near any fighting. Do you know what happened to him? He tripped over a tent-peg in a camp in France. It was enough to curtail Fotheringay's brief outing into the real world. He came limping (literally) back to Oxford with his tail between his legs.

And what about your war work, I asked?

Ah well, I signed the Official Secrets Act, he chuckled. So I have a good excuse for being discreet.

No wounds, I asked?

Not visible ones, smiled Wynters. Nothing to detract from my natural good looks.

You weren't in uniform then, I asked?

Oh yes, I had a uniform, said Wynters, standing up from the chair as if proudly wearing the uniform in our cell. I was a Colonel, he chuckled. Not a full Colonel, but a Colonel all the same.

I suppose you were in Intelligence, I said.

Ah, that would be telling, laughed Wynters. But then you could probably guess by looking at me that I wasn't in the Commandoes.

It was a joke he found so funny that he had to sit back down in the chair and start hugging his sides as he rocked to and froe with laughter.

Back in the prison farm office with another envelope of press-cuttings, I found that Wynters' 'Officers' first job was to identify the 'soldiers'. Wynters gave them the steer they needed. Wynters' requirement for 'soldiers' coincided with the British Army's. It was the beginning of the Korean War and there was a Recruiting Office in central London. All that Wynters' 'Officers' had to do was to hang around on the street and identify, by their slightly slumped shoulders and the way they walked, those who'd been turned down by the Recruiting Office. Some through lack of experience, some because their War Record had been less than unblemished, others just because they were Polish refugees, determined to fight Communism but unwanted by the British Army in Korea. The 'Officers' did a good job, finding the right sort of people, taking them for a drink in the Pub, weeding out those they judged wouldn't make the grade.

When they had a dozen 'soldiers' selected, the 'Officers' gave them their train fares and an advance, told them to pack a bag for a week and told them when to be standing on a specific street-corner in Croydon ready to be collected by a lorry with a grey canvas hood.

Safely down in the privacy of Wynters' estate, the 'Colonel' gave them the uplifting lecture on the secret campaign against Communism and described his own very-secret self-funding Unit. He outlined the jewellery robberies that would pay for the Unit, recces for which had already been carried out by his 'Officers'. The rest of the first week was spent in physical fitness training, interspersed by classroom lectures by the 'Colonel' on Communist aggression across the world. Quite quickly, the two Poles and a former Army Corporal from Lewisham stood out as the obvious NCO material.

Wynters and his 'Officers' were pleased with their first week's work as they loaded their 'soldiers' into the lorry with instructions for a Monday pick-up on a different Croydon street-corner. As Wynters put it, the bonding had begun.

I have to say, said Lance, there was something of genius in Wynters scheme, as described by the prosecuting barrister. Take the jewellery robberies, for instance. The 'soldiers' listened in silence to Wynters' account of how they'd approach the target shop on mopeds. Well not mopeds exactly but 125cc James ML motorcycles that one of the 'Officers' had bought second-hand with a wadge of notes supplied by Wynters. On their James motorcycles they'd carry out the smash-and-grab (diamonds for preference) and then scoot a half mile or so to the pick-up point where the lorry would be parked with a wooden ramp already down ready to scoop up men and motorcycles. It was the James motorcycles the 'soldiers' objected to. Why couldn't they use proper motorbikes?

Because, said the 'Colonel', I don't want you crashing on the way to the lorry. Thirty-five miles an hour is all you'll need.

It's the surprise and the planning that will win the day, not an extra thirty miles an hour. They had to agree that the Colonel knew his stuff. The escape routes as well were superb. The weaving between bollards down quiet pedestrian alleyways, all the tricks to stop a car from following. The 'soldiers' could tell from the routes that their 'Officers' had walked them all. It was the thought and planning that had gone into it that they admired. It made them feel somehow invincible.

The jewellery thefts went like clockwork. Whether it was Bond Street, Kensington or the Burlington Arcade, each 'operation' was executed with precision. The lorry would collect the 'soldiers' at the pick-up point and one of the 'Officers' would drive them back to Wynters' estate where the jewellery was handed over to him for the Unit's funds. Like all soldiers, they liked a job where the Officers got you from A to B without mucking you about along the way. That was a Unit worth belonging to. And the pay was good too. Every Friday Wynters would hand them the cash. Like their Unit, the cash would be untraceable.

I couldn't help but admire Wynters as I read these newspaper cuttings, said Lance. My nondescript and fat old cellmate had shown himself to be on top of his game. He'd won the admiration of his 'Officers' and his 'soldiers'. The Unit was truly his and would march to his command. Or so it seemed.

Which was as far as I got that day before the warder came to tap me on the shoulder and lead me respectfully back to the cells.

Later that evening, after lights-out, when Wynters and I were safely under our blankets on our bunks with nothing but sleep before us, he turned the conversation to proverbs.

I have always considered proverbs to be the greatest distillation of wisdom, said Wynters. Don't you agree?

It was not something I'd ever thought much about but, after a fifteen-minute disposition on the subject from Wynters, I had to agree that he was probably right.

Why else would they survive, said Wynters, if they weren't hard-won lessons for the future, something for people to pass down to their children? I think the educational system could save itself a lot of trouble if it just got schoolchildren to learn their proverbs off by heart.

What's your favourite proverb? asked Wynters.

It's a Russian one, I said. "Life is not as simple as a walk across a field."

A complete course of philosophy in a single sentence, laughed Wynters.

And yours, I asked?

I think it's probably one I heard from a central European refugee in the War, he said. "When a donkey gets too happy, it walks on ice."

And Wynters chuckled to himself before turning over in his bunk to go to sleep.

From the evidence presented at the trial, it became clear that the problems for Wynters began when his Unit of 'Officers' and 'soldiers' moved to Stage Two, the knee-cappings. One of the 'soldiers' was a bit of a psychopath and took to it like a duck to water. The others, though, were outside their comfort zone, as we'd say nowadays. Walking up to an unarmed person and firing rounds into them is not what someone normal does.

The first two 'operations', however, went ahead without a hitch. It was probably because of the nature of the 'targets' and the strong motivational pre-operation talk delivered by the Colonel. The first man they knee-capped was a senior figure in the small British Communist Party. 'Officers' and 'soldiers' alike nodded in unison as the Colonel described their first 'target'. This was precisely the sort of man they should be warning.

The second 'target' was a Conservative Party MP. The troops found this one harder to understand but were won round when

Wynters traced for them the man's long-term secret links with the Communists back to his years at Oxford University before the War. He had been recruited by the Russians during the War, said Wynters, and was now one of their most highly placed agents in British politics. And so the knee-capping went ahead and the Police were left baffled as to who could have perpetrated such an outrage.

It was the third attack which really rocked the Unit and revealed the divisions that would threaten its future. The psychopath amongst them was happy enough to carry out the order, but the 'operation' left most of the others feeling thoroughly sick. Wynters had come up with the same argument that the 'target' was a Russian agent and had been since her secret war work in London and Cairo in World War Two. To the 'Officers' and 'soldiers' of the Unit, however, she was a Society hostess, an Earl's daughter who spent her life in good works for Charities. She was on the board of the WRVS. She may have been upper class, but she was a housewife all the same. And surely the Unit hadn't been set up to knee-cap housewives? Would anyone want to work for a government that did that? It's what you'd expect from a dictatorship, not a democracy.

The Corporal from Lewisham took it particularly badly. When he'd been home the weekend after the shooting, his wife had been in tears. She worshipped this Earl's daughter who'd been helpful and kind to her when she worked with her in the WRVS. What kind of scum would do something like that, his wife had asked? The Corporal said nothing to his wife, but he put family first and voted with his feet. He didn't turn up to meet the lorry on the following Monday.

Wynters shrugged off the Corporal's departure when he next addressed the Unit. The hard road was not for everyone. That was just a fact of life which they had to accept. As far as he was concerned, the Unit had done well. They all deserved two weeks' paid leave before he briefed them on the next 'targets'. They'd be given a bonus as well to spend during their holiday. They should look on their work with pride. They'd earned a rest.

For the psychopath, however, Wynters had a private message which he passed on when the two of them had a moment alone. The latter was to deliver the Lewisham Corporal to the Estate. The 'Colonel' and the psychopath would have to deal with this treachery on their own.

It was the Corporal's subsequent disappearance which proved Wynters' undoing. He was too obsessed, too arrogant, too detached from the real world to reckon with the persistence of a very ordinary abandoned housewife. It was her evidence, extracted one sentence at a time in a hushed Courtroom by the prosecuting barrister that put the nails in Wynters' coffin, so to speak. For she was such an unassuming force of justice and truth. She admitted herself that she'd never really liked it when her husband had nicknamed her 'mouse' during their courtship. And she hardly found her married title of 'Luv' much better. But she did love him and, because of that love, felt she had no choice but to find him when he disappeared. She knew he wouldn't just walk out on her. Something had happened.

All she knew for certain was that he'd tried to sign up again, for the Korean War this time, against all her protests and pleading, and that he'd been devastated when he was turned down because of the limp in his left leg, itself a left-over from the War. However, he'd turned up all smiles one evening a couple of weeks later. He'd been accepted for another job, he'd said, for the government. The pay would be good. All she'd been able to get out of him was that he was collected each Monday by a lorry in Croydon somewhere and that he'd spend the week working at a big house out in the country. What he did there, he wouldn't say. He seemed very proud of himself, though.

The Corporal's desertion, however, had rocked the Unit more than Wynters had first realized. When they returned to his country estate for their next briefing, they were restless and on edge. The psychopath apart, they understood why the Corporal had gone. They didn't want to be shooting any more housewives. When the 'Officers' took Wynters aside and explained the mood in the Unit, he decided to stand them down for three months on half pay, paid in advance. Half-pay was a lot better than none, so they were happy to take it, cash in hand. A few of them had already made up their minds that they wouldn't return.

As for the Corporal's wife, there was only one place she could go for advice on what she should do next. With the Earl's wife still in hospital, 'mouse' (or 'Luv' as she'd been known since she'd married) went to see another of her senior colleagues in the WRVS. The advice she got was to report her husband as a missing person to the police, which she duly did. But the kindly senior WRVS colleague admitted that, with the police so stretched, there was little they could probably do. The colleague, though, had a brother, ex-Army and now setting himself up as a private detective. He might be able to help.

He'd obviously been tipped off by his kindly sister because he agreed to take on the case on a no-results, no-fee basis. The Corporal's wife was just relieved to have someone on her side in what seemed a hopeless quest. She passed on every little thing she could about her husband's rejection for the Korean War, his subsequent mystery recruitment and about the weekly Croydon pick-ups for his secret work. She honestly didn't expect the private detective to come up with any results, but at least she didn't have to find the money to pay him in advance.

From what emerged at the trial, there were, for reasons which would become obvious later, gaps in the prosecution barrister's knowledge of how the private detective had worked his way painstakingly from establishing contacts in the Korean War recruitment office, to the list of the rejects and to the subsequent movements of those few who had been suddenly taken on by the 'government' for another job. What seemed clear was that he'd managed to find one of Wynters 'soldiers' and pay him to talk. However, he'd done it and it was a fine piece of work. The private detective had identified Wynters and his country estate as the heart of the mystery. It was there that the private detective would have to seek answers for the Corporal's disappearance.

The private detective had shared his knowledge with his client, little expecting that she would act on it herself. And it was by chance that the private detective was already there on the day that the Corporal's wife arrived at Wynters' estate, by Green Line coach and a brisk walk along country lanes, with her late father's service revolver weighing down her handbag.

Determined to find out what had happened to her husband, she'd forced her way through a slight gap in the boundary hedge and made her way through the trees towards the big house. And it was by chance, on the way there, that she saw her own private detective being forced along a path away from the house, forced by a small fat man holding a pistol to the detective's back.

Keeping her distance, she'd followed the pair of them until they disappeared into an old low brick-built building in the trees. When she got there and found the heavy door ajar, she slipped off her shoes, took out her father's gun and walked as silently as she could along a damp stone corridor.

What she could hear was a one-sided argument with the short fat man's high-pitched triumphant voice breaking out into laughter as he mocked the detective who was standing silent in front of him. When the fat man stopped talking and the silence became unbearable, the Corporal's wife had fired. There was an enormous explosion of sound and both men suddenly disappeared.

It seemed from the subsequent police reports that she had shot Wynters in the back at the same time as Wynters had shot the detective. The force of the bullets sent both men over the edge of the pit in what was a disused Victorian Ice House. But in one of those perverse twists of fate which always seem to give the evil of this world a second chance, it was Wynters who survived and the detective who died.

And the detective's was not the only corpse the police found there when they finally arrived. The Corporal, shot in the head and dead some weeks, lay there with him, resting on a bed of diamonds and other jewellery, the proceeds of the Unit's robberies, tossed down there unwanted by Wynters for whom the robberies had just been a step along the way.

At the trial, with Wynters and his victims in the witness-box, the prosecuting barrister was able to unfold and lay out for view the motivation, the 'rationale' (if that's not completely the wrong word) for the three knee-cappings carried out by Wynters unit. For Wynters, of course, like many people of his type when their career was over, was very keen that the world should know of his cleverness.

It seemed that the first victim, the British Communist, had worked alongside Wynters during the War in Cairo. It didn't take him long to see through the bombast and charade that was Archibald Wynters and he'd had a quiet word with their superiors, hoping that that would be sufficient. Wynters. though, had his friends and supporters in the Cairo office and they pointed to the Communist's known left-wing views, of which he made no secret. His warning about Wynters was just bad gripes against a right-wing colleague. And so the Communist found himself moved sideways to another job while Wynters survived and prospered.

The second victim, the Conservative MP, had been one of those superiors in the Cairo office. But even he had come to realize over the course of the next year that Wynters apparent skill at conspiracy was in fact a manifestation of his fundamentally flawed and twisted way of thinking. In short, you just couldn't trust him. He wasn't so much working for the British government as for himself. And God knows what he was up to. The result was a transfer to a more mundane branch of army service, a transfer which Wynters had never forgiven. He regarded it, he said in the witness-box, as a betrayal.

As for the third victim, the Earl's daughter, she found it hard even to remember Wynters name. The records proved they had worked in the Cairo office at the same time but all she could recall was a small, strange man who seemed to be full of himself. He might have asked her out for a drink once, but then everyone there had, and she certainly didn't remember accepting his offer. She didn't know why she would have been on his list for retribution.

When I got back to the cell after I'd read this final batch of newspaper cuttings on Wynters trial, I found him sitting on the bottom bunk of the bed with a sly grin on his face.

Sorry for pinching your seat, old boy, he said, but I find it useful sometimes to sit where the other chap sits. It helps one to understand their position, if you know what I mean. It's so important to see the other side in life, don't you think. We can't go making snap judgements on how the other half act, can we?

And, with that, Wynters raised himself from the bunk and took two steps across to settle himself back onto the chair. He looked self-satisfied, like Lord Lovat in Hogarth's print. That was the worst thing about him.

With the full details of Wynters trial still fresh in my head, said Lance, I didn't know what to say. Or rather, I didn't know how best to say nothing. So I plonked myself down on the bottom bunk and, for want of a better word, sulked.

It was Wynters who broke the silence.

I've been working on a little plan, he said. Something that might enliven your time here in my cell.

Wynters reached down under the bunk and pulled out what looked like strands of rope.

Bedsheets, he said. A tried and tested method.

To escape, I said?

Well, after a fashion, he laughed. I spent a lot of my spare time in Cairo, in the dead hours of the afternoon at least, in one of those Arab coffee shops in the old market part of town. It was opposite a furniture maker. 'Furniture' is probably too grand a word. What they turned out there were 'angareebs', those wood-framed beds with a mattress made of plaited rope stretched across the framework. I'd sit and watch the boys plaiting the ropes while I drank my coffees. It's always therapeutic to watch someone else work, don't you agree?

And with that, Wynters set to work and spent the rest of the day till lights-out plaiting the strips of torn up bed sheets, working them into a short rope, a rope with a simple but effective-looking noose at one end. When he'd finished his work, he turned it over in his hands to appreciate his own craftsmanship and then got up and shifted the chair against the wall beneath the barred window. With some difficulty, he hoisted his bulk up onto the chair and tried his rope for length, making sure that he would have enough to tie one end around the bottom bar and leave the noose hanging down free, checking that the noose would slide easily.

Just testing, he laughed. One likes to get one's tools ready.

At lights-out, he remained sitting on the chair with his rope coiled and tucked beneath him. He made no move to get into his bunk when I'd climbed up for the night.

I lay there in the silence, said Lance, knowing that I should have spoken out, banged on the door, called the Warders. That was my duty as a human being, but I didn't do it and that was the longest evening of my life. I'm ashamed to say, though, that I did eventually fall asleep. After what I'd read of his trial, I was sick of him and I was happy to let him get on with it. Wynters was someone the world would not miss.

What woke me in the middle of the night was not a noise but the feel of the noose being slipped carefully around my neck. A few seconds later and I wouldn't have had time to get my fingers in between the rope and my neck. Without those seconds, he would have killed me.

A suddenly very athletic Wynters was standing on the bottom bunk, the rope around the metal bed-pole for leverage, his foot wedged against the metal side of the bed, pulling on the rope with every ounce of his strength and more. He was a man inspired, driven you could say, and he had Physics on his side. All I had was youth and, luckily for me, youth told in the end. As soon as I'd freed myself and knocked Wynters to the floor, I did go to the door and bang for the Warders.

The following morning, some hours after Wynters had been escorted away, still grinning, to another cell, I found myself sitting with a china mug of tea in my hand in the Governor's office.

I was rather hoping you'd get under his skin, said the Governor. I suspected that your intelligence would be enough to provoke him into doing something. Of course, it's always hard to know in advance what that 'something' will be. Perhaps the psychiatrists will now finally accept that he's insane and I can be rid of him.

But he could have killed me, I said.

Only if you'd let him, replied the Governor.

But how did you know he wouldn't commit suicide?

In my, albeit limited, experience, said the Governor, psychopaths have too high an opinion of themselves to commit suicide.

Lance paused in his account, looked round the table at us and asked if he might have another glass of port.

Did the Governor plan the whole thing, we asked?

Well, put it this way, said Lance, I was too inexperienced then to know better. But it's the only cell I've ever been in with a wooden chair that can be placed under the bars of a window.

I'm afraid I've had you here under false pretences, said Lance. It's hardly a ghost story as such. Professor Archibald Wynters is long-dead and has never come back to haunt me. As I said, I couldn't even detect his presence when I did finally go to that country house of his in Surrey, now a National Trust property. But that may be just a weakness on my part. For if he has lived on as a ghost, it would have to be there in that Ice House, chuckling to himself as he empties out those sacks of diamond jewellery from the robberies, tipping them into the pit, watching all those brilliant flashes of light disappearing down into the darkness.

No, if he does come back, it's been to help me in a way. Whenever I'm getting ahead of myself, getting too confident in life or too happy, I'll suddenly wake in the middle of the night in a cold sweat and all I can remember of my nightmare is that donkey on the ice.

# ABOUT THE AUTHOR

While many of these stories draw on places where the author has lived and worked, they are not drawn from life.

# AUTHOR DISCLAIMER

This is a work of fiction. Unless otherwise indicated, all the names, characters, businesses, places, events and incidents in this book are either the product of the author's imagination or used in a fictitious manner. Any resemblance to actual persons, living or dead, is purely coincidental.

Printed in Great Britain
by Amazon

29861333R00128